THE DE-CODING OF JO

BLADE

OF

TRUTH

Ascending Angel Academy II

LALI A. LOVE

Published by Ravens & Roses Publishing LLC
Book Cover Design by Larch Gallagher

eBook ISBN: 978-1-7372998-0-6
Paperback ISBN: 978-1-7372998-1-3
Hardcover ISBN: 978-1-7372998-2-0

Award-Winning Publications
Heart of a Warrior Angel: From Darkness to Light (2019)
The De-Coding of Jo: Hall of Ignorance (2020)
The Joy of I.T: Infinite Transcendence (2020)
Ananda: Poetry for the Soul (2021)

TESTIMONIALS

"Wrapped in a young adult story, *Blade of Truth* is a guide for the evolution to one's higher self. It is a story that transports the reader to higher consciousness, tapping into energy that lights the path towards goodness. It is an examination of the existence of good and evil, where humankind continually battles the forces that drag it down to lower realms.

Delving into the heart and mind of the adolescent psyche, Ms. Love examines common struggles with sensitivity and compassion. The characters battle substance abuse/addiction, body image, and self-esteem. As each character is developed, Ms. Love reveals their individual paths and draws the reader into their lives, leading us to care deeply about them and root for them along their journey of self-discovery.

Having taught high school for thirty years, I believe that Lali A. Love captures the essence of the adolescent experience—self-doubt, the need to connect with others amidst feelings of isolation, and the fear of rejection. All this depth is encased within an action-packed adventure where the heroine learns of the power she holds within. Ms. Love presents visions of a utopian world of beauty and peace, where love and acceptance are unconditional. She reaches beyond our cultural and historical norms embracing diversity with no division or hatred.

There are so many profound messages in the *Blade of Truth*, but one strikes me the most—the importance of aligning with our inner truth, not letting outside forces, opinions, or energies get in the way of self-love, our journey, and life purpose. If we are true to ourselves, the world would be a better place."

—Dr. Mario Dell'Olio, Ethics Professor, Author of *New Men*

"It's a relief and a thrill to be back with Jo and the gang. In book two of the stellar Ascending Angel Academy series, the stakes are sky-high. The story sparkles with crystalline clarity as our main character, Jo, continues her celestial education.

With *A Wrinkle in Time* and *The Matrix* vibes, *Blade of Truth* will feed your mind, body, and soul. There is a treasure trove of brilliance here, a wealth of information nestled inside a hugely entertaining tale; it's truly a story to savor.

A cosmic tapestry of science, spirituality, history, and myth weaves the next level of this epic saga. Lali A. Love expands the world and intensifies the battles, gripping the reader with intrigue and action from the very first page. We reunite with old friends and meet many new ones in Jo's beautiful found family. The representation is superb; there is a reflection for every reality. The author champions a revolution in inclusion across the full spectrum of humanity. Her characters are not only diverse; they are accepted, and this acceptance paves the way to normalization.

Lali A. Love threads together brilliant strands of math, music, art, and universal patterns in a genius and ingenious tale of harmonic oneness and existential unity. Jo undergoes a transformation, and you will, too, throughout this book's riveting, restorative transcendence.

Galaxies of wisdom await you. What a stunning, powerful message."

—Halo Scot, Author of the *Rift Cycle Series*

"In book 2, *Blade of Truth*, Jo continues the ascension journey while recovering from a devastating loss. Jo is tasked with the quest of saving Roma, the Custodian of the Galaxy. The challenges Jo and Roma face along with her group of friends form the crux of this YA sci-fi/fantasy adventure. Although the book is a part of a series, it can also be read as a standalone.

The author, Lali A. Love is a fantastic writer with influence and wisdom in her words. Through her powerful prose, she manages to show the reader the power of healing through love, acceptance, and self-realization. She created a captivating, mesmerizing world through this story that feels as real as our everyday life. The author has used a superlative technique of telling this story by combining the spiritual, fantastical, and scientific aspects of writing.

I must also point out the exceptional job of diversity and inclusion in the book. The characters are vivid, talented, and from diverse backgrounds. It was heart-warming to see the author include characters from the LGBTQ+ community without stereotyping or side-lining them. As a YA book, this makes for an excellent read specifically for teenagers battling mental health and self-acceptance issues. If I must describe this book in one word, I will say it is *Entrancing*! If you love reading YA sci-fi/fantasy that leaves you with a powerful message, then this book is a MUST read for you!"

—Rashmi P. Menon, Author, Editor,
Owner of *Confessions of a Writeaholic*

"In this brilliant second installment of the Ascending Angel Academy series, the journey to enlightenment hastens as the eternal struggle between good and evil intensifies. Readers of young adult fantasy will delight in the rich, multidimensional world-building that masterfully intertwines teen angst, struggle, and a higher calling.

The Blade of Truth grabbed me from the first page and, as all good series do, left me wanting more. Our benevolent hero, Jo, skillfully balances her sometimes complex friendships while facing a dark multidimensional seize on the Earth. A tall order, but she is far from the quintessential teenager.

This book is a page-turner, but what shines through is what Lali A. Love does best; inspire, include, and speak truths. You cannot read this book without being energized and optimistic for a better world. Make room on your shelves for this important series."

—S.P. O'Farrell, Author of the *Simone LaFray Mysteries*

"As someone who devours books (fiction and nonfiction) centered on mystical forces, I loved Lali A. Love's newest work. This novel comes after *The Decoding of Jo*, and it is a unique type of sci-fi/fantasy or magical realism. In this book, Jo is enlisted to battle entitles with nefarious intentions for Earth and its citizens. On one level, this book has science fiction overtones because of these bad entities. At the same time, mysticism plays an important role in Love's universe, which could also be classified as magical realism.

The *Blade of Truth* is about young adults and their search for identity and independence. I would also recommend the novel for people who want coming-of-age stories with a mystical focus. In sum, people who enjoy detailed fantasy, and magical realism about astral realm, lucid dreaming, and humanity's role in the larger cosmic context, will likely enjoy Lali A. Love's latest work."

—Anya Pavelle, Author, *The Garden of Stone Houses*

"The absolute journey that I was taken on while reading the *Blade of Truth* had me in awe. Lali A. Love captures every realm of not only the characters and their daily lives, but the journey, both mental and spiritual, that they are on. And she does it in a way that is just gorgeous flowing prose.

This story picks up where the first book left us off and offers enough insight to be comfortably involved in getting right back into it. Jo and her friends are typical high school kids by day, dealing with the serious situations of family dynamics, friend dynamics, teenage alcoholism, drugs, etc. The other half of the story is the enlightened side that captures the truth of situations, of people, of their vulnerabilities and their emotions, and comforts the reader to know that both are working together.

It was a journey that taught me about myself, about what I see in others, and gave me a lot of knowledge of trust in ourselves and our bodies. Again, this was a joy to read, and I can't wait to get my hands on what Ms. Love brings forth next!"

—Ash Knight, Author, *The Gravity of Shooting Stars*

DEDICATION

This book is dedicated to all the brave Star Seeds and Light Warriors that are currently holding space for Mother Earth with love-consciousness. You are powerful, magnetic, free-willed, multi-dimensional beings, whose purpose is to expand into the truth of love and rise to your full potentiality with self-mastery.

"The shadow is merely the illusive absence of light, a catalyst seeking to be acknowledged by your remarkable radiance."
—Lali A. Love

MASTERY

Life is for the living, to embrace the struggle,
Without avoiding or bypassing our emotional rubble.

The pain is an energetic tide that allows us to feel,
Exposing an awareness unseen that needs to heal.

By acknowledging the shifting seasons of our heart,
We drink the potion of recovery that will never depart.

This emotional capacity affects our changing flow,
Riding the surge of conditioning, diminishing the glow.

Our higher self guides the path to this understanding,
Aligning our minds, bodies, and Spirit without branding.

We keep fighting our battles with blades that endure,
We cry a million tears, but our eyes remain pure.

We have been abandoned, rejected, betrayed, and broken,
But we rise, integrating our warrior scars as a token.
A calamity is an experience where we were wronged,
But it is not our entire identity to be prolonged.

The Light has divulged, unearthing our shadows,
Revealing the darkness that feasts on our wallows.

Behold our inner radiance that consumes the night,
Reflecting our innocence and integrity with delight.

We take back our power, combating conformity,
Making choices that don't insult our Soul's uniformity.

Upgrading, releasing, and clearing our density,
With majestic galactic light code intensity.

We honor our strength and truth with gratitude,
Connecting our unified hearts with greater latitude.

Bridging our spheres by respecting Mother Earth,
Entering a new paradise with humanity's rebirth.

We assist our collective journey with gentle peace,
Focusing our heartfelt intentions, breath, and actions with ease.

Evolving our natural balance with harmony and self-love,
We remember our mastery graced by the Creator above.

Lali A. Love

CONTENTS

PROLOGUE

un! The voices in her head thundered as panic took over her entire being. She could barely feel her legs. The weight of the metal fringe bore its cold, jagged claws into her shoulders. Without her sword, Roma was doomed.

The putrid stench of the Draco Lizzies assaulted her senses. She squeezed her eyes shut as forceful arms dragged her battered body along the lush island shrubs. Her powers were weakened by their dark crystals.

These ancient extraterrestrial entities represented the Dark Forces and had finally found her on the Earth plane, proving she could never outrun them. The vicious onslaught by the cold-blooded Lizzies on her beloved planet, Avalon, still haunted her Soul from a parallel timeline.

Welcome to your galactic initiation. Roma had waited lifetimes for this epic battle. As she pondered her past existence on Lemuria, Roma was determined to attract a much favorable outcome in this timeline, to change Goddess Gaia's fate. She would not allow the vile Lizzies to continue their assault on Mother Earth.

The Galactic Council had summoned Roma to help humanity evolve through the density of the fourth-dimensional astral plane, launching the mighty StarSeed Quest.

The Sacred Light had activated millions of enlightened beings known as StarSeeds on Earth, dispensing them with their secret missions. These humans awoke at specific times around the world to remember their higher vibrational Galactic roots.

Each of them lit up with their encoded missions that originated from parallel Universes, star systems, and other planes of existence. Their rise in this timeline was to eradicate the unseen, sinister entity that plagued Mother Earth, and loomed in the shadows, feasting on humanity's negative thoughts, emotional anguish, and rancorous behavior.

Roma knew that the Lizzies were desperate to maintain their dominance over humans—especially after the demise of the Lord of Darkness. Their determination to enslave Gaia and drain her supreme plasma life source was a priority that exceeded all other nefarious agendas.

The Lizzies were unyielding in their plan to further their galactic reach, and so were their relentless attacks. Without any intrusions, they infiltrated planet Earth's fourth-dimensional astral plane.

This realm contained the density of trauma-based reality—an illusory veil of existence with a lower vibrational rate of recurrences. Their fortitude to succeed with their treacherous conspiracy within this timeline triumphed over every other Galactic agenda.

Humanity continued to dwell in the menacing shadows, emitting negative thought forms by involuntarily abdicating their sovereignty. They relinquished their power to the artificial malevolent systems of perceived external realities. This evil existed in the dark aspects of duality that resided within the specters of the physical realms.

As Roma surrendered to her captives, she recalled the story of how these beasts originated within her galaxy.

Approximately five hundred and seventy million years ago, several massive spaceships appeared in the Lyran star system timeline. From the Constellation of Draco, the Alpha Draconis disembarked, causing the Lyrans to be suspicious of the alien beings. The two opposing races that once considered themselves alone in the galaxy were faced with an accidental confrontation.

The Draconis was the first known race in the galaxy that possessed interstellar space travel abilities for four billion years. Once they realized that they had access to the natural resources of the Lyrans, they birthed the desire to conquer and control every similar planet in their path.

As such, with the endorsement of the Dark Forces Program, the Draconis slaughtered millions of Lyrans from Roma's galaxy, destroying innocent civilizations.

The lower-tier Draconis Lizzies, the Ciakar, soon discovered multiple solar systems hosting a variety of phenomenal planets—all of them lush with resources. As a self-serving race operating on a separative principle and fear-based consciousness, they began to view humans as fodder.

The Draconis took control of the space route, and in doing so, they established their dominance on the Galactic transport of resources to Lyra. War ensued—and the Ciakar relished the taste of human flesh.

To further their domination agenda, the Lizzies stripped the nation of all hope and prospect of redemption by enslaving their youth, the divine feminine and masculine Lyrans.

The prisoners were used as sex slaves to breed future generations of the Ciakar broods using various methods of gene manipulations and cloning. This was the advent of the Galactic entanglements and struggles which began the conflict between Light and Dark Forces—humans and Lizzies.

The aftermath of the Lyran-Draconis Galactic War served to be the largest catastrophic event that had occurred in this galaxy—possibly even the entire Universe.

Using the vigorous galactic loopholes, these malicious entities time-traveled to the present-moment reality on Earth in the calendar year twenty nineteen.

Feasting on the trauma-based reincarnation cycles, and karmic looping of perpetual conflict, the Lizzies controlled the collective thought patterns of the fourth-dimensional astral plane with psychic manipulation.

Roma understood the Lizzies were behind the fear-based belief systems, blood rituals, human trafficking, intergalactic slave trade, and childhood-wounding programming matrices. The chemical compound adrenochrome, released during mass human suffering, provided these entities with enhanced psychic capabilities upon consumption. Since they were missing this organic life force energy, the invaluable external source was crucial for their endurance.

As such, the Lizzies were determined to prevent Gaia and humanity to shift and cross over the ethereal bridge, into the fifth-dimensional love-consciousness existence of Sacred Light, where their powers would become futile.

Roma vowed to never allow the same horrific history of her beloved home to repeat itself, not in this timeline. She was summoned by the Lemurian High Council to drive out the dark shadows and protect sacred Goddess Gaia from extinction.

After all, she was a celestial delegate of the higher intelligence quantum Source energy—a cosmic survivor, a Warrior of Light, a Custodian of the Galaxy, and the defender of StarSeeds.

In captivity, Roma commenced the light code activation, a beacon, that would reach the Lyran High Council. Without her Blade of Truth, she had no choice but to surrender to her destiny and began channeling her location telepathically to the StarSeeds, Indigo Children, and Celestial Earth Angels.

Roma prayed to all that was pure and holy that the high-pitched sound waves were undetected by the demonic, callous Lizzies and their evil leader, Ciakar, the Wizard of Bondage.

This will not be the end, so help me Ka-ha-lee!

CHAPTER 1
THE RISE

"Who looks outside, dreams. Who looks inside, awakens."
— CARL JUNG

Jo

I gazed in shock and utter bewilderment. The Council of Creation spoke to me in light codes as my ethereal form transformed with iridescent light wings. I couldn't believe I graduated from the Hall of Ignorance during my first stage of the Ascending Angel Academy.

It had been a tough battle, but it was worth every ounce of nervous energy. With the help of my friends, I had succeeded in my mission of rescuing my classmates by vanquishing the Lord of Darkness into another dimension. The struggle between Light and Dark was unnerving.

Thank goodness the pressure of the terrifying experience had lifted when my classmates were saved from enslavement as sleepwalkers within the elusive matrix.

"Your journey has just begun, dear beloved. If you choose to continue into the Hall of Truth and Learning, your cosmic powers will accelerate at higher octaves on the Earth plane. You must go through each of the initiation processes to fully accept your own mastery, Jo. You have successfully completed the activation stage with grace. The next two levels of integration and embodiment will challenge your ability to tap into the healing energy of Angelic forces."

The Council paused as I diligently observed their every move. "It is time for you to recognize that we are agents of Divine authority stepping back in time to visit ourselves, and we commend you for saving humanity from the Lord of Darkness."

The illustrious Council embodied the celestial representations of many star systems that exemplified the Galactic Light. They were Ascending Masters, Spirit Guides, Galactic Shamans, and the Custodians of the Great Cosmos.

They were responsible for transmitting plasma light infusions through their energetic portals, advocating unity and love-based consciousness for our Solar System, including Earth.

I was so excited to discover these higher-dimensional beings during my Galactic initiation. Their prime objective was to help humanity and planet Earth evolve from the duality, trauma-based physical existence, into higher states of conscious perception.

They offered guidance for all sentient beings on planet Earth to anchor, receive, and emit heart-based frequencies of love in the zero-point neutral state, into the quantum magnetic field of oneness.

The Council was upgrading humanity with light codes, empowering our collective awakenings and Soul-based remembrance. They provided introspective modalities for daily meditative practices to help connect our spirits back to Source, revealing magical spiritual realms.

Some of the information of existence were seeded in my awareness through downloads, to assist with specific cosmic missions. I regarded them as precious gifts of revered knowledge, which were released slowly within my DNA, contingent on my elevated state of heart coherence.

It was the connection to Spirit that I had always craved on a deeper level. This allowed me to become more mindful of the negative thought patterns and survival hormones that didn't serve my higher truth and purpose in my daily life.

My celestial lesson on Earth was to help me remember this aspect of my essence by healing my traumatized human ego, which operated from conditioned beliefs and external attachments through self-centered desires.

As they concluded their communications, I marveled at their beauty and elegance. Their auras radiated loving energy of pure wholeness that surrounded me like a warm, cozy blanket. They faced me directly and removed their illuminating masks. I gasped in astonishment and disbelief.

They all looked like me!

The Council mirrored my physical resemblance since they were a representation of my higher self, an eternal, unified omnipotent intelligence that transformed all my physical lives in every timeline.

The shock of this knowledge woke me instantly in the safety of my bed, my heart thudding out of my chest. It was another night filled with lucid dreams. I was only recalling the incident of the time travel when I visited the Council over six weeks ago.

I hadn't experienced any downloads since that occasion. I felt relieved for the time out—winter break could not have come fast enough.

I needed some time to process the events of our first semester. I never imagined my experiences from grade ten would be so ethereal and psychologically charged. I had to quickly learn to manage my emotional reactions with contemplative tools and practices after the devastating loss of my friend, Rey.

The emotive triggers were an opportunity for me to elevate and connect with my inner power, which enabled me to transform my human Light Body into an ethereal form to travel beyond the physical planes—using my Galactic Compass.

Who knew that the basement in my high school's library harbored a holographic portal with access to a black hole? The event led me to this incredible discovery of my celestial powers and the rich history of the Ascending Masters.

In my first phase of Ascension, I embraced my galactic mission. I had to obtain the light codes needed to secure the Akashic Records and decode the artificial matrix where the Lord of Darkness had enslaved the minds of my classmates—the sleepwalkers. It had been quite a feat to forgive the actions, the horrific assault of the bullies and the mean girls.

Thank goodness for my best friends, Nisha, Daphne, Zax, and Flynn. I could not have survived the encounters without their tenacity and assistance. They were instrumental in my mission's success, and I cherished their unconditional love and unyielding support with my entire heart.

The intensity of my headaches had been unbearable as I continued to process my human upgrades. The pain had enabled me to clearly examine the matrix grid of toxic programming, karmic debris, and all limitation scripts running our world.

The absorption of my higher Soul expression and increased sensory perception allowed me to merge the cellular template of my physical, emotional Light Body with the innate wisdom held within my higher-dimensional master field.

My mind wandered back to the moment I found the courage to divulge my celestial experiences to my best friend Nisha.

"What in the world are you talking about?" Nisha remarked, staring at me as if I had two heads.

"It was incredible, Nish!" I responded. "I have discovered extraordinary powers of intuition, astral projection, and time travel through the twelve cosmic dimensions! They were like these amazing, holographic spheres, these orbs of light. I can't even explain its magnificence!" I shouted in excitement as she backed away from me in confusion.

"Okay…so does that mean that you have magical powers?" she asked with curiosity and disbelief.

"Yup, I learned how to teleport from one location to another. As long as I have my galactic compass on me, I can travel through time and space!" I closed my eyes and within a millisecond, I appeared behind her out of thin air.

I tapped Nisha on the shoulder. She jumped in bafflement. "Oh my gosh…how did you do that, Jo? This is so freaking cool!" she squealed with delight.

It was such an extraordinary feeling to find the courage to share my mysterious secrets with the rest of my friends. Having their assistance on my quest meant the world to me, especially knowing that I was not alone on this peculiar, ethereal mission.

My celestial powers grew throughout my initiation phase. I obtained and used the cosmic plasma source of the Akashic Records as my friends helped me battle the sleepwalkers to prevent the Lord of Darkness from demolishing the Light. Otherwise, all of humanity would have been enslaved into a third dimensional matrix of darkness and oppression.

Thinking back to that fateful day during the school's Winter Formal Dance, it all felt so surreal. The fire instigated by the sleepwalkers had severely damaged our gymnasium, but thankfully, no one else had been hurt. During the epic battle of good versus evil, I developed a deep appreciation and gratitude for my gift of music. Using harmonic healing frequencies and my sound system at the formal dance, brought peace and concord to the chaotic environment.

I had to admit, it was the best DJ gig of my life!

My entire focus over the past few weeks had been on my music. I tried to hang out with Nisha and Daphne as much as possible, keeping Zax company while Flynn rehabilitated for six weeks. For once, I was hopeful that he would overcome his addictions and reckless behavior.

Unfortunately, past experiences didn't miraculously heal my friends from their anxiety and depression. The truth was that Daphne continued to struggle with her eating disorder, but she was more aware of the triggers. I couldn't be prouder of her. Daphne took back her power and worked tirelessly on her worth with self-love and emotional healing.

Nisha was my anchor, my strength, and my guiding light. Facing her truth liberated her from feelings of anger, guilt, shame, and sabotage. She felt empowered to be her authentic self and had since become an incredible role model among her peers.

I loved my friends and felt a deep sense of gratitude every morning for their soulful connections.

"Excuse me, some of us have lives, you know!" Liz yelled, banging boisterously on the bathroom door.

"Calm down! Give me a few minutes, Liz. You don't even live here anymore." I replied as my older sister giggled under her breath—she knew exactly how to push my buttons.

Liz was staying at home to prepare for her upcoming university exams. It seemed like campus life got a little too chaotic at times.

"You're acting like this is your first time in this house. You know damn well there's another bathroom on the other side of the floor. Why aren't you using that one?" I teased her.

"I couldn't haul everything from campus, could I? Besides, we use the same type of shampoo." Liz maintained a half-smirk as she nudged me out of the way and rushed into the bathroom, slamming the door behind her.

Despite being four years younger, I felt more mature than my sister. After what I had been through, I gained decades of wisdom and incredible discernment. I went through a magnificent quantum leap in my ascension journey, bending the very fabric of time and space.

Over the past few months, I discovered something crucial. For most of my life, I had operated from a space of unconsciousness, where I identified with my egoistic narratives, my mindset, and limiting perceptions perpetuated by society. This rigid and fixed belief system drove my thoughts, emotional intelligence, and behaviors, stemming from an overactive and fragile survival-based ego and identity.

When I finally developed an awareness of this perceived reality, I began to practice self-observation and realized that my thoughts or mindset did not define my true essence. This fundamental understanding was incredibly profound when I discovered that I was more than just physical matter. All material creations that I could see, hear, taste, smell, and touch came from the same source of energy.

Enlightenment taught me that consciousness was the infinite life force within the unified field that was beyond the familiarity of the five senses of the physical world.

With this knowledge, I unearthed the power of boundless originality through my creativity, the conditions to manifest different experiences according to varying sensory perception.

I learned that all reality was governed by masculine and feminine energy consciousness within every human. The balance of the brain on both sides triggered the opening of the pineal gland. Since I had always been a pragmatist, I required a logical and scientific understanding of my metamorphosis.

From a biological perspective, this tiny gland located between my brows produced melatonin, a neurotransmitter hormone responsible for regulating sleep and wakening phases.

This intelligence further demonstrated the interconnectedness with all things within the cosmos, providing a correlation between my body and spirit.

With this insight, my neurons were completely re-wired, decrypting my DNA through enlightenment, initiation, and harmony. Upon graduation from the first stage of the Ascending Angel Academy, I was equipped with the full potentiality to temper and balance the edges of the collective human life force emissions.

I realized that life in the third dimension was measured by experiences that were set into motion by time. This elusive observed phenomenon was merely a construct since time was linear, calculated by day and night cycles. We based it on the period planet Earth required to circle the sun in a flowing continuum, moving along in its trajectory. This was how we recorded environmental changes on our planet.

I was always diligent in my practice to ensure that I didn't get caught in the daily grind and conflict of the physical realm, routinely stopping to appreciate the present moments consistently aligning my heart, mind, and Soul in stillness.

I understood the Universal Law of Vibration quite well. This energy encompassed all fundamental forces, gravity, strong and weak nuclear forces, and electromagnetism, which was predominately light.

The infinite mandala-creating Universe was a magnetic hologram, formed by geometric laws of light. And light particles could be converted into motions, cycles, vibrations, and electricity. My feelings and emotional reactions were the conscious awareness of these specific pulsations within the present moment of experience.

I also grasped that time could be perceived as a movement of thought and memory continuity, using the ego as the eternal reference point. Once I broke through the barrier of the personality, I began to experience the unseen spiritual time.

This was the stillness I maintained daily, attempting to remain impartial, regardless of how much linear time had passed. Every morning, I acknowledged the likelihood that I could be activated at any moment for the next phase of my ascension mission.

A nervous flutter thumped in my chest as I compelled myself to drink some water. The coolness eased the dryness in the back of my throat. I preserved my true self, without any masks—pure, vulnerable, everlasting, and constantly flowing. I was an immortal being.

Immortal.

I would have never used that word six months ago, let alone understood its significance. Every choice I made as a human—breathing the fresh, crisp air of vitality—determined my ascension path. At least I had the freedom to choose, and for that, I was extremely grateful.

Although my mind wandered to recollect my knowledge and downloads provided by the Council, I pulled over to text Nisha that I was parked outside her house.

"Yo! What's up with you?" she yelled. "Took you long enough to get here." Nisha broke my concentration as she sat in the front seat of my beamer. "I suck at physics, and you know that, Jo. I can't afford to get a late slip—I'm not smart like you." Nisha said, reprimanding my tardiness.

"Girl, please! You're a freaking genius and I guarantee that we're not going to be late," I replied as we set off.

"How was your night with your special friend?" I asked with a grin. My excitement over Nisha's date was written all over my face. "Come on, give me the tea!"

"Oh, please! It was hardly a date. We just studied, that's all... It was good, though," Nisha replied, turning her head toward the window. I witnessed the look on her face, as her smile reflected on the side-view mirror. She couldn't help but blush with exhilaration.

Nisha became quite fond of a band member, Alicia, a talented musician who played the violin. Her twin brother, Theo, also in our band, was a master on the electric bass. I briefly recalled that Rey was never comfortable with Theo, but I never did understand their reason. Perhaps it had something to do with how confident Theo was in his sexuality as a transgender male.

I sensed Alicia had romantic feelings for Nisha as well, and the thought of my best friend finding her first love melted my heart.

"Changing topics," Nisha said, "What about you and Conrad, Jo? When are you going to sleep with the poor guy? It's been months. You're blue-balling the life out of him."

"There's no rush, Nish. I'm just taking my time." I replied. "When I'm ready, it will happen." As much as I adored Conrad, I was not certain if I wanted an intimate relationship. After all, we were only sixteen and had all the time in the world. Ever since I was young, my mother had coaxed me to treat my body as a sacred temple for my spirit.

As we drove up to Daphne's house, I heard a faint whisper calling my name. The rustling in my ear puzzled me, so I parked my car on the side of the road.

"Did you say something, Nish?" I asked in confusion.

"About Conrad?" Nisha asked.

"No, I heard someone whisper my name…wait! There it is again!" I turned off the music and focused my attention on my third eye.

All that practice on sharpening my pineal gland to strengthen the power of my telekinesis seemed to be taking effect. The hair on my arms tingled as the goosebumps grew in anticipation. The faint voice spoke again.

"Can you hear me? I need your help!"

I took deep breaths to calm my nerves. "Okay, so, remember I told you that it's been like six weeks since I had a download?" I asked. "Well, I think I just got the call, Nish."

Nisha's face lit up in astonishment, "What do you mean the call? The Council has downloaded your next mission?" She seemed nervous

11

and excited at the prospect of another unknown event that was about to occur in our teenage lives.

"I'm receiving a telepathic message, but I don't understand who or what it's for, to be honest. But someone is in trouble, of that I am certain." Just as I finished my sentence, Daphne hopped into the back seat of my car.

"Hey ladies. How's everyone today? Are you excited about band practice? I can't wait for our spring performance at the Annual Sleep Fest." Without catching her breath, she quickly turned toward Nisha and said, "Oh wow, Nish, I love what you're wearing! Your septum piercing really ties it all together! Anyway, what did I miss? I—Jo, is something wrong?"

Daphne's vitality seemed to diminish with every word as I filled her in. I couldn't help but wonder what type of event was about to ensue as we barely made our first class of the second semester.

I instinctively knew that my little break from the Ascending Angel Academy was over.

❖ ❖ ❖

Daphne

Daphne had learned so much from Jo over the past few months. She was completely in awe of her best friend's strength and devotion to her Angel Academy mission.

She helped Daphne establish a daily practice of inner work meditation, alchemizing her pain into love for herself one step at a time. It was important for Daphne to reflect on her upbringing and explore the trauma buried deep in her subconsciousness.

The assault she had suffered at the high school party before the winter break, compounded her abandonment issues. Daphne's Soul split from the violation of her innocence, refusing to acknowledge the discord and fragmentation.

It was an incredibly difficult and scary path to revisit her memories. But Daphne needed to find the courage to face the pain to commence her healing process. It was the only way for her to liberate herself from the cruelty and suffering she had endured.

Although her mother did the best that she could as a single parent, Daphne craved stability and guidance from a father figure.

Daphne neglected her emotional needs, repressing her feelings of abandonment from her younger years. This manifested into sentiments of low self-esteem and self-worth that most likely contributed to her poor nutrition and eating disorder.

Jo provided a safe, judgment-free zone, a loving environment for Daphne to express her authentic thoughts, acknowledging and honoring her pain. She encouraged Daphne to articulate her suffering without criticism, enabling a breakthrough in her healing journey.

As she sat in the back of the car listening to Jo's next mission, she couldn't help but reflect on their crazy celestial experiences. Jo's words, sprouting with every prompt as they chilled one night, binging on a series, were etched on Daphne's mind.

"Daph, it's okay to feel scared or sad. And if you want to go punch a bag to let the anger out, I'll come with you. Goodness knows I need to release some steam!" Jo laughed.

"Are you sure? I don't want to bring you down, Jo. Nobody likes a negative, air-sucking whiner," Daphne responded.

"First of all, you are not a whiner. I am here for you because I love you, Daph. Look at me and all my flaws. I'm a mess, one foot in the human world and the other in the cosmos. You wouldn't want me to stop sharing my feelings with you right?" Jo asked.

"Of course not, Jo. You better tell me every detail about your cosmic predicaments!" Daphne teased.

"You are so special to me, Daph. Honestly, you have the most incredible, kind heart. Of all the billions of Souls, we have connected at this moment to experience life together. How lucky am I?" Jo expressed her gratitude, wearing her emotions on her sleeve.

"You're incredible as well Jo, I couldn't manage high school without you, honestly! I just wish I could find a healthy, happy relationship like you and Nisha seem to have with Conrad and Alicia." Daphne sulked, her body language projecting her self-deprecating beliefs and inadequacy-based mentality.

"Daph, you don't need anyone else to make you feel worthy or fulfilled. You can fill that void with your self-discovery. Don't forget, as humans we tend to attract situations, people, or things that validate our views. We don't want to sabotage ourselves from a dualistic space, emitted from negative neurons. First and foremost, you need to recognize your value and demonstrate self-love and kindness. We also need to remember to be mindful of our words and memories; they carry a distinct energetic signal. So, speak what your heart desires, and before you know it, you will magnetize that same frequency of love into your reality," Jo reiterated as Daphne tried to grasp the concept of self-actualization.

"You are so worthy of joy and all the luminosity of the stars and the moon combined, Daph," Jo persisted by holding her in a warm embrace. "I truly feel blessed that you trust me with your feelings. We have each other to lean on, always. You put up with my celestial confidences, and I couldn't do it without you and our friends."

Daphne felt grateful to have forged such a deep, soulful connection with her best friend. She continued her mindful practices with positive affirmations of self-love, acceptance, and developed a deep reconnection with her inner child.

Jo explained how Daphne's innocence replayed the loop program of pain and suffering since she continued to focus her narrative on the traumatic events, reliving the hurt unknowingly. By forgiving her absentee father, she released herself from the perpetuated heartache of the past.

Daphne permitted herself to feel everything she had craved from a father figure through vulnerability, including holding compassion in her heart for everyone she loved.

After all, Daphne realized that real relationships were not about forming long-term, egocentric, narcissistic attachments in misery and numbness. Once she learned to love and value herself wholly, Daphne's heart desired to establish a similar bond with another person—a partnership based on improving and celebrating each other, that resulted in a thriving, collaborative union.

❖ ❖ ❖

Jo

My high school, Forest Hill Academy was a preppy co-ed private school for privileged scholars, funded by old money in Toronto's wealthy district. The annual tuition ranged from twelve to twenty thousand dollars, depending on whether the student attended the advanced programs.

The school flourished financially and attempted to give back to the community by providing subsidies for students who couldn't afford the yearly fees. While academics were a high priority for the institution, the school also placed an intense focus on extracurricular activities such as sports, music, and the arts.

The faculty boasted of hiring the best, most qualified teachers compared to the public systems. However, the rigid educational structure was outdated from its initial standardization over sixty years ago.

Many of our classes required us to memorize information that was only useful for the massive amounts of archaic testing. The undiversified content didn't really prepare us for adulthood or higher education as required for the innovative twenty-first century.

Most of the students in our privileged institution were unchallenged, and the old problem-solving techniques to address truancy, classroom disorder, and passive resistance were failing under the male-controlled leadership of our principal, Mr. Grey.

"Excuse me, Ms. Rolland." Nisha raised her arm in defiance in our history class. "There are only ten history books on the syllabus for this term."

"Yes, Nisha, is it? I expect a review in the form of a synopsis for each one before the end of the school year," Ms. Rolland replied, lips pursed. She was new to our school.

Nisha continued her grievance. "I'm just wondering why we are reading literature that is predominantly written from a white male perspective. Am I to expect the one black author to serendipitously crop up just in time for Black History Month?"

The entire class broke out in laughter at her eruption. Pulling in a shallow breath, I glanced back at my best friend, who had found her voice, fighting against patriarchy. I was both proud and nervous for her while the teacher searched for her words carefully.

"I don't appreciate your tone, young lady. What exactly are you implying?" Ms. Rolland retorted with a tinge of coolness.

"I'm extremely serious about my education, Ms. Rolland. You may be new to Forest Hill Academy, but you need to understand that it is not my wish to adopt an ideology based on the outdated, irrelevant point of view," Nisha said, barely blinking.

"I feel that it is eradicating my voice and my heritage as immaterial. As such, I am informing you that this curriculum does not stimulate me intellectually," she concluded.

Scanning the room, I felt the temperature rise as my classmates snickered at Nisha's boldness. Unease bloomed in the pit of my stomach, sensing an energy shift around me. It had a vaguely familiar eerie texture that I recognized from defeating the Lord of Darkness.

"I will not tolerate disrespectful outbursts and showboating in my classroom at the expense of your peers, Nisha. You have been warned," Ms. Rolland sternly replied, while diverting her eyes to another student. "Yes, Alicia?"

"With respect Ms. Rolland, I agree with Nisha. I am also concerned about my subconscious consumption of the white privilege superiority viewpoint," Alicia said. "Also, may I be excused? I'm experiencing my monthly cramps." She chuckled, winking at Nisha.

"That's enough! I think this surprise pop quiz should keep you all very stimulated," Ms. Rolland countered. "It's worth fifteen percent of your final grade."

The whole class conveyed their complaint loudly. We weren't prepared for the test, but I deeply admired Nisha's tenacity to state the obvious conditioning of our outdated educational systems.

As we answered the questions in silence, I couldn't help but reflect on my previous ethereal lessons that helped me emerge from my state of obliviousness. The academic curriculum of my posh private school paled in comparison to the celestial transcendent teachings and downloads that I genuinely craved for my ascension.

My initiation was quite an awakening as I crumbled with teenage angst while barely passing the first semester of tenth grade.

The Council was primarily governed by a galactic Society of Light Beings that were the flawless expressions of the unified Source energy. They directed the higher truths of the Universe and were the guardians of the Akashic Records, where every Soul's existence and imprint were archived.

I had discovered that originally, these higher plasma Light Beings emerged from the star cluster located in the constellation of Taurus the Bull. They existed within the twelfth dimensional astral plane of celestial wisdom that included the Pleiadeans, Lyrans, and Arcturus beings. They were the keepers of the Sacred Light and regulated the peace agreements throughout the Galactic Union.

As I reflected on my time-travel experiences, I couldn't help but yearn for that familiar feeling of belonging within these higher realms that boasted the radiance of the Cosmos.

The Pleiades were also known as the Seven Sisters. It was the brightest and most radiant of star clusters located near planet Earth. They performed a significant role in humanity's advancement, as they continued to guide our planet through the ascent from the third-dimensional density.

I marveled at the supreme intelligence that existed within every living organism on our planet. If each human could realize their supernatural potential, I was convinced that we would live in a different reality, projected by our collective experiences.

I recalled the Council's explanation about humanity's amnesia.

"Every Soul embodies the knowledge of Creation, which is forgotten at the arrival into your human vessel. This is for your protection and well-being in the third-dimensional existence."

"In the beginning, there was the eternal, infinite Light of Love frequency Source, the Prime Creator, who had always been aware of its ever-expansive and creative intelligence. As an expression of that oneness, a colony of energetic forms were created for that Source to interact with itself, as the clear and absolute reality."

"Is it true that every Soul reincarnates back to Earth to continue their lessons?" I inquired, eager to learn about humanity's true origin.

"Yes, that is called the Oversoul; it's the first place each state of consciousness travels from Source into form and is returned to the Pleiades before going back home to the Source," they said, continuing their teachings.

"We, the Pleiadeans, have evolved as a Society of Light Beings intending to experience and feel like the Source energy. We have progressed to reach a certain level of consciousness as clear reflections of the Prime Creator. To play in this realm, Source transformed one of our Light Beings, Goddess Gaia, into a holographic planet known as Earth."

I continued to absorb the intelligent downloads like a sponge.

"The intention was that this energy of our civilization would enter the atmosphere of planet Earth like a Golden Ray, connecting us to the holographic planet. To cover a wide surface area of the Earth plane, the Light energy formed into a third-dimensional polarity, divided into two equal parts that sprinkled the energy into the soil. This new civilization began to accelerate quickly and had to upgrade their consciousness to absorb our Pleiades vitality. This rate of recurrence became encoded in the cells and the atoms of the human DNA as they began their celestial and cosmic upgrade process."

The Council transferred the information, and I was enraptured by this sacred knowledge. It was a far cry from anything I had learned in our school system.

"When our civilization entered Earth in a different form, we provided enhancements and energetically transferred new frequencies and technologies into the hard-wired DNA of the collective human experience. To cover more surface area of the planet, one section of Earth carried divine masculine energy, and the other section of Earth carried divine feminine energy. Over time, that masculine energy evolved into the Atlantis society, an advanced civilization centered in technology and power. As a result of the negative charge and imbalance, the overly masculine manifestation perished."

I listened intently, recognizing the fate of the fabled lost city of Atlantis, as the Council continued to transmit their invaluable wisdom into my ethereal form.

"The sacred feminine energy of planet Earth formed a family of wholesome Society of beings, called Lemuria, filled with harmony and mysticism. To ensure balance, they were disintegrated into a microcosmic model, and the two energies cross-pollinated throughout the world to form the Ancient Egyptian civilization."

"Humans were the living aspect of the Prime Creator, to experience their true nature as multidimensional expressions of spirit. Humanity went through many incarnation cycles to discover their true potential through endless lifetimes. In your world, the result of male and female fragmented energies began to integrate into their Light Bodies, to become known as relationships."

As I recollected these transmissions very clearly, I realized their value and the effectiveness of the coded data for my next mission.

"Too many humans are caught up in the external, material struggle of life. They will perceive this evolution as a time of desolation, sadness, and despair. But don't dismay, dear one. The mindset of the industrial age will not fail to provide the wisdom required for the collective evolution. This integration of mind, body, and spirit will elevate humanity's emotional bodies toward clarity, truth, and opportunity for growth."

The Council further clarified for me that as a sentient being, the mission to progress through the three stages of celestial ascent was my choice and entirely consensual. I couldn't wait to integrate with my genuine Higher Self.

I affirmed my commitment, acknowledging my duty and intention before commencing my second path through the Ascending Angel Academy.

"I devote my Soul's eternal existence to serve the Sacred Light, with truth, compassion, forgiveness, hope, and peace throughout the Universe."

As I time-travelled back through the cosmos, I remembered the most incredible mystical and surreal experience of my entire existence. I was lucky enough to have witnessed the five spheres of Creation. The sheer beauty, radiance, and magic of the Planetary, Solar, Galactic,

Universal, and Cosmic spheres enveloped my entire being with the presence of the Prime Creator.

It completely removed any previous doubts of higher intelligence, the power of Divine Source, that presented itself as a deep resonance of pure bliss.

When I closed my eyes and focused on my breath, I was able to feel the majestic and magnificent blueprint of the ultraviolet blue and violet rays emanating from the Galactic Sun frequency.

In this dreamscape, I floated into the center of the spheres, and I noticed a circuit made from plasma light transmitters. They resembled a holographic numeric dial pad, using the three-six-nine ratios. I instinctively entered the downloaded light codes with my mind, without touching the iridescent light.

The numbers 1113, 1111, 1110, and 444 transmitted by the Council simultaneously shifted the astronomical, interstellar plates of the five spheres of creation. A tiny archetype was revealed in the shape of a hexagram hidden within the circuit. This modest representation of humanity's existence completely shocked me.

It consisted of seven overlapping circles resembling the most magnificent twinkling stars with the same diameter. Six of the circles were regularly spaced within the seventh, producing a rosette-shaped petal. That's where I found the secret location of the Akashic Records.

I realized that the sacred archives were a representation of unified consciousness that contained a vibrational profile of every Soul throughout its incarnation cycles since the beginning of time.

This hexagon of light spheres represented the seed of life as a recurrent archetypal pattern of creation, which manifested all fractal reality. I was completely enamored by its ultimate expression of the geometry of vibration. It included the wave interference patterns of light, electromagnetism, and sound forms, found throughout all scales, from atoms to minerals, vegetables, flowers, fruits, and galaxies.

I couldn't believe that I held humanity's existence in the palm of my unearthly hand! I gently hid the radiant, powerful archives inside the chamber of my transcendent Galactic Medallion. I fiercely protected its location from the clutches of the Lord of Darkness or any other malevolent force that desired its powers.

As I sat in my History class, reflecting, I stared blankly at my completed quiz. I anticipated my next mission into the Hall of Learning with veracity and a ferocious appetite. Suddenly, this projection sparked a surge within my intuitive energetic field found in my pineal gland.

This was the sixth spinning color wheel within my electromagnetic vortex of light that every human embodied on Earth. It was a representation of the Soul's energetic vibration based on the level of awareness. It projected with radiance within my mind's eye as a purple hue from the cosmic reel, governing the door to higher dimensionality.

The light codes embedded by the Council began to harmonize and awaken my inner aspects of Source, unifying my fourth field within my center. This generated a heart-mind coherence that acted as a bridge to anchor in new timelines.

While I calmly waited for the lunch bell to ring, I prepared for the next wave of oscillation within my energetic vortex. Scanning the room, I made sure no one was paying attention to me as my Light Body went through another crystalline upgrade—detaching from separation and distorted co-dependent identification narratives that created toxic templates within the matrix.

As I quietly purged these dense patterns lingering within my cellular memory banks and the collective subliminal programs, a labyrinth of autonomy and retrieval codes from the Source blueprint recalibrated my being with tiny electrical currents.

No matter what obstacles lingered in my path, I vowed to remain faithful to the mission and rise to the challenge. My instinctive radar alerted me to prepare for the next stage of my ascension and mastery—without knowing the details, I felt its potency within every fiber of my human container. A battle of epic cosmic proportions was about to arise.

❖   ❖   ❖

"My world it moves so fast today, the past it seems so far away. And life squeezes so tight that I can't breathe."—The Miseducation of Lauryn Hill by Lauryn Hill

CHAPTER 2

RAINBOW BRIDGE

"Music is the mediator between the spiritual and the sensual life."
— LUDWIG VAN BEETHOVEN

Jo

I couldn't sleep last night. I meditated until my anxious energy subsided. The expectation of the foreboding unknown kept me on high alert. Somehow, I floated through first-period Physics and found myself back in Ms. Rolland's history class.

I was in no mood to learn about Napoleon's war strategies. My mind drifted to my energetic upgrades that had occurred over the past three months.

Was I really that different?

I felt like the same person, had the same basic physical appearance, apart from possessing intense intuitive powers. It was incredible how much I had grown and matured spiritually.

After every transmission and upgrade, my human vessel projected physical symptoms as I expanded my auric field with light frequencies. The pain within my crown and brow area increased with every download. This pressure intensified immensely with every celestial expansion of my consciousness, but I managed to breathe through the tension.

I noticed a distinct strain in my heart. It continued to open pathways to plasma waves as I detached from externalized validation projections. The metallic taste in my mouth indicated an energy recalibration within my solar plexus to align with electromagnetic shifts.

This often made me nauseous and wobbly as my sensations aligned to the powerful gravitational fluctuations. It triggered some of my old feelings of annoyance, releasing the inner teenage self-sabotage programs.

The high pitch in my ears further amplified with every DNA upgrade. I focused my breath on my third eye as I exhaled gratitude for the knowledge. It wasn't pleasant, but every time I experienced these sensations, it was another opportunity for me to elevate my psychic abilities and connect with my celestial being.

Ever since my awakening, I had been careful in managing my emotions. I refused to allow anything, or anyone, to break my inner peace. I decided to divert my attention from negativity since it only brought me down from my heightened perspective. I no longer resonated with feelings of hate, gossip, or judgment.

After all, the opposite of love-consciousness was fear, a disempowering, shrinking and contracting energy. It was the absence of Divine truth that existed from the choice and acceptance of a reality based on deception, manipulation, lies, and illusions.

Sometimes, this ascension made it difficult for me to enjoy normalcy in my youthful years, surrounded by hormonal, moody teenagers. I became a magnet, attracting their emotional density.

Yup, I am a full-blown empath.

I had to continuously remind myself that, energetically, our entire reality was founded on archaic and divisive belief systems, perceptions, traumas, and childhood conditioning. This facilitated the occupation of a different version of life by each Soul, depending on the frequencies emitted within our existence.

It was so fascinating to me that the unified Source, the Prime Creator, provided each Soulful expression a unique Universe to manifest distinctive experiences based on our awareness and projection.

The underlying essence of this creative force expanded our state of being. Pure love was whole, and it magnified, increased, and blossomed our consciousness towards greater levels of self-awareness, a remembrance of our true nature and the world we inhabited.

As my mind continued to roam, whatever little concentration I had about the Napoleonic era immediately disappeared when I heard it again—the faint whisper.

"Can you hear me, Jo? Focus your attention on this frequency range. My name is Roma, I'm on a StarSeed Quest, and I need your help. Tune into my signal, please!"

The Council wouldn't communicate with me through ESP. They only provided downloads with light code data. I shifted with trepidation in my seat, hoping that Ms. Rolland wouldn't notice. I closed my eyes and tried to focus on the voice. Unfortunately, silence was the only thing that followed.

I continued to ponder over the nature of the message. My phone, which I hid on my lap, began to vibrate. I had to be careful—I didn't want to get caught breaking the rules.

The teachers were strict about the "no phones during class" policy. I looked around to see if anyone was looking. Fortunately, the coast was clear, and everyone was half-asleep listening to the boring history lecture.

I discreetly slid my hand down to unlock my phone and noticed a message from Zax in the group chat.

"Hey, guys. Flynn gets back home today, and I am super excited to throw a little homecoming party for him. Don't be late, it's a surprise!"

This had totally slipped my mind. Zax told me like a dozen times that I was in charge of providing the decorations and the snacks.

Unexpectedly, the cold, piercing voice of our new history teacher jolted me in place. "Are we keeping you from something important, Josephine?"

The last thing I wanted today was to lose my phone. "Sorry, Ms. Rolland. It won't happen again."

She glared at me intensely. There was something mysterious about her aura. For some reason, I couldn't read Ms. Rolland's energy.

"Let this be your first and last warning, Josephine. In fact, for everyone. If I see any of you using your cellphones during class, I will confiscate them, and don't expect to see them again until the end of the semester!"

My classmates glared at me with contempt. Someone tossed over a note with terrible penmanship. *Way to go, Jo. Thanks for ruining it for everyone.* They all looked pissed.

A strange awareness brushed over me, starting as a stinging sensation along the back of my neck. It increased with every passing second. I felt like I was being scrutinized, but by whom?

I tried to concentrate on my lesson, but my mind diverted to our history teacher. Something about Ms. Rolland didn't sit right with me. I couldn't quite put my finger on it, but she emitted a rather precarious presence. I secretly sought to search her on the internet, but there was no digital trace of her existence.

She was a tall, slender woman probably in her mid-fifties. A sharp dresser, always prim and proper, with her dark hair slicked back in a tight bun and eyes intense enough to put Medusa to shame.

I attempted to read the aura surrounding her energy fields to determine her true nature. This intuitive gift aligned me with people, spaces, and situations. I understood why colors were associated with emotions. Red represented anger, white meant tranquility, blue signified a glum outlook, dark green implied a jealous streak, black with a purplish hue denoted a feeling of anxiousness, depression, and so on.

Even if I didn't recognize the significance of a particular hue, I felt the energetic resonance that the person emanated, with specific tones and textures. If their emotions changed in a moment, so did their dynamic field.

Unfortunately, Ms. Rolland only emitted a neutral hue of grayish white—no emotion, which was quite perplexing.

Despite my best efforts, my mind continued to stray toward my pineal gland. I couldn't help but recall my studies about the brain inside this biological computer of my emotional Light Body.

I found the human anatomy to be quite remarkable, teeming with unseen intelligence. The celestial lessons have taught me that my consciousness was everything in the virtual hologram of my experiences. This was brought into awareness by my brain that was forever viewing streaming codes of knowledge and interpretation. It was almost like watching a movie, projected on a large HD screen.

But what is telepathy, and how does it work, exactly? Is it like tuning into a radio station?

I pondered this thought as I searched online for its definition. I was amazed at what I found. It seemed that this psychic phenomenon was much more common than I initially realized.

Someone had been trying to communicate with me from a considerable distance. I wondered if this person belonged to an advanced society from an Alternate Universe or timeline that was harnessing mystical and psychic abilities known as premonition and clairvoyance.

I wasn't aware that this type of brain-to-brain communication was developed to construct more complex interfaces for modern technology. Unfortunately, I worried that humans would eventually use this expertise to manipulate radio devices to control the masses.

Our planet was already deploying ultra-violet wireless networks that operated on the same radio-frequency bandwidth of the electromagnetic spectrum.

My gut told me that the risk of exposure to non-ionizing radiation would cause a multitude of illnesses, from brain tumors to chronic headaches and calcification of the pineal gland.

I couldn't allow myself to get worked up about this unfathomable, emerging issue.

Just breathe, Jo.

I needed to focus on enhancing my telepathic abilities. Thank goodness for Science class, it was my favorite subject, where I'd learned that my brain was an elaborate network of neurons that transmitted electrical indicators. Amazingly, these became my memories, commands, and ideas. When these neurons transferred data back and forth, they created brain waves that accumulated and assigned information across different segments of my intellect.

I quickly realized that there was a link between quantum physics and consciousness. This was an important revelation since I'd been quite the pragmatist before my celestial awakening. Nonetheless, I discovered that science and spirituality had finally forged an agreement regarding evidence of a unified quantum connection to Source energy.

So which Light Being was trying to contact me? I required answers about this mysterious clairvoyant. I reached into my backpack and grabbed the magical Galactic Medallion. For safekeeping, I quietly hid it in the pocket of my favorite hoodie before entering the girls' bathroom.

To ensure I wasn't followed, I swiftly teleported from the bathroom stall on the third level of the school building into the basement hall just outside of the hidden portal.

It was just as I remembered. The walls around the aged door were lined with exposed brick, enveloped by a mist. I recalled this quite vividly from my previous battle with the Lord of Darkness.

After graduating from the Hall of Ignorance, I observed how humans had always felt insecure and detached from our life force energy. As a result, our civilization was controlled by the darkness that extracted this negative charge with domination. This struggle accounted for much of today's human conflict and anguish.

Inexplicably, the black hole in our high school's basement housed the memories of all false belief systems, ignorance, nightmares, and negative thought patterns. They included the emotional discharge of all suffering, fear, anger, jealousy, competition, oppression, misery, and systematic discrimination amassed over thousands of years.

I knew that the energies of separation and duality existed here in the blackness. It was the residence of sinister entities that created fear-based programming since the fall of the ancient civilization of Atlantis. It was not a myth, as we were led to believe by external systems.

I discovered that it also included the negative karmic modalities held within the unconscious grid matrix. Only the infinite light and unconditional love could shift the framework from fragmentation, back into a state of oneness.

As difficult as it was to believe, I found out the matrix on Earth had been hijacked and dominated by dark galactic forces that controlled humans through the frequency emitted by malevolent behaviors. It served as a vibrational match to patterns and belief structures of fear propaganda.

Even after all my experiences, I found the inception of the crystalline grid template fascinating. This cosmic framework was the light body of the awakened planet Earth, known as the higher vibrational, multidimensional ascension web of Gaia, Mother Earth.

I had learned through my downloads that the translucent grid functioned by anchoring light codes and cosmic intelligence within the multidimensional Earth plane. It was pure interstellar awareness that received the vast and infinite voltage wave energies directly from the Source and the center of the galaxy.

When the breakdown of the false illusory systems was initiated during my last mission, the crystalline field had been reactivated within the heart of Gaia as the triangulated stargate systems opened and aligned to planet Earth.

It was incredible to observe how it raised the frequencies through the gemstone generators' harmonic pitch and realigned the planet with a Lemurian timeline that seeded the blueprints into the emerging love-based quantum field.

This miraculous event had activated 144,000 beings aligned to the StarSeed template. They had been suspended on Earth until planetary events and the collective consciousness transcended karmic distortion imprints from previous Atlantis timelines.

Standing in the school basement where we had accidentally discovered the portal, I once again followed the geometric symbols that were cleverly etched into the wooden door's borders. I traced my fingers along the grooves, and the dust lined my fingertips. I found the repetitive patterns that epitomized a complex system of symbols and structures involving space, time, and form.

I looked around and intuitively noticed a minuscule beam of light from the top of the archway, which was not visible to the human eye as it reflected on the opposite wall across the hall. After I waited patiently, the second beam mirrored and collided back with the manifested light of the first beam, forming a holographic plate.

My heartbeat elevated as the excitement grew into an adrenaline rush. It echoed in my ears—all my six senses were fully stimulated.

I'm going back to the Pleiades again!

This feeling of pure euphoria was unlike anything I had experienced on planet Earth.

I quickly moved away from the portal that led into the black hole to examine the etchings on the opposite side of the exposed brick wall. The sacred patterns in the cold stone were well hidden. I realized that it was another form of holographic simulation that united and created all realities.

I reached into my pocket and removed the Galactic Medallion adorned by luminous jewels. I couldn't help but marvel at the patterns around the gemstones as if it was my first time. The crystals were loaded with amethyst, surrounded by white topaz. It was brilliant! The glow from the center quartz seemed to radiate with every minute I held it in my hand outside the portal.

The exquisite rainbow pendant was unique in its beauty and seemed to capture the essence of the cosmos. It simulated mystical powers to help me navigate between the natural and cosmic realms.

The captivating stone was wrapped with a sterling silver Galactic Compass, designed to direct and guide me toward my celestial ascension journey, in search of wisdom.

The gemstones and crystals included the fundamental elements of the natural world, Air, Fire, Water, and Earth, which allowed me to receive assistance from Gaia's guiding forces of nature.

The Galactic Medallion also included harmonic infusion frequencies that I had tapped into—the Sound of Sun, Sound of Earth, and OM, the Sound of Creation. I placed the Medallion into the hidden divot within the wall, rotating it clockwise until it clicked into position.

I removed the pendant and dug my fingers into the crack to open it wide enough for me to enter. As soon as I squeezed myself inside, I was flooded with immense blue and white neon lights. Shielding my eyes, I recited my cosmic code, *I AM Light, the Light that I AM* as I transformed into an ethereal Light form, shedding my human structure and carbon mass.

Clutching the Galactic Compass, I proceeded toward the beautiful holographic hallway. A long, brightly illuminated path presented itself to me—lined with electric florescent light orbs that represented each of the twelve-dimensional planes of consciousness. I was immediately mesmerized by the feeling of calm serenity, harmony, and magic. I commenced floating through space, much like in my dreams.

As I traveled through higher dimensions, I noticed the narrow tubes of energy that stretched across the entire length of the ever-expanding Universe. These thin regions of cosmic strings presented themselves in loops with no ends.

Transforming into my ethereal light form allowed me to move through the strings, bending the space-time continuum. These hidden dimensions were tightly wound using elementary particles, providing a cosmic superstring gravity wave energy that stretched across the vast distances of the Universe.

The cosmic compass guided me back to the Pleiades to meet with the Council of Creation. The twelfth-dimension emulated heaven as humans would have described it on Earth. It was the headquarters for the Oversoul, a unified field of consciousness, where the Soul would journey before their experience and incarnation on planet Earth.

I witnessed the different timelines of existence encapsulated in the multiverse much like a movie projection. These parallel worlds included an infinite number of cosmic patches, repeating several multi-dimensional realities through particle activities many times over.

Since time did not exist in these realms, I traveled past the Ancient Egyptian civilization, marveling at the great pyramids and the fluorescent Nile. I observed the lost City of Atlantis with its fabulously affluent and scientifically advanced, divine masculine civilization that had been swept into the sea.

Finally, I viewed the thermo-nuclear blast that heralded the demise of the enchanting continent of Lemuria. It was the home of magnificent magical creatures such as Pegasus, Centaurs, Griffins, and Unicorns.

They really did exist!

The peaceful continent had been filled with fertile, lush greens, blues, violet, and soft pink lands that exemplified the divine feminine energy. It was a vivid and captivating paradise.

I felt ecstatic to be greeted by a magnanimous Pleiadean presence of plasma light again. There were no words to accurately describe the majestic beauty of these celestial Beings, with their bluish-violet tinge of energy that exuded pure love. They took my breath away as I gazed in total awe and appreciation, with feelings of total bliss.

They spoke to me in light codes and telepathy that did not resemble human language. I observed with humility, knowing this experience superseded time and space—this was the highest expression of the Universe; it permeated absolutely everything in Creation.

The Pleiadean Beings regulated the Council of Creation and were not governed by the past, present, or future, nor any karmic intersections. Their radiant energy pulsated with the Universal Core, rotating as sparks of light or consciousness units thrust directly from Creation.

They existed in a perpetual state of connection with the Source power supply, occurring as the spiraling experience of Creation within the Cosmic Order. They connected and communicated with other beings through filament-like strings of light energy.

They acknowledged my presence with a warm, peaceful embrace and I felt all the sensations of belonging and acceptance, without limitations or expectations.

In a unified expression, they simultaneously communicated with me. "My Soul honors your Soul, dear blessed one. Welcome home."

They did not hide their faces this time as I recognized my mirror reflection in their representation. My holographic memory related and intertwined with every other segment of remembrance since Creation. I could only begin to perceive the frequency of reality through the perceptual filter of my uncrystallized pineal gland.

"We acknowledge that you have been evolving on Earth, transforming your perceptions and beliefs of the collective mindset. As you work on controlling your emotional reactions to the experiences of the physical world, you will obtain more appreciation for humanity's history. Through compassion and understanding, the sacred Light will continue to radiate the Divine's expression of unconditional love with every experience. It will flow through your auric field and energy points, then will continue to upgrade your physical DNA. Only with rest, healing and meditation will you be able to integrate the increase of plasma light enhancements into your awakened state of consciousness."

The Council paused as they deliberated my next steps in my ascension journey. They proceeded carefully, not to overwhelm my system with celestial knowledge.

"You will have to develop and fine-tune your intuitive gifts at your own pace, beloved. We will not be able to guide you through the Hall of Learning. Your next mission is to locate the truth about humanity's integration."

"To do this, you must cross the rainbow bridge of the fourth-dimensional realm, where you will be called to challenge outdated belief systems operating in separation. You will encounter malevolent entities that have dominated humans on Earth. To defeat them, you must remember your history and continue to seek answers within to align with your higher purpose. Only the truth will set humanity free from the bondage of duality existence."

I listened with intent and managed to reply, "How do I locate the bridge and sharpen my telepathic abilities?"

"Surround yourself with StarSeed energies that nourish and awaken your Soul, mind, and body. As your physical vessel becomes stimulated by the increased influx of crystalline light, a clearing process will continue to activate your DNA, to ensure spiritual detoxification. You must heal and clear the collective wounds, conditioning, distortion, imbalance, and energy blocks that are still running fear-based programs of victimhood within your vessel."

There was an edge to their energy exchange that I couldn't pinpoint for the first time. *Was it a warning?* I wondered.

"Once these vitality fields are processed and integrated, the emotional trauma stored within your nervous system will be released to make room for the light expansion, synergy, and elevation. Only then will your awareness deepen, allowing you to tap into powerful gifts."

I listened attentively with all my being as they continued to download their wisdom.

"Rest, be patient, and trust the process. If emotional triggers arise, and you are concerned you might be falling back into old patterns, do not be afraid. Embrace your feelings fully, beloved. Embody your divine feminine energy and allow yourself to integrate and process the traumatic events before you resolve them. This is how you will heal your ancestral wounding patterns. Find ways to express what you are feeling through creativity, music, and conscious movement. Continue to explore your authentic, individual expression to allow for celestial expansion."

As the Council prepared me for my galactic mission through the Ascending Angel Academy, they blessed me with Sacred Light protection.

"There are multiple timelines in your existence that may arise in the quantum moments to guide you toward future potentials. Take time to cultivate your innermost feelings of love and tranquility. Allow the intelligence of life to flow through you in whatever way it chooses. May the rainbow bridge empower you to elevate and ascend from your perceived realities. Find your voice and express your truth when crossing the dimensional overpass into infinite transcendence, dear one. Everything you desire is within you. You are ready. Embrace your power and knowledge."

The Council concluded their communication in cosmic codes, fully aware that the light language was beyond human perception.

And so began my ascension mission through the Hall of Learning.

In a blink of an eye, I found myself back in the stall of the girls' bathroom, before I'd teleported from reality. I composed myself while looking in the mirror, processing the magical experience of my time travel.

Breathing heavily, I left the bathroom and sprinted toward my locker, only to be stopped by Daphne. "Jo! Where have you been?" she shouted from across the hall. "For goodness' sake, Nisha is still looking all over the school for you! You should text us before disappearing like that."

"I'll fill you in after school, Daphne. Are you coming with me to the store? I need to pick up some stuff for Flynn's homecoming party. Sorry, I look so jaded. I have a lot going on—I totally forgot it was today!" I responded.

Daphne was determined to keep up with my pace. "I can't believe you of all people forgot! Of course, I'll come with you, Jo. As long as you don't mind stopping off at my house for a bit so I can get a quick change of clothes—I feel totally huge in this outfit."

"Stop it, Daph. I think you look fabulous!" I responded. I didn't appreciate when she referred to herself disparagingly.

"Well, you know that guy, Matt?" she asked, ignoring my comment.

"From our math class?" I recalled a shy classmate with thick glasses.

"Yup, he was texting me all week nonstop. He kept chasing me, so I started responding over text, and we were having amazing conversations. But when I suggested that we meet up to see a movie, he totally ghosted me." Daphne sighed, her insecurities on full alert.

"I'm sorry, Daph. That must have felt really shitty. Do you think he might need some more time? Maybe Matt's just intimidated by your magnetic charm?" I smiled, holding her hand as we walked toward my car.

"Or maybe he thinks I'm too chunky and is too embarrassed to be seen with me," she responded quietly.

"Nonsense! You are a queen, and he would be so lucky to spend time with you. Matt's probably projecting his own unconscious insecurities, Daph. Your energy is rising, and perhaps it's too much for him to handle." I supported my friend, sensing that her radiance was exposing some of Matt's unprocessed shadows.

As we approached my car, I couldn't help but admire my sweet friend's essence. My heart swelled with the immense love I was feeling for her. "Daph, you are so worthy of finding someone that will appreciate your kind and generous heart. Don't let anyone dim your light, my beauty."

As much as I wanted to continue this conversation, I realized what time it was. "We have to hurry. Zax has already texted me a few times. He's both excited and nervous. What a cutie!"

Changing the subject, Daphne expressed her concern. "Let's just hope Flynn stays sober this time. Are you worried Jo?" she asked attentively. Daphne struggled to play off the seriousness in her tone with a nervous giggle.

We all cared about Flynn, and I hoped that he accepted his past behaviors and chose to rise above their energetic influence. I realized that Flynn's recovery would take time. We needed to be loving, supportive, and understanding. After all, this was his journey, and we would honor his path without any preconceived notions or judgment. I couldn't help but feel an exuberant amount of compassion for his innocence.

"I think we should be mindful around him, Daph. I've decided not to smoke weed or drink any alcohol when we're together. It will be hard enough for him to be surrounded by reminders and cravings at parties. Everyone can make their own choices, but I choose to refrain from all external stimuli completely." I declared.

"Actually, I don't even yearn for bong hits anymore. It's awesome!"

"Ya, I should probably lay off the weed too. It's not even enjoyable anymore," Daphne responded.

I grinned with relief as my mind drifted to the past couple of months. "Gosh, time really does fly, huh Daph?"

"Pfft! You're telling me! This dress used to be loose!" Daphne retorted.

As I circled the school parking lot and headed toward the exit, my mind drifted back to Rey.

Oh, how I miss you, sweet friend, but I know your angelic Soul is at peace.

❖ ❖ ❖

Daphne

Daphne inhaled love and exhaled gratitude. Walking through the school hallway still gave her anxiety. The inner work that Jo had taught her helped ease her emotions, but she had to be diligent with the practice.

As she passed the popular girls, with the perfect thin bodies and flawless skin, her heartbeat elevated. Her hands became clammy, sweat formed above her lip.

Daphne had always identified herself through others' perceptions of her physical attributes. This lack of worthiness and self-confidence had shaped her illusive reality as the toxic thoughts lingered in her mind. The focus on her limitations fueled her emotions of uneasiness, stress, and worry.

Lately, Daphne had become more aware of these festering thoughts and was able to stop them before spiraling back into the void of despair. She didn't wish to attract these potent views into her daily reality any longer.

To gain back her power, Daphne decided to step out of the box of conformity with her limited, self-deprecating beliefs. She chose to rise above her fixations on others' views of body image and to embrace her unique gifts and beauty. She realized that breaking old habits would be difficult, but she was determined to take the first step—to feel comfortable in her own skin.

Before class, Daphne decided to remove her social media accounts completely. She recognized that she had developed an unhealthy dependency on technology. Daphne spent too much time on her phone, echoing the mainstream media's perceived reality.

Her obsession with trends that glorified the beauty industry with impossible standards was part of the problem.

Throughout her adolescence, Daphne was sculpted like a malleable soft piece of clay by her surroundings. Her mother's opinion of her imperfections completely distorted her view of self.

From her mother's perspective, the messages were emanating from a space of love, however, it was the unintentional subtle behavior and harmful words toward Daphne that had built up into conflict. Her mother was simply perpetuating a cycle of generational conditioning of her upbringing, projecting her Asian beliefs of striving for an elusive reality of perfection.

Daphne's mother was obsessed with maintaining control over her only child. She treated Daphne as an extension of her own identity and was filled with shame when her community viewed them with unfair judgment and disdain, based on Daphne's physical appearance.

Over the past few months, Daphne understood the existence of energy and how darkness resided in everyone's vibratory field of perception. These negative energetic charges were frequencies that existed in the thoughts, behaviors, or actions of everyone around her.

Although her mother loved Daphne, she violated her free will by unconsciously projecting her inadequacies onto her only child. She did not possess the emotional intelligence required to positively communicate her feelings with Daphne. Without these abilities, her mother was unable to relieve her stress and overcome the onslaught of challenges to defuse their ongoing conflict.

As part of her therapy and healing, Daphne wrote her intentions in her journal. She stripped down to her very core, facing her truth with vulnerability.

Her unhealthy relationship with food was a symptom, a defense mechanism, that consoled her inner child who only yearned to be accepted, loved, and acknowledged.

She longed for parental security and reassurance, seeking to be cherished unconditionally, protected, and emotionally nurtured.

Daphne partly understood why her mother had such unrealistic expectations from her only daughter, projecting her insecurities and failures. She began to appreciate her mother's sensitive needs, paying more attention to her emotional cues. Daphne was determined and motivated to resolve the ongoing conflict with her mother.

This was the primary mother-daughter relationship that required healing in her life if she desired to stop operating from a fragmented and disempowered state of existence.

Moving forward, Daphne wished to resolve her struggle in a healthy manner. She didn't have any control over their past experiences, but Daphne recognized that she had the choice to settle the mother-daughter issues with respect and by setting healthy boundaries.

Daphne recalled one specific session with her therapist that had stuck in her mind.

"Daphne, our emotions are vital pieces of information that inform us about our feelings. However, stress takes us out of our comfort zone.

When this happens, we become overwhelmed and lose control of our actions," she explained.

"By learning how to cope with pressure and anxiety due to external tension, we provide ourselves with an opportunity to remain emotionally present. This means, no matter how upsetting the situation or information that we receive, we can compose ourselves without allowing the stress to override our thoughts."

"Yes, I'm aware of the importance of self-chatter and negative thought patterns," Daphne replied.

"Wonderful, so when you are cognizant, you are empowered to manage your emotions by adapting to changing situations," her therapist further clarified.

"Dealing with your stress hormones is just the first step to developing emotional intelligence as you progress through life experiences. We know that your attachment patterns reflect your childhood perception. As you work on healing yourself from the past, you must continue to manage your fundamental feelings of sadness, resentment, and panic."

Inspired by her therapy and Jo's support, it took Daphne a few days to find the courage to speak her truth. She unearthed her voice and confronted her mother at the right opportunity.

"You look like a stuffed marshmallow, Daphne. Take off that outfit. I have something more suitable for your physique," her mother remarked.

"No," Daphne replied in defiance, with a quivering voice.

"Excuse me?" She snapped back in disbelief. "Do as you're told, young lady. I don't have time for your insolence this morning."

"Mom, I am almost seventeen years old. I don't need your inappropriate comments. It's painful." Daphne swallowed hard, gulping the sobs forming from deep within her core. She forced herself to continue, by taking deep breaths to calm her nerves. Her entire body shook with trepidation as she broke old patterns and relayed her emotions.

"I'm sure you don't intend to hurt my feelings, but as my primary caretaker, you were responsible for my childhood emotional experiences. Since I found your derogatory words confusing, I learned to distance myself from my feelings because I didn't know how to process them. But it needs to stop now."

"I am your mother and know what's best for you. I'm not trying to hurt you, Daphne. I'm trying to protect you from the cruelty of the outside world." Her mother stood in astonishment as the bitter chill of truth shocked her system.

"Well, I don't need you to shred me down first thing in the morning. If you want to help me, please keep your negativity to yourself, Mom. I'm already judging myself, believe me." Daphne let out a sniffle as tears stung her eyes. She was determined to refrain from crying, but her resolve was faltering.

"I....I never meant to be disparaging. I just want the best for you, Daphne. You are my world; I love you, my baby." Her mother broke her stoic exterior, tears flooding down her face. It was unusual and heartbreaking to witness her cry.

For the first time, Daphne felt heard, acknowledged, validated. She opened her heart to let her mother into her sympathetic embrace.

"I love you, Mom. Please don't cry. Let's just focus on our communications from now on. I just hope you will be conscious about the words you use to relay your emotions, okay?" Daphne hugged her mother tightly as she acknowledged her request.

With this simple act of kindness and by relaying her honesty, she had changed the nature of their mother-daughter relationship and reality.

Armed with this solace, Daphne found her resilience to overcome her insecurities when surrounded by football players and cheerleaders at school. She still had a lot of healing to do to process the distress she endured a few months ago at a house party. But Daphne knew that with time, she would emerge stronger, wiser, and out of victimhood.

Jo had spent hours on the phone with her, sharing her understanding of self-realization attitudes. Daphne recalled a specific message that really resonated with her during their chat.

"Daph, I have learned that our thoughts dictate our feelings, which are expressed through our bodies. How we think and how we feel create our state of being. If we stop in the moment and become aware of our stress-induced hormones, we halt the pattern of behaviors. We begin to understand that operating from this space causes us to unconsciously focus on the worst-case scenarios. This contracts our energy, resulting in self-sabotage and negativity. We then magnetically attract these types of experiences back into our reality," Jo explained.

Daphne felt an intense shift in her momentum when she heard those powerful words. They were seeded in her mind, flourishing with every opportunity to expand her perception.

She realized that every time she focused her attention on negative events that insulted her Soul, she lowered her energetic tone.

In those moments of anxiety, she regained control of her inner dialogue, learning to cultivate her state of being. By taking deep cleansing breaths, Daphne was empowered with tranquility, calming the inflammation of her central nervous system. She learned to take time to process her feelings before reacting from a fight or flight state. This was done by exercising self-love, kindness, and empathy for herself.

As Daphne prepared for her classes, she made a crucial decision. She was no longer interested in unnecessary drama caused by unprocessed trauma.

❖ ❖ ❖

"Come on baby, light my fire. Everything you drop is so tired. Music is supposed to inspire, how come we ain't getting no higher?"—Superstar by Lauryn Hill

CHAPTER 3
LIFTING THE VEIL

"The unexamined life is not worth living."

— SOCRATES

Jo

I woke up feeling bogged down by the previous day's download during the time travel. The wisdom of the Council and the presence of the Pleiadeans were a cosmic high. I was still feeling the warm embrace of the magnificent Beings as they welcomed me home in my Ethereal form.

This ascension schooling was no joke. It required most of my vital force energy. Training my pineal gland to expand the connection of my physical emotional body and spirit had become an active practice that flooded most of my mental space. It was partly the reason I forgot about Flynn's homecoming surprise party.

After making a quick pit stop at Daphne's house, we picked up Flynn's favorites snacks and cute decorations. I hoped that he felt special, loved, and accepted as we welcomed him back with open arms.

It was our responsibility as his friends to give him the support he needed while battling his dependencies to stimuli. In a group chat, we decided to keep all forms of drugs and alcohol away from the party, including cigarettes.

I was filled with optimism and pure joy as I witnessed Flynn and Zax together as a couple. Ever since Zax confessed his true feelings for his best friend, he was like a different person. There was an energy of serenity around him, and I could sense the relief projecting from his core. The affection for each other was evident, and it brightened both of their faces.

"Is this a coincidence, or did you two lovebirds pre-plan on color coordinating?" Daphne pointed to Flynn and Zax's purple shirts, teasing them.

"Why, are you jealous, Daph?" Zax laughed sassily.

"Yes, go ahead, avoid my question. Your refusal to answer says it all, my dude." Daphne snickered, and the rest of us joined in the harmless banter.

My heart warmed, observing their beautiful, loving auras. They held hands throughout the evening, demonstrating their affection. The teasing elicited smiles and rosy blushes from Flynn, displaying Zax's happiness and tranquility. It was a sight to behold! What a transformation since his liberation.

I decided to leave Flynn's homecoming gathering earlier than normal. As I drove home, passing the beautifully lit and manicured lawns of suburbia, I couldn't help but reflect on my meeting with the Council. I was tired from the day's adventures, feeling emotionally drained.

Once I finally reached the sanctity of my bedroom, I felt a surge of energy ripple through my body. *So much for sleep.* I could only focus on accessing my third eye to tap into the mysterious clairvoyant messages.

The urgency I had received the day before triggered my unease. A feeling of upheaval and doom had crawled up into my chest, rocking my state of peace and stability out of equilibrium.

I needed to realign my energy fields and resolve the imbalanced emotions. The Council had tasked me to exercise control over my expressive reactions, no matter the obstacles that came my way.

However, I felt my mind wandering back to Ms. Rolland's unreadable energy. The grayish-white aura deeply puzzled me, and it kept me from teleporting to her residence. For some reason, my magic didn't work around her. It was interesting to me that she was the first person to repel my powers.

Her aura stuck in my mind like sticky toffee, trying to massage and process the information. As I observed the chaos of my thought patterns, a feeling of foreboding took hold of me. Doom was about to unfold in our reality. Whatever was coming, my salvation for this experience rested with the enigmatic, StarSeed named Roma.

❖ ❖ ❖

Flynn

After spending six weeks in rehabilitation, Flynn was determined to change his life. He didn't wish to end up like Rey, accidentally overdosing on recreational drugs. He was determined that this time it would be different.

With some extensive reflection on his past, Flynn had time to focus on his inner work and the underlying triggers behind his real feelings. The rehab facility provided him safe, caring, and nurturing therapy, which was vital for his healing and recovery.

Growing up, Flynn had always been a rebellious child and as such was criticized for his conduct. His parents often disapproved of his behavior when he acted out, damaging his self-esteem.

This led to codependent, self-destructive mannerisms as he grew up, using them as defense mechanisms to mask his pain. Flynn projected his feelings of humiliation on others as a protective shield.

He recalled his last session in rehab with his therapist and remembered his oath. He was fully invested in his mental health and well-being journey. Flynn had too much to lose to screw it up again.

"Why are you so hard on yourself, Flynn?" The therapist inquired.

"Hard on myself? I think it's important to acknowledge the truth. Isn't that part of rehabilitation, Doc?" Flynn asked with a grin.

"Yes, but it doesn't need to be done with self-criticism. Why so harsh?" she asked again.

"Well, I guess it's because I feel like my entire life has been a lie. I've been a liability to everyone who ever cared for me—my family, my friends," Flynn whispered in remorse. "I put so much emphasis on other people's opinions on their version of who I'm supposed to be. That person isn't really me, you know?"

"What does that mean? Am I speaking to an avatar? Where's the real Flynn?" the doctor inquired.

"I don't really know, to be honest. I've been pretending for so long. It's the only way I can hide from my pain. How do I discover my true self?"

"First, we have to acknowledge your feelings and ordeals hiding under the masks. Have you ever thought of hurting yourself, Flynn?" The subject was broached carefully.

"There's a huge difference between thinking about it and wanting. But there have been occasions when that gap got too close. Especially after my benders," Flynn admitted. He'd made a promise to Zax that he would be honest in the therapy sessions while he was in rehab.

"Somehow, I have always thought of puberty as this irreversible metamorphosis. Terrifying. Stuck in conformity and expectations, just like my mom. I just want to be free," Flynn said, relaying more than he expected.

"Is that how you perceive your mom, Flynn? Stuck?" the doctor persisted.

"I don't really want to talk about my mom right now. Or my dad's trust fund," he replied, shutting down the conversation completely.

Flynn was the prodigal son of his wealthy family, born the last of six children. His family owned a big construction company that provided them with a lavish lifestyle, which earned Flynn the title of the "Trust Fund Kid" at school.

He proudly embraced the title. If anyone was looking to party, they only needed to approach Flynn. He always provided generous partying gifts for any event. His carefree attitude had led him to develop many unhealthy habits and dependencies.

Having unlimited access to cash provided plenty of opportunities to experiment with hard-core drugs at an early age. Flynn had developed a compulsion for painkillers, alcohol, and cocaine in his teenage years.

He had spent the past summer in rehab, managing sobriety for an astounding sixty days. Yet he relapsed on the first day he returned to school. Flynn possessed a despairing mindset and he always felt that life was too short to be taken seriously. That had been his motto.

"I have no set agenda, Flynn. We can discuss whatever you wish. Do you want to talk about Zaxden?" the doctor asked, fully immersed in gaining Flynn's trust.

"Zax is my best friend and the love of my life. No one has ever looked at me like he does. He sees me, like underneath all these layers of crap. He notices the real me," Flynn said with a glimmer of hope in his eyes.

"Can you articulate how he makes you feel?" the doctor pressed.

"Umm…I think the best way to describe it is that he makes me feel like the ocean—strong, secure, and in constant free motion. I've never known a love like that. This probably sounds cheesy." Flynn attempted to laugh it off, blushing with embarrassment.

"I think it sounds lovely and like a huge relief," she replied.

"It was so surreal when Zax finally admitted his feelings for me. I was stunned. Growing up together, there were so many moments when I wanted to kiss him. But he always portrayed himself as this strong, masculine guy. I was too afraid that my best friend would reject me. I'm completely in love with him, and it makes me feel really exposed, vulnerable." Flynn admitted.

"Isn't that a good thing, knowing how much Zax loves you? You don't have to pretend anymore," the doctor said, trying to get below the surface.

"Honestly, I'm afraid. Once I leave rehab, he will see me without the drugs and alcohol masking my pain. He may not love the messy, weak, frightened little boy inside." Flynn unleashed his truth for the first time.

"It's okay to be scared. We are all afraid of rejection and abandonment to some degree, but you can't allow that worry to rob you from having healthy and joyful experiences. You just need to acknowledge the fear, and it's important not to bypass your emotions," the doctor explained. "Can you describe what the word *pain* means to you, Flynn?"

"Do you mean physical or emotional pain? For me, they both feel the same. It's anything that hurts or is uncomfortable, whether it's my broken arm or my broken heart, it just doesn't feel good. And to be honest, I'm too scared to go through the suffering, to feel the distress," Flynn admitted, revealing a truth that had surfaced for the first time.

"That's understandable, and I like how you described it, Flynn." The Doctor smiled, commending his ability to communicate his feelings.

"In my experience, I have learned that pain is a label we use to describe something that doesn't feel good. It's another form of energy that is designed to move through our bodies. When we have a traumatic event during our childhood or young adult years, the energy of this experience attaches to our physical body. We then formulate certain thoughts, beliefs, and patterns around this particular experience we refuse to feel, so it gets stuck," the doctor explained.

"This builds up a crust of dense energy, and it grows as we continue to avoid or bypass the process of feeling the emotions. So, as we get older, there's this cemented mud that gets stuck along the walls of our interior body and blocks our energy fields. When we decide to finally acknowledge that crusted traumatic event, we start to feel the discomfort as it's dislodging from our emotional body."

"So, every time I do my inner work and identify the causes of my pain that's behind my addictions, I eliminate the cemented crust from my system?" Flynn asked.

"Yes, as long as you don't affix to it or judge the process of purging the extreme distress of your past. This is a necessary step toward your healing journey, Flynn. The more you feel your emotions, the faster you release the blockage. Going through this process requires lots of courage. It's like a band-aid when you first remove it, there's an immediate sting and then you don't feel it anymore," the doctor said, continuing to connect with Flynn.

"It's perfectly alright to feel your pain—embrace it, normalize it, and then detach from it. Don't label it, don't identify with it, and just allow the energy to flow through you. The pain wants to be acknowledged, honored, and liberated from your heart." The doctor concluded her advice before changing subjects.

"Thanks, Doc, you have definitely given me lots to think about. I'm excited to share this information with Zax, I think it will resonate with him as well." Flynn replied.

"It sounds like Zax knows you quite well. You two have been friends since you were young kids, right? It seems to me that you have quite a solid bond, and you trust him," she said with a warm smile.

"What if I relapse again because my sobriety is completely reliant on Zax and his acceptance of my authentic self? I don't want to put him through that again. It's too painful. And let's face it Doc, life can be a real letdown." Flynn distrusted the prospect of true happiness and freedom of self-expression.

"What do you mean, Flynn?" she asked.

"It's just so much easier to hide in my room and connect with people online. The relationships are these fantasies that I concoct in my own head. That's why I fall so easily for boys, girls, men. It doesn't matter in the end because it's not real. I'm safe in my bubble when I don't let anyone in. They can't hurt me," Flynn confessed.

"Wouldn't you rather spend that precious time with your best friend, instead of the illusory fantasies you narrate in your mind?" the doctor asked blankly.

"Of course, I would! I just don't want to lose him. What if he can't handle my physical and intimate connection? He has never been in a relationship with a guy. I just can't live without Zax," Flynn said, his mind automatically racing with worst-case scenarios.

"You know that having a codependent relationship isn't healthy, Flynn. You can't allow perceptions and fear to dictate your choices," she reiterated, peering over her reading glasses, perched low on her nose.

The doctor decided to wrap up the productive session. "Perhaps you can give the twelve-step program a real chance this time. Take it slow, one day at a time. What do you think?"

"I will, Doc. As part of my recovery, I have already begun to make amends with my family for putting them through the nightmare." Flynn responded.

"Just remember to be patient and kind with yourself Flynn, and most importantly, forgive yourself. Give yourself the compassion and empathy that you are seeking from others first. That's the only way to move forward," she continued, reminding him about self-love after every session, over the six weeks.

The doctor's words were etched into Flynn's mind as he prepared for school. Forgiveness had been a lot tougher than he had originally anticipated. The intrusive, self-disparaging thoughts still lingered. But he was determined to take back control of his life and heal one day at a time.

Flynn felt profoundly thankful to be surrounded by Zax and his considerate friends while he was recovering. He felt open and extremely vulnerable without his fake persona. Whether he believed he deserved it or not, they did not judge him for his past regressions, and for that, he was extremely grateful.

Jo

The backs of my legs and arms tingled with invigorating fervor. Today was a fresh start, a new day. With prolonged mediation practices, I was determined to focus and expand my pineal gland to receive more information from Roma. I had this unexplainable, magnetic pull toward this mysterious stranger.

I had to speak to her. I knew she'd have the answers I was seeking for my next mission. The swelling and pulsations in my third eye acted as a radio receiver to tap into the right station. I hoped that my consciousness had increased to the level required to obtain the clairvoyant messages.

Just as I grabbed my favorite black hoodie, I received a message from Conrad.

Will be waiting for you outside of school, hurry up gorgeous!

His texts always put a smile on my face. It significantly brightened my mood.

As I drove to Nisha's place, my mind strayed toward her growing relationship with Alicia. They both seemed compatible and into each other. Their blooming friendship filled me with the hope that she would finally find a loving, worthy companion who would challenge and accept her fully.

"Hey girl, why the heavy dark circles?" Nisha plopped down in the front seat, throwing her backpack in the back.

"Well hello to you. Must you toss around your belongings in my car?" My greeting caused her to grin, one side of her mouth raised higher than the other as she rolled her eyes.

"Come on, tell me. You left early last night to catch some sleep, but the moon craters have worsened. What happened?" Nisha nudged, her smirk subsiding into a concerned frown. This was why she was my best friend. Her ability to keep track of my appearance and moods always surprised me and made me appreciate and adore her even more.

"Yes, that was the plan, but my mind wouldn't shut off…" I began to explain my portal crossing and visit with the Council. Once Daphne joined us, I decided to get their views about the new history teacher, who continued to baffle me.

"By the way, what do we think about Ms. Rolland?" I inquired as the thought swirled in annoyance, demanding attention.

"She seems very strict, a no-nonsense instructor," Nisha said nonchalantly. She didn't have much regard for our archaic educational institutions.

"I think she's going to make history seem more boring than it already is, to be honest Even her appearance portrays the typical uptight master that wants to control with surprise pop quizzes." Daphne brought my attention to her astute observation.

Why did adults like to exert their control over other beings? Disempowering behavior was a nasty virus that needed to be extinguished, as I learned from the Hall of Ignorance. I discovered a significant lesson—nothing was really how it seemed.

I was getting tired from playing in this holographic interactive, video game of life that responded to outdated belief systems we held within our vibratory fields. It was time for humanity to shift our dimensional gears.

So, why had I pulled myself into the same types of events? Was it a dominant frequency that was residing somewhere in my blind spot within my consciousness? I wondered if there were residual negative convictions encased within my emotional body that had not been addressed? Or was this my intuition guiding me with clairvoyant signals?

As I progressed between the physical and spiritual realms, I found it challenging to maintain the balance between my ethereal being and the human form. Lately, it had been a constant struggle, questioning and doubting myself.

Driving up to our school, I noticed Conrad's tall and lanky silhouette waiting for me anxiously. A warm sensation arose from my heart center in excitement.

"Someone's caught the love bug. No wonder you were driving faster than usual." Daphne teased. I grinned at her through the rearview mirror, unable to say anything in my defense. Blood rushed to my cheeks as my face gave me away.

I barely had time to park when Conrad ran up to get my door like a true gentleman.

"Hey, you," I greeted him. My lips curled up in a warm smile. He reached out and pulled me in for a sweet embrace. Wrapping my arms around his neck, I gave him a light peck on his cheek and continued to press my forehead in the space between his neck and shoulder.

"Hello, how are we this morning?" Conrad asked. His fingers wove through my curly hair, pushing it back to reveal the smooth skin of my neck. With a gentle peck, he let go of me enough to lovingly stare into my eyes. His hand cupped my cheek, his thumb slightly grazing the dark circles beneath my green eyes, signaling that he noticed the lack of sleep.

"We are better now." I cracked a grin which was then mirrored on Conrad's handsome face. The chuckle momentarily evaporated my fatigue, replaced by the jubilation of his warm welcome.

The freshness of our interaction provided me with a brief escape from the ongoing tension tethered to my Soul. It brought me emotional balance and stability, at least temporarily. I relished these human moments with Conrad. Lately, my mind was always fine-tuned to function according to my ethereal form.

Uneasiness began to fill my essence again, but I grounded myself with deep, conscious breathing techniques, through my nose, channeling down to my solar plexus. I visualized the vitality expanded and aligned through my spinning electromagnetic fields.

The balance and connectivity of my mind and spiritual self were crucial. To graduate from the second level of the Ascending Angel Academy, I had to train myself to keep my emotions in a neutral state.

I was momentarily distracted from my troubles as Conrad, and I gleefully hopped toward the archaic entrance of our school. The stone gray and black building stood tall like a cryptic ancient edifice. It was built in the early nineteen hundred, and the existence of a mysterious portal that led to the black hole within the universe added to its overall charm.

Conrad and I discussed yesterday's homecoming gathering as we walked to the main hall. Words flowed easily with him. It felt natural, spontaneous, and uncomplicated.

We had built a strong connection over the winter break, with frequent dates and hang outs with friends. Our compatibility only enhanced our relationship, and he made me feel respected and appreciated.

"I am getting excited about spring break. Can you guess where we're going?" I asked curious about his preference for the two-week vacation.

"I'm not sure yet…there are many possibilities. It depends on which teacher is assigned to the trip." Conrad mused, his eyes squinting slightly at the prospect of our intimacy.

"It will be a voluntary trip for the teaching staff, and I heard through the grapevine that we're going to the mystical Canary Islands in the Atlantic Ocean. Since the island has a strong link to ancient history and the Legend of Atlantis, Ms. Rolland will be responsible for coordinating our trip," I replied, nonchalantly.

"Oh really? I was personally hoping to see the white lions' wildlife reserve in South Africa." Conrad laughed.

"Africa? That would be such an incredible experience, especially to bond with Mother Earth." Conrad was familiar with my esoteric lingo.

"I thought Atlantis was just a myth. Imagine the gorgeous coastline. I could really use a tan," he joked.

"Greek legend has it that Atlantis used to be larger than Libya and Asia combined. It was the dominion of Poseidon, God of the Sea. It was inhabited by royalty and immense wealth. They observed their laws of justice and were a peaceful, generous society. Unfortunately, they degenerated, due greed and war," I said.

"How did the entire empire perish?" he asked, amused by my enthusiasm.

"Well, according to our history books, Zeus, King of Gods punished Atlantis with disastrous volcanic eruptions and tidal waves. Legend has it, the only reminiscence of this ancient civilization is scattered at the bottom of the ocean in the Azores, Madeira, Canaries, and Cape Verde. Imagine finding its golden palaces and temples?" I could barely hide my excitement as I thought about the true saga behind this mystical society.

"Wow, how do you know so much about this, Jo? Honestly, you amaze me every day," Conrad gushed as he squeezed me affectionately.

If only he knew my truth. As we walked through the hallway hand in hand, I noticed Daphne standing by Flynn's locker. Judging by their demeanor, I could tell they were arguing. I felt immediately alarmed at the sight of my best friends criticizing each other.

"So, you think I'm weak? You think I won't be able to handle it?" Flynn tried to control his anger, his lips setting in disappointment.

"When on Earth did I say that, Flynn?" Daphne stepped back; her movements reflected her defensive tone.

"Didn't you just say that you guys deliberately didn't bring any alcohol or weed to the party yesterday?" Flynn raised his voice extremely agitated. I stepped in, trying to defuse the tension as I pieced together the reason for the argument.

"Hey, guys, what's all the fuss about?" I stood between the two of them, with my back to Daphne. I didn't want her adding fuel to the blazing fire.

"Daphne said you guys think I am too weak to handle myself around substances." Flynn's tone was accusatory. I flinched by the energy exchange of his word as it speared a twinge of hurt to my heart.

"Oh my God, Flynn, I literally never said that. We just wanted to support you that's why we didn't bring any alcohol to the party!" Daphne expressed with disappointment.

"Well, that's what Pierre said right before he took off with Lavender," Flynn argued, as I paused in confusion.

"Wait, who is Pierre?" I asked.

"So, you'd rather believe someone you literally met ten minutes ago, but you won't trust me?" Daphne ignored me, struggling to hold back her tears.

I decided to become the voice of reason and prevent this argument from blowing out of proportion. We had been through way too much together over the past semester, and I wouldn't let anything, or anyone tear us apart.

"Guys! Stop fighting!" I stomped my foot on the floor, the motion releasing my energy in a rippling effect.

It created an aura around me, palpable enough to jolt Daphne and Flynn as they stumbled back into their lockers. Shocked at the sudden interruption, both looked at me with eyes wide in astonishment.

"Jo…your eyes…" Daphne stammered.

"Good, I appreciate you letting me finally get a word in!" I didn't need a mirror to confirm her words. My eyes were blazing with bright shades of sparkling emerald.

"Jo! Someone will see you!" Flynn glanced around, trying to hide the pulsating energy orbs around me.

"It's the only way to get your attention. Don't worry, the momentum will dissipate in a minute," I reassured them.

"Now that we have all calmed down, who the heck is Pierre?" I asked again in a composed manner.

"Pierre and Lavender are siblings, fraternal twins to be exact. They transferred here at the start of the second semester. There! That's Lavender," Daphne pointed toward a brown-haired girl with glasses toward the end of the hallway.

I turned to observe this newcomer and eyed her through my peripheral vision.

"That's strange…I am unable to read her energy," I said. "The funny thing is, I was not equipped to decipher Ms. Rolland's aura in yesterday's history class as well. It was grayish-white, which signifies blankness."

"Is it because she's new?" Flynn asked innocently.

"No…I don't think that matters, Flynn. So far I've been able to read the auric fields of all the humans I've come across." I paused, realizing the significance of my words. *All humans I've come across. Humans!*

I glanced at Lavender who was now standing by her locker, texting someone. The prospect of Ms. Rolland and Lavender possessing extraterrestrial properties sounded ridiculous, but I had seen worse. However, it would be accusatory of me to be suspicious of innocent people without facts or evidence.

"Are the siblings related to our history teacher? Oh my gosh, what if they are not descendants of the human race?" I cracked a smile, unable to stop my excitement from seeping through. It certainly made for a fun conversation. I turned toward Daphne and Flynn who were staring at me wide-eyed. Their reactions made me laugh out loud.

"That's…a little extreme, Jo…" Daphne trailed off as she tried to make sense of my response. She glanced back at Lavender who was getting ready to attend a class like a normal teen.

Daphne seemed to share my twisted humor and chuckled. Even though I wasn't completely joking, I was still relieved to see her smile.

"You guys are ridiculous! Of course, they are human. Look, she's texting. Would aliens use Wi-Fi?" Flynn mocked, shaking his head.

"Hey! I'm a supernatural being, and I know how to text!" I replied. His rationale made me laugh. I faked being offended at his words, causing some major eye-rolls. I pushed him playfully by the shoulder into his locker. Daphne giggled at our banter, which relieved the tension between them.

"So, what exactly did Pierre say that caused the fight?" I asked again, trying to get to the bottom of the argument. The fact that this Pierre had so much power over my friends rubbed me the wrong way.

"They looked lost, trying to locate their class. Somehow, we ended up talking about last night's party for Flynn, and I mentioned that we were being supportive by staying away from alcohol and drugs. I have no idea why I felt the need to share that with them, to be honest," Daphne stated, exasperated.

"Pierre questioned the real motives behind this decision. He thought you guys left out substances because you think I'm pathetic," Flynn added. I understood why he would feel hurt by such an atrocious accusation. He had just returned from rehab and wanted us to believe in him. He was in dire need of our encouragement, trust, and compassion.

"Flynn, I would never invalidate your feelings. I just wish you had asked us first. We are in this together, remember?" I reasoned with him. "Our intentions were pure, we just wanted to show our support. I'm really sorry for any misunderstanding."

I tried to read his mood, hoping my words softened his energetic inflammation.

"Also, Pierre is new. He doesn't know us, or what we have been through together. Don't give anyone the power to affect your well-being, okay? We are always going to care for you and have your best interests at heart," I continued, hoping to satiate his feelings.

I opened my arms wide, reaching for an embrace. He accepted the notion and drew me in, stress releasing from his body.

"Yeah, okay. I'm sorry, Daph." Flynn turned toward her, pulling her in for a bear hug.

"Aw, it's okay buddy. All good in the hood." Flynn let out a chuckle at Daphne's goofy wit, and she echoed his laugh, hugging him tighter.

Immense relief washed over me at the resolved conflict. I suddenly realized that Conrad had been waiting for me patiently, standing five feet away from us. His right shoulder was propped up against his locker as he browsed through his phone. I walked over and gingerly tugged at his shirt to signal that the friend drama had been contained. At least for now.

After our morning classes, I had a chance to quickly update Nisha on Flynn and Daphne's squabble.

"I don't know, Jo. I don't trust this Pierre guy. It was so easy for him to convince Flynn to turn against us with just one false statement," Nisha said. She held a strong opinion about the morning occurrence and strongly believed that we should stay away from the puzzling siblings.

"I get your point, Nish. I felt weird about that too, but maybe we are overthinking it? We don't want to make quick assumptions." I tried to defend Pierre and Lavender, not wanting to add more fuel to the fire.

Even though my gut agreed with Nisha, I didn't want to feed her skepticism. I had to practice patience and emotional stability, and for that, I needed to stay non-judgmental and impartial no matter the obstacle.

As we entered the cafeteria and walked to our usual table, we were both surprised to find Flynn and Zax sitting with Pierre and Lavender. Nisha turned toward me with a frown of disapproval.

"Hey, guys." I took a seat beside Flynn and Zax, opposite the twins. I dragged Nisha down beside me, and she huffed into her chair, her face set in a sulk.

"Jo and Nisha, this is Pierre and his sister Lavender. They are new to our school," Zax greeted enthusiastically.

"Hi. Nice to meet you," I responded politely, not letting the situation get any more awkward. I gently pinched Nisha on her thigh, prompting her to reply.

"Hey." Her tone was off, but at least she managed to utter the word without sounding too upset.

"Which classes have you been assigned this semester?" I continued to make idle conversation as we ate our gourmet meals.

"We have Calculus, History, Music, AP Physics, Neurobiology, and…" Lavender swiftly answered. She seemed to be the nervous type, fidgety, refusing to make eye contact.

"…Chemistry, Psychology, and American Literature." Pierre completed her sentence with a smug attitude and dark piercing eyes.

"You're both in the exact same classes?" Nisha asked, astonished that the siblings had matching schedules.

"Yeah, we're just not comfortable being apart. They didn't have any issues approving our application since our mom works here," Lavender replied, not giving much notice to Nisha's icy tone.

"Oh really? Who's your mom?" Zax asked.

"Ms. Rolland. She teaches History," Pierre replied, glaring into my soul with his smoky black eyes, sending shivers down my spine. And not the good kind.

❖ ❖ ❖

Nisha

Ever since she could remember, Nisha had always been distrusting of the opposite sex. She realized that she wore her childhood wounds on her sleeve, sometimes judging boys unjustly. However, she clutched her daddy issues like blazing armor.

The experiences she endured over the past few months had helped her navigate through her panic attacks. Nisha was grateful for Jo. Even after the huge fight they had before their Barcelona band performance, they were still able to patch up their friendship. Their shared experience of loss formed a deeper level of connection and trust.

Nisha's best friends provided her with a safe space to process her issues of anxiety stemming from her upbringing.

Her struggle to fit into a prescribed world continued to plague her. However, Nisha had decided to stop questioning her self-worth based on the opinions of others and the void she had felt from her father's neglect.

She was tired of playing the same worn-out narrative of her isolated existence. As she reached adolescence, Nisha grew distant from both of her parents, harboring feelings of resentment from the emotional abandonment.

Nisha's parents had vastly different backgrounds. Her mother was accustomed to the luxuries and privilege of her ancestral wealth, and her father only knew the struggle of poverty from his upbringing. He prioritized work over his family time, disregarding both his wife and daughter.

However, Nisha loved her father, but she bitterly felt his absence from her childhood. By the time she turned thirteen, her parents could no longer tolerate each other's company. Neither of them realized the distress they had caused their daughter, and when their marriage fell apart, the pressure of the divorce had devastating impacts on Nisha.

Her anxiety and panic attacks worsened through puberty as she developed a rebellious nature of a pre-teen. Nisha's mother dismissed her mood swings and erratic behavior, expecting it would dissipate. Her father avoided her emotional outbursts, hoping to bypass the uncomfortable stages of adolescence.

Unfortunately, Nisha's panic attacks were legendary at school. During the summer, her chest pain, shortness of breath, and heart palpitations sent her to the hospital.

With Jo's guidance, the shocking experience of loss when Rey passed away, snapped her out of her victimhood mentality. Nisha realized how precious life was, and she vowed to cherish each day on the planet. She began to educate herself on ecological issues and championed the significance of climate control.

During band class, Nisha bonded with Alicia discussing environmental reform with enthusiasm. They were bandmates, but the subject of planetary action brought them closer, as they shared similar passions.

For Nisha, Alicia had been a gift from the Universe, and she clung to that lifejacket for dear life with a grateful heart. She brought her a sense of belonging and inner peace.

Alicia embraced Nisha's intelligence, her shadows, listened to her conspiracy theories, and cherished her exuberance without any conditions or expectations.

However, Nisha didn't connect as easily with Alicia's brother, Theo. He was a totally different mood.

"Thanks a lot, Nisha. I probably failed that damn history quiz!" Theo complained as he passed his sister and Nisha in the dining hall during lunch.

"That's not my problem, dude," Nisha snickered back.

"Don't pay any attention to my brother. He can be a jerk sometimes," Alicia stated, sending Theo death glares.

"Sorry to say this, but Theo can be quite intense. He's giving off real asshole vibes right now," Nisha replied.

"He's harmless, really. Do you want to eat our lunch in the park?" Alicia quickly changed the subject.

"Sure, that would be great actually." Nisha smiled bashfully.

"So, how the heck are you two so different? Isn't Theo your twin?" Nisha asked, still unable to shake off his negativity.

"Yes, fraternal. However, I take no responsibility for his actions." Alicia laughed nervously. Her brother didn't leave a good impression on any of her friends.

"Did something happen to make him so miserable?" Nisha asked.

"Theo was never the same after our boating accident when we were kids. Our biological father passed away," Alicia explained, taking deep breaths to guide her through the painful experience.

"I'm so sorry, Alicia. That's horrible. I had no idea." Nisha was stunned by this revelation. She reached out and gently clutched Alicia's hand in comfort. "It's very difficult growing up without a father figure."

Nisha understood this feeling too well. She was in awe of Alicia's positive and uplifting outlook on life despite her traumatic loss.

The connection she felt for Alicia was sacred and motivated Nisha to purify herself from the prescribed medical toxins that she had been voluntarily ingesting to numb herself from feeling pain and anxiety.

After all, she had touched evil, came face to face with the Lord of Darkness, and survived. Since then, Nisha vowed to protect her loved ones, and her best friends from anyone that intended to cause them harm.

Meeting Pierre triggered her, instigating her defensive nature to bubble to the surface. There was something dangerous about him that Nisha couldn't articulate. She just knew in her gut that he felt like death.

❖ ❖ ❖

"Every time I've tried to be what someone else thought of me. So caught up, I wasn't able to achieve." —The Miseducation of Lauryn Hill by Lauryn Hill

CHAPTER 4
ARCTURUS STARS

"The Way is not in the sky; the Way is in the heart."
— B U D D H A

Jo

My friends and I hung out in my parent's family room after school, doing our homework. Everyone seemed uptight, juggling our grades, extracurricular activities, and unrealistic expectations. Life seemed hectic as we continued to perpetuate the cycle of perceived perfection.

"Guys, I'm so stressed. I have hives in some of the weirdest places! It's not much fun, I tell ya!" Daphne complained, scratching her lower back. "The thought of volunteering for more after-class programs on top of homework, band, school, and rehearsals makes me want to scream."

"I feel you, Daph," Zax responded. "Between football practices, championship games, and getting tutored so I don't flunk tenth-grade algebra, I'm feeling burned out."

"Stop complaining, guys. We are lucky to be going to this school," Nisha interjected, annoyed at the whining. "This extra crap that we have to do for university prep, is pointless anyway. A psychology de-gree will be totally useless when the planet finally implodes in twenty years."

I agreed with my best friend, however, I wanted to provide Daphne with a sympathetic ear and a safe space to unload her feelings. "What are the pre-requisites for your program, Daph?"

"I have to volunteer in Machu Picchu and win a mock science com-petition!" she exclaimed in frustration.

"Yo, we only have two more years left before graduating, guys. That's just craziness. I don't think I'm ready to adult," Flynn added, exasper-ated by the prospect of mundane responsibilities of life.

"I'm not sure we need to rush the process, Flynn," I replied, hoping to soothe everyone's nerves.

"And perhaps, we should re-examine our future paths, guys. Why do we need to follow in our parent's footsteps if that's not what we want to do? We have the right and the freedom to choose our authentic experiences and to follow our passions, don't you agree?" I planted an interesting alternative for my friends.

All of us had been conditioned by society and our parents to follow a prescribed path that fed into the broken and unreasonable systems, prioritizing the value of money over basic human needs and our planet's welfare.

"My parents will freak out and cut me off if I don't get into univer-sity!" Flynn laughed. "Maybe that wouldn't be such a bad thing."

"Well, I don't know about you guys, but I'm pretty certain that I want to go to med school. For that, I need top-notch grades," Nisha replied, while simultaneously texting Alicia.

"You would make an incredible doctor, Nish!" Daphne giggled. "I can just picture you in your white overcoat with a stethoscope around your neck, bossing all the male attendees."

"Ya, you can treat my head injuries from my pro football games," Zax said, looking solemn.

I could feel the tension rising in the room. The expectations of this distorted reality to strive for perfection was an increasingly difficult measure for our generation. The angst and anxiety emanating from my friends sucked the oxygen from the room as we silently sat around the warm fireplace, contemplating the rest of our lives. We were barely seventeen.

How many of us had compromised our mental health or conceded our integrity to enhance our qualifications to get into the perfect school? How much did a university degree prepare us for a balanced and successful life in today's environment anyway, when our planet was weakening?

It all seemed very archaic, rooted in competition and division as we continued to fight each other for the esteemed honors. This whole notion insulted my soul. The quest for perfection was unhealthy and stemmed from external sources of limitations and scarcity.

There was nothing wrong with high-achieving people who excelled at challenges, but the difference was that they didn't harbor the delusion that they had to be good at everything.

My sister Liz was a perfect example of a high achiever. She valued constructive criticism as an opportunity for self-improvement and growth. Liz didn't crumble with the prospect of failure; she simply overcame the setbacks with a healthy attitude, which motivated her to work harder.

However, my friends and I continued to strive for reinforced perfection in every aspect of our lives, thinking that it would guarantee success in obtaining the constricted opportunities. This lack-based belief further propagated our level of worthiness and value unless we met the impossibly high self-imposed standards.

We continued to discuss how our perceived imposter syndrome stifled our creativity for innovation, music, and arts in general. What we needed most from our educational system was to equip us with emotional intelligence and tenacity. This would be incredibly helpful to prepare us for the realities facing our generation, coupled with tangible, shared skill sets, and leadership qualities.

Most of us craved the challenge and strong work ethic to contribute with solutions that evolved our future for the betterment of humanity and our planet.

My heart stirred with empathy and compassion at this profound understanding of these disputes facing my peers. Collectively, we all desired to belong to a culture that accepted and celebrated originality, diversity, and creativity, not suppressed it.

Life as we knew it was about to change. Even as I submerged myself in the warm, healing embrace of my bubble bath, there was a deep resonance of inner knowing. I closed my eyes, deepening my breath as I focused on the rhythmic thumping of my heart. It pounded into my ears; almost immediately, a sense of serenity overcame me.

As I entered my transcendental meditative state, I saw the white plasma light pulsating in changing forms. The colors began to reflect my mind's eye in hues of blue and soft purple. I could feel every fiber of my body activated by the transmission. The etheric blueprint light codes released my fourth-dimensional structure and caused geometric spins within my emotional, mental, and physical forms.

My body absorbed the plasma light like a sponge. The changes began to manifest rapidly as I started to feel the heaviness of the fatigue in every aspect of my being.

The blueprint enabled my emotional Light body to act as a transducer; a decoder of higher frequencies, connected to the pulsing rhythm of Mother Earth, Gaia. We were now one, bonded, with our hearts aligned, our breath in symphony. I could feel her angst, her pain, her burning rage.

We, humans, had ravaged our planet, its resources, leaving truly little for the rest of the ecosystem. It was so sad to realize that we had infested the wild natural habitats with our greed, pestilence, and disregarded our environment, leaving Gaia vulnerable to pollution, disease, and exploitation.

How did we allow this to happen? I wished people could feel and sense her desperation. Perhaps then, humans would put aside personal desires to seek fortune, fame, and power from external stimulation. We all carried the collective responsibility for our children's future. It was not too late to save our planet.

Gaia was undergoing a mass extinction, including the threat of survival of mankind. Unfortunately for our race, we were not as important as we believed. Mother Earth would recalibrate and renew herself as needed in her evolution. She would endure, outgrow us, and new life would eventually arise.

"It's not too late, Jo. There is still hope."

The exotic voice in my head jolted me out of my meditative state. I sat up in the lukewarm tub, my heart racing. *Could it be, have I tapped into the secure telepathic channel?*

"Roma?"

"*Sorry to disturb your reflections, Jo. You were having quite a conversation with yourself.*"

Was she taunting me? I couldn't tell, but I was liking her sense of humor.

"*Oh my God, I have been trying to reach out to you for days. Are you okay?*"

"*Listen Jo, I am using a protected bandwidth frequency that the Lizzies are not aware of. We must be careful and keep this pathway safe from the insidious Wizard. They are hijacking humanity's thought patterns to poison and enslave the race. Can you hear me clearly?*"

"*I'm trying to focus on your energetic wave, Roma. This whole telepathy in real time is a new experience for me. Who is this Wizard? Is he the Lizzie that has captured you?*" I inquired, heart racing.

"*Yes, but they have no idea that I'm transmitting above the veil of density that encapsulates the Earth's atmosphere.*"

"*So, you're here, on planet Earth? How can I help you? Do you have a location of where you're being held? Maybe I can ask the Council for assistance. It sounds like we may need some celestial muscle to defeat this Wizard if he's anything like the Lord of Darkness,*" I replied with optimism.

"*No, Jo. It's against the galactic law for the Council to intervene on the physical plane. Consider me your teacher for this stage of the Angel Academy. I'm here to guide you through the Hall of Learning toward your mastery. By conversing with me, you will strengthen your psychic powers and discernment. But we don't have much time.*"

"*Why, Roma?*" Before she could answer me, I felt the ominous flares in my gut. I quickly dried myself and got dressed. I continued to focus on her sound wave, as though I was tuning an old radio station for the less static channel.

"You are right to worry about this planet. We must help Gaia. She has called all the StarSeeds to awaken to their mission in this dimension. We are here to sound the alarm. A wake-up call to help humankind toward urgent action to save Earth from imminent destruction. I am here with the Blade of Truth to unchain humanity from the density."

I took a deep breath, grounding myself while I sat back in bed and listened to this incredibly wise soul. I didn't know much about Roma, but there was a familiarity about her. A kinship from another lifetime perhaps. I was so curious to hear her story.

"Gaia is trying to transmute this heaviness and smog of putrid waste. The Lizzie forces have poisoned the air, water, and food sources to dumb down humans. They have been dictating the future of mankind through mind control and brainwash," Roma said.

"You have graduated from the Hall of Ignorance within the Angel Academy. That is the only reason you can hear me, Jo. Congrats by the way!"

As she spoke, I closed my eyes, taking deep, cleansing breaths. My pineal gland burst with explosive light as her transmissions were received without unwanted static.

"I don't understand, Roma. We extradited the Lord of Darkness into another dimension, away from our star system. How did the Lizzies succeed so quickly?" I asked.

"The Dark Forces have many agents enlisted to perpetuate their sinister agenda. They have the technology to time-travel and have quantum leaped into this timeline through portals to seize Gaia's plush resources," Roma answered.

"Are they behind all the environmental conspiracies?" The revelation about how chemtrails accelerated global warming and caused pandemics deepened my resolve further.

"This galactic war began with the great experiment millions of years ago, Jo. The descent into physicality was placed right next to a much bigger constellation, called Draco. It contained ancient dark, service-to-self Lizzie entities, known as the Draconians. This began the great conflict between the Light and Dark Forces, commencing within the Lyrian timeline."

"I thought humans were a free-willed race?" I questioned with naivety.

"As sentient beings, we gave away our inherent freedom through patriarchal, disempowering belief systems. There was a loophole within the galactic agreements where these low-density entities have taken advantage of humans to dominate and control the masses. They feed off the collective thought patterns of every Soul that has existed within the Akashic Records. This allows them to enslave beings that have been zombified and have forgotten their truth, Jo," Roma explained.

"You see, humans have been conditioned with limiting programs installed into their DNA emotional Light Bodies. This presented an opportunity for the Lizzies to become more insatiable and driven to defeat all light beings that represent the Prime Creator, the Source of love energy, once and for all."

"So, this is much more severe than the sleepwalkers that acted as hosts for the Lord of Darkness?" I asked. The Council had imparted some of the historic teachings in my first stage of ascension, but at the time, I was not ready for the entire truth behind creation.

"Are you sure you can handle this history lesson, Jo? Once you peek through the elusive shroud of existence, there's no going back," Roma warned.

"I am ready, Roma. Bring it." I chuckled nervously telepathically while my mouth went dry in anticipation.

"Well, for the sake of time, I'll have to give you the SparkNotes version. So, the Prime Creator, the Source, split itself into two aspects of duality consciousness. There is the Alpha Mother galaxy, known as Andromeda, and the Omega Father galaxy, the Milky Way. This is also known as the Antares Stargate, where the Galactic Center exists around the Grand Central Sun. This Center is managed by the OverSoul Groups, called the Founders."

"Are the Founders responsible for the great experiment?" I couldn't get the information fast enough. Suddenly, I had this unquenchable thirst for the truth, for the narrative that had eluded humans since the beginning of time.

"Yes, the Founders created two races on the tiny constellation of Lyra, a star system close to the Galactic Center. They discovered it had optimal conditions for physical life. Here, they created the Feline and Avian races. Their new blue planet, Avyon, was a beautiful paradise, lavished with mountains, lakes, streams, and oceans. It resembled planet Earth with a variety of vegetation and several life forms," Roma explained, helping me visualize the enchanting utopia.

"Did they incarnate into the human race on Avyon Planet?" I asked, ensuring that our connection was still tethered.

"Well, the Felines experimented with a genetic program that crossed their DNA with mammals, giving them Souls. After millions of years and genomic upgrades, they formed the Nordic race, which represented the Omega male consciousness, and the blue Vegan race, inhabiting the divine Alpha female consciousness. The Nordic race created the Adamic humanoid. The Lyrans played an important role in seeding the first Nordic Souls onto Atlantis," she explained.

"*So, is that why the inhabitants of Atlantis were an advanced species? The Council downloaded that intelligence to help with their technology?*" I tried to refrain from interrupting her, but I needed to know.

"*The Lyrans contributed immense knowledge of physical energy to Atlantis. The society mastered the powers of the divine masculine energy and were experts in agriculture and nature. The citizens of Atlantis lived in abundance and peace for over forty million years,*" Roma replied.

"*So, who were the blue Vegans, and where did they live?*" I was transfixed, trying to mentally follow the timelines while Roma communicated her knowledge.

"*That's my ancestry, Jo. The Vegans were a darker, blue-skinned group who upheld mother consciousness with their femininity, creativity, and spirituality using thought and intention setting. They were a peaceful race, focused on kindness and service using their healing powers. They created my planet Lemuria, the only fifth-dimensional civilization that had ever existed to date. Lemuria was colonized by the Arcturus extra-terrestrial beings who exist within the twelfth-dimensional plane. They were joined by a collective colony of consciousness that included Lyrans, Sirius, Pleiades, and Nibiru.*"

"*Sounds like a beautiful place to live, Roma. Did you grow up there?*" I asked, feeling her nostalgia.

"*Yes, Lemuria was a majestic, enchanting paradise that existed on a large continent in the Pacific Ocean. It was home to magnificent magical creatures like my best friend, Pegasus. My peaceful continent embodied the divine feminine energy of Love. Our culture explored imagination, celebrated artistic expression, and evolved through Dreamtime, interdimensional travel, and astral projection.*"

"*What happened to Lemuria? They were a peaceful, loving nation, right?*" I didn't want to admit that the Council showed me the destruction of Roma's beloved home. Even using telepathy, I could feel her energy of pain and loss.

"Long story short, Atlantis, driven by greed and world domination, destroyed our gentle nation during the big war. We were outmatched with our limited technology. And this was how Gaia plunged from the fifth-dimensional realm into the third-dimensional existence. Even today, remnants of Lemuria can be found splattered across the Hawaiian Islands, New Zealand, Easter Islands, and parts of Australia," Roma clarified.

"I'm so sorry, Roma. That must have been devastating for you." I hoped she could feel my sincerity. Her story of Lemuria sounded way too familiar. My heart seized at the thought that the same fate awaited our beloved planet Earth.

"So, how did the Lizzies emerge in this galactic formation?" I changed the subject, sensing her emotions filtering through the static connection.

"The ancient Draconian beings originated from a completely different Universe, Jo, a much larger star system. They represent a deceptive fear-based consciousness and polarity, vibrating on a lower density frequency that contains dark, sinister energy. They were known to leave nothing but destruction in their path and were physically expunged from their constellation by higher-dimensional beings." Roma paused for a moment, centering herself back in alignment.

"They were deposited in this Universe on the Orion star system, in the constellation of Draco. Their original pedigree was the Ciakar, a genetically mutant race that also embodied the Lizzie consciousness of separation. They have the power to swing from darkness to light, depending on their desires. They are mysterious, reclusive, yet powerful adaptable beings that can shapeshift into matter easily. You need to know that they resemble alligators and enjoy feasting on human flesh."

"*They sound alarming, Roma! Who are the other StarSeeds? Can we organize a group to come save you?*" I pinched my leg in frustration. I sounded defenseless and weak.

"*The Lizzies are powered by limiting belief systems, fear-based conditioning, and victimhood programming. They are determined to prevent Gaia and humanity from crossing over the bridge to the fifth-dimensional existence of Light, where they cannot hide or exist in the shadows, due to the Galactic Law.*" Roma continued to explain.

"*This matrix of humanity's perceived reality is a network of systems that provides the celestial Light of goodness with a physical representation of consciousness in the form of a human body. The grid template on Earth has been seized and dominated by the Ciakar, who have controlled humans by emitting malevolent behaviors into the quantum field. This reality serves as a vibrational match of patterns and belief systems of disconnection from Source. Humanity has been dwelling in the specters of the Lizzies' self-projected, fear-based programming since the demise of Atlantis.*"

"*Do you know where they are holding you?*" My skin crawled at the thought of these creatures existing in our world. I prayed that Roma's physical location wasn't too far from me.

"*Unfortunately, I don't have the specific coordinates. I have fought these monsters many lifetimes, Jo. I'm not afraid of them, but I did lose my Lemurian sword. It is the only weapon powerful enough to destroy them in this realm. My Blade of Truth contains the original crystalline gemstones, embodying the Light of Source,*" she explained.

"*I battled the Lizzies during the great war, but I failed. The planet Avyon was destroyed by the Ciakar. They slaughtered over fifty million Lyrans, enslaving the young females as a food source and sex slaves for breeding purposes. They are nasty and have permeated planet Earth for their next conquest. This is the reason that Gaia has sounded the alarm, activating the StarSeed Quest and Light Warriors to awaken to their destiny and mission in this timeline. We cannot fail this time and allow Lemuria's history to repeat."*

"So, what's the plan, Roma? I'm not sure I alone can save you, never mind the entire planet." I took deep breaths to lower my anxiety and bring myself back in alignment. I wanted to believe and trust the process.

"I need you to locate my blade, Jo. It was created by the Arcturus, using the pureness and truth of their sacred star crystals, located in the Bootes constellation. They are the most advanced extraterrestrial civilization of our galaxy, mastering metaphysics, quantum physics, and healing modalities of the conscious mind," she replied.

"The Arcturus work closely with ascended masters of the Brotherhood, who are allies in this quest and known to be highly analytical. They have integrated their emotions and intuitive powers, becoming the protectors and guardians of the Universe. I have reincarnated many times to ascend and elevate my consciousness as one of the Custodians of the Galaxy."

"Wow, is that why the Lizzies have captured you, Roma? Are they looking for other Custodians with similar missions on Earth?" I could feel her determination and resolve to defeat these malevolent beings. I got the sense that Roma was a feisty galactic warrior, and I was in complete awe of her vitality.

"Yes, but I am protecting their identities. The only way we can defeat them is to heal and clear the collective wounds, triggers, and energy blocks that are still running programs of blame and judgment. Once these energy fields are processed on a mass scale, the emotional trauma stored within the collective nervous system of the grid matrix will be released. This has to occur to make room for Gaia and the sacred Light elevation into the fifth dimension."

"*Have they harmed you, Roma?*" I held my breath, waiting for her response.

"*Don't worry, Jo, they can never break me. However, I do need you to find the sword. It's lost somewhere in the bush, off the shores in the Canary Islands. Goddess Gaia will lead you. They are coming, I must go! Remember to trust your instincts!*" Roma concluded.

"*Wait, where on the Canary Islands? Roma, are you still there?*" My heart sank as I realized the connection was gone. I managed to say a prayer for Roma and humanity before I plunged under my covers, drained from the overload of information.

It dawned on me that our two-week school trip for spring break was also booked in the Canary Islands. Could this be a total coincidence?

I had to recharge and eliminate any doubts or anxiety that was trying to worm its way back into my awareness. I would not permit the darkness of the old paradigm back into my auric field.

I inhaled deeply, allowing the shard of white light to infiltrate my mind's eye as I recited my affirmations, downloaded by the Council for protection.

I call my power back. I choose to break free from the expectations placed upon me by family, friends, or society. I exclude myself from the narrative of the false matrix. Having sovereign free will is my birthright. I am not here to abide by the limitations set upon me.

I remember who I am. I am infinite light; I am limitless love. Any other definition would only confine my real essence of spirit. I am here to co-create my reality and to ignite the sacred fire within me. I am here to be my authentic self and to help break the cycle of conformity.

I am here to awaken the masses from the dream state that dims their light and rips their Souls apart. I break the cycle of submission of those who set these foundations and limitations. I shed the light on all atrocities and upheaval that's been swept under the rug by previous generations, exposing its veracity through forgiveness and healing.

When I ascend from my heart-centered awareness to meet myself in every form of each multi-dimensional realm that comes to be, the true reality of divine love arises within my vortex.

The Council of Creation ignited my remembrance. The Source expression of creation comes alive in my being. As such, all cellular imprints of darkness and shadows are transmuted in the presence of my eternal light. This is the integration process of Collective Awakening.

I understand that I always have a choice to approach my life either as a victim or a master of my existence. The Universe will grant me the capacity to rewire my subconscious mind and clear out the cellular debris. As such, I discover my emotional freedom, and even moments of heavenly revelation.

This choice of free will and self-reflection will lead me toward wholeness, oneness, and unity. My mission is to help integrate the density of our collective emotions and develop a more cohesive, loving connection with humanity. The more I radiate high frequencies of love, the more my physical reality manifests in my Celestial training.

I AM grateful to be here in the now. I AM loving awareness. I AM THE LIGHT THAT I AM.

As I drifted off to a much-needed sleep, I couldn't fathom the menacing scheme and level of devastation that was about to ensue on my beloved tribe.

Theo

Theo fixated on his notes, simultaneously tuning his electric bass. He enjoyed the after-school band group that included his eclectic classmates. Aside from his sister, Alicia, he didn't particularly appreciate anyone's company outside of the posh school. Even she annoyed him on most days with her righteous demeanor.

Alicia focused most of her attention on saving the planet, and Theo was supportive of her passions to a degree. As long as she respected his space and moods, they didn't have a problem. He liked to be left alone with his thoughts.

He was an introvert, masking his pain stemming from his identity crisis and the perceived social injustice all around him. For Theo, his twin sister exemplified the goodness of humanity, while he personified all the grief and suffering of an effeminate boy.

His upbringing was mired in childhood trauma and mental health issues. Adding to his fragile mindset was his handicap, his physical disability. He didn't feel whole or worthy to pick up the torch and fight for just causes like the environment or radical queer activism, like his sister.

For Theo, his battle stemmed from within, his perceptions of scarcity, limitations, and self-judgment. Theo was exhausted from the daily chronic pain he felt from losing his limb. As he grew into his teens, the hormones further agitated his emotional well-being. This caused him to give up on joy, trapped in a brooding transgender shadow of his inner child.

After a second suicide attempt, his parents were forced to confine him to a psychiatric institution. He hated himself for causing his family so much misery. But the experience left him feeling bitter and cynical, causing a great deal of tension with his loved ones.

Theo's stepfather didn't support his choice of identity. After all, he was brought up with limiting conservative beliefs, deeply rooted within his Hispanic ancestry. Although Theo felt loved by his mom and sister, he lacked the same emotion about himself.

He couldn't fathom living in this reality of inequality, persecution, systematic exploitation, and abuse of underprivileged populations. The repression of gender-nonconforming individuals, women, and minorities fed the structures of oppressive forces.

The more Theo learned about free enterprise through the lens of the institutionalized educational systems, imperialism, colonization, and genocide of innocent people across the world, the more he withdrew from life. He functioned on a survival-based autopilot, on a day-to-day basis, zombified by his medication.

The only reason he chose to exist every morning was Alicia. Theo had given her his word that he would not harm himself again. Alicia was quite intuitive and felt his pain as well as his internal turmoil. They were both trauma survivors, and the thought of safety consumed their daily realities.

Especially for Theo. The anxiety perpetuated by bullying and mob mentality in his school further devoured his state of being, fragmenting his Soul. There was solace in the familiarity of this pain. It validated his mood swings and feelings of shamefulness, sequestered within the chambers of his heart.

Alicia was the only person who didn't judge him or his morbid thoughts. She listened and provided a safe space for him to release the emotional storms, to prevent them from consuming him entirely.

Theo appreciated that about his sister; she didn't reject, abandon, or violate his freedom of expression. She provided a loving, nurturing environment without humiliation or guilt. He admired her strength and resilience to love him without conditions or expectations at such a young age.

Both brother and sister considered themselves as gender fluid, and Alicia understood his desires, as well as his fears. He deliberately stayed away from any type of relationship with classmates, due to his mistrust and fear of rejection.

Theo didn't believe any stranger could create a nurturing environment for him to express his intimacy, not until he dealt with his shadows with acceptance and self-love.

After all, pain and agony established a residency within every bone in his body. Only Alicia saw him fully, with his broken parts, respecting his boundaries, without preconceived expectations.

His sister provided him with a beacon of hope for a better world, where they could both dream of someday developing external relationships without discrimination, ridicule, and toxicity. Perhaps even joy.

Theo understood that the connection of radical queer kinship ran deeper than their bloodline. They both envisioned a world and a future reality where they celebrated each other's uniqueness, gifts, and radiance with kindness and a loving embrace. Where every person was acknowledged and accepted, despite labels and associations.

For Theo, Alicia was his lifeline, his support system. He held on to her with a tight grip, fighting the urge to drown in the bitter, cold storm of life's unyielding waves. Her adoration and faith in his redemption were his salvation. Theo's entire existence hinged on her safety, well-being, and happiness.

Jo

The Forest Hill Annual Sleep Fest was an esteemed tradition, dating back fifty years. It was an opportunity for students to socialize and release some steam from academic pressures, under tight supervision.

This year's theme was Star Wars, and the gymnasium was aptly decorated with fun memorabilia. As my friends and I entered the lavishly embellished gala, I felt transported into the galactic realms. The feeling was surreal as I marveled at the twinkling stars above me. I chuckled to myself at the magical significance of synchronicity.

"Holy crap, this Sleep Fest is on crack!" Daphne exclaimed, barely able to hide her excitement.

"Okay, so I scoped out the place and came up with an amazing game plan," Zax interjected, holding Flynn's hand.

"Awesome! But for now, let's go get weird my dudes!" Flynn laughed, pulling us all onto the dance floor as the Shuffle came on the sound system.

I loved dancing with my friends. These were the moments I cherished, the innocence and laughter of our youth. Although I was on hyper-alert, I allowed myself to get lost in the human experience.

After ten minutes of jubilation, we were all parched. We consumed the fruit punch that overflowed from the champagne fountain, fully aware of its non-potency. As I observed the smiles and auras of my beautiful friends, I felt elation and gratitude in my heart for the present moment.

Zax and Flynn were determined to take adorable couple pictures in the photo booth, both giggling at their silly expressions. Nisha and

Alicia continued to dance to a slow love song, gazing into each other's eyes in adoration. Daphne was vividly engaged in a discussion with other bandmates over the quality of our performance, dissecting the flaws related to our musical harmony.

As I stepped out of the gymnasium for some fresh air, I noticed Theo sitting by himself at the end of the hallway, under a homemade sign that read "Love Yourself, Don't Drug Yourself". He looked miserable while we were all enjoying ourselves, and it broke my heart.

"Hey, what are you doing out here, Theo? You're missing all the fun!" I said, fully aware of his aura.

"The Sleep Fest is lame. I was forced to attend so I could keep an eye on Alicia," he explained.

"Come on, it's one of the highlights of our preppy high school. They give us the night to relieve some of our stress. We should take advantage and let our hair down a bit," I prodded.

"This school doesn't care about us, Jo. They just want our parents' money, as long as we fit into their grand design," Theo complained. "If we don't take six AP classes, then we're labeled as underachievers. I'm sick of taking Adderall just to keep up with mediocrity. It's totally savage."

Pushing aside my intuitive suspicions, I opened my heart to sense Theo's underlining pain that seemed to stem from grief. It was the kind of anguish that caused a person to become resentful, damaging their ability to enjoy the simple pleasures of life.

"Well, you don't have to take any medication if you don't want to, Theo. Have you talked to your parents about this?" I asked, hoping that he had a loving support system.

"Nah, don't worry about it. It's not your problem. Everyone has shit to deal with. Don't let me ruin your night." And just like that, Theo shut me down and left me standing in the hallway to ponder his auric energetic projection.

Feeling saddened by his dense emotions, I shielded myself from Theo's anguish as its energy tried to attach to my essence, attempting to drain my power.

I turned back toward the blaring gymnasium, and my stomach dropped at the sight of Darth Vader's statue ominously guarding the doorway. It sent electric pulses down my spine. Something sinister was afoot, and it was coming for us.

❖ ❖ ❖

"Now tell me your philosophy, on exactly what an artist should be. Should they be someone with prosperity and no concept of reality?"—Superstar by Lauryn Hill

CHAPTER 5

SPRING BREAK

"Nothing is, unless our thinking makes it so."
—WILLIAM SHAKESPEARE

Ms. Rolland

Ms. Rolland stood beside her desk as the first bell rang, prompting the students to make their way to her history class. She stared at the heavy wooden doors that framed the entrance to the classroom. She straightened her pencil skirt, removing the creases. Her hair bound tight in a sleek bun and with rectangular glasses, she represented the perfect stereotype of a strict, private school teacher.

Jo walked into the class with her friends, laughing at some errant joke. Ms. Rolland's sharp shifty eyes focused as her Lizzie energy tuned into Jo's emotional Light Body. Her mind regurgitated the galactic plot tasked by the Wizard, Ciakar.

As she reminisced, Ms. Rolland's Lizzie body stood tall on two brawny legs in front of a throne carved out of limestone. A nine-foot, menacing, muscular body with thick, scaly porous skin perched in command, with yellow gleaming eyes.

The upper echelon Draconian's oversized head resembled that of a massive gator, showcasing a precious black crystal crown that was propped on his head. The Wizard's green Lizzie scales shimmered in the cosmic light penetrating through the shadowy surface. The putrid scent wafted through the darkness. Unlike humans, Lizzies didn't defecate or urinate, as their scaly skin naturally excreted the waste.

The shapeshifter bowed, remembering the hierarchy of her middle-class status. "My King, you summoned me?" she asked in their native Draconian tongue.

The mysterious and reclusive Wizard barely acknowledged Ms. Rolland. He slithered his massive, formidable, lengthy tail. The menacing sound alone was enough to break the strongest of their Lizzie warriors.

The Wizard Ciakar rose from his seat slowly, standing tall over the shapeshifter's bowing body. He walked down the steps, every movement threatening Ms. Rolland's existence.

He snapped his tail, pounding the cement ground. A lower-class Lizzie servant immediately approached the throne, carrying an opened container that revealed a tiny, pearl-sized black crystal. It shimmered like corrugated metal under the sunlight.

"Take this precious stone to help you access the Earth realm. It will allow you to blend with the humans and go undetected on your mission," Ciakar ordered.

"I command you to bring her to me to the fourth-dimensional astral plane. Do not disappoint me, Lizzie," the Wizard warned as he glided away.

"Yes, my King. I understand. I will not let you down." Ms. Rolland took a deep breath, realizing the gravity of her task. Failure was not an option. She had too much at stake.

Back in the classroom, she stared at Jo, scheming and plotting ways to capture her target and destroy her once and for all. After all, it was Jo who had ruined her alliance with the Lord of Darkness.

She could taste the sweetness of revenge as she envisioned gnawing on her human bones.

Ms. Rolland was still unaware of the Wizard's human identity when he shapeshifted on Earth. Ciakar had retained that secret from all his Lizzie Warriors for a reason.

This mystery kept Ms. Rolland on edge and suspicious of everyone who crossed her path. She had to be extremely vigilant with every human she encountered. She assessed their thought patterns and latched onto the low vibrations, hijacking their ideas and perceptions for the cause. World domination.

❖ ❖ ❖

Jo

I had no idea how I managed to get through the last two weeks of school with stability. I teleported through time to get my schoolwork completed while I continued to astral travel to other worlds during the night, in preparation for my mission.

Roma and I had a few psychic discussions through telepathy but couldn't maintain the frequency for too long. She was incredibly careful not to risk losing our secure energetic line.

One thing had become increasingly clear: I didn't possess the same ethereal abilities in the physical world. Even though my angelic light wings had blossomed, my human body needed to acclimate to higher frequencies of energy by anchoring the plasma light codes. This transition had to happen organically over a period of time. It was necessary to prevent shock and trauma to my DNA through this fourth-dimensional ascension process.

As such, I focused my energy on rest and meditation in solitude. To contain my vitality, I decided to refrain from creating more music and listening to my beloved Tupac soundtracks. I was aligning my energy fields and increasing my strength in silence and stillness, preparing for what was to come.

Roma clarified that the Galactic Council had learned from their past interventions with humanity. She explained that over seven thousand years ago, the higher-dimensional Light Beings managed to create an interdimensional layer where they were able to interact and communicate with humans. This was known as the fourth-dimensional rainbow bridge, which connected the ethereal and physical states of existence.

I reveled at the knowledge that the Galactic Light Beings designed the pyramids of the world, Machu Picchu, and the sacred sites of Stonehenge to help evolve our race. Their light beams raised the frequency of those to allow humans access to the higher intelligence without risking the health of their physical form.

However, the level of energy required to work with the Galactic Council had drained their human bodies, leaving them vulnerable to the lower dimensional Lizzies to evade our world.

They permeated the fourth-dimensional loophole, seized human minds that harbored the lower realms. They continued to destroy the civilizations that were taught by the Galactic Beings, removing any trace of knowledge and advanced technical abilities of ancient Egypt.

No wonder our ancient history was skewed, leaving no evidence behind. The Galactic Council was devastated by these atrocities, passing a law that prohibited their Celestial interference on Earth.

As such, the Draconian agenda for domination of Gaia and humanity propelled in full force under the new world order.

My mind fixated on getting to the location where Roma was being held and tortured. The stronger I got, the more perceptive my psychic powers had become.

I really wanted to teleport to the island by myself, but that was forbidden by the Angel Academy. There were no shortcuts for this mission. My path had been set.

Our trip to the Canary Islands was coordinated by Ms. Rolland. I was surprised our school principal, Mr. Grey, appointed her to lead this excursion. After all, it was a great responsibility, especially after the incident in Barcelona last fall. With Rey's accidental overdose at the music festival, I thought there would be a bit more pushback from the School Board of Directors to ensure suitable supervision. I was astonished that he trusted her with his precious student body.

Ms. Rolland didn't bother hiding her disdain for me, but I removed her from my awareness. I couldn't spend much time with my best friends, but they were hyped for Spring Break. We were extremely fortunate to be travelling to such a luxurious tropical destination.

As I packed hastily for the flight, I noticed my mother hovering over me. I sensed her electric verve as she dabbled casually around my room under the guise of providing a helping hand. She was quite attuned to reading the collective energy and had her perspective about humanity's great awakening.

"Everything will be all right, Mom; you don't have to worry," I said, hoping to address the elephant in the room.

"I know, my love. I'm not concerned. All will be well. You are such a strong and capable young woman, empowered to manifest your own reality. I am excited about all the adventures ahead of you. I just wish the Council would provide you with more Celestial guidance to find Roma on the remote island." She paused to find the right words.

"Do you even know the location where she's being held?" she asked. "You know, I don't mind accompanying your classmates on this school trip as an extra volunteer. I could offer my wisdom and intuitive abilities to derail the Wizard."

"We have plenty of parents supervising our trip, Mom." I took her hand and gently soothed her apprehensions with my energy.

"You of all people know that I alone must follow the prescribed path for this mission. Our planet is decimated, and Gaia is in agony. Reducing my carbon footprint is not enough anymore. The success of this quest is vital to save Roma and our planet. Once we defeat the Lizzie Wizard and cross this dimensional realm into safety, then we can focus on phasing out fossil fuels, restricting meat consumption, converting agricultural farmland to wilderness space, and eliminating non-biodegradable items."

"I understand this is your journey, Jo. I honor your path, my love. However, the entities that you are about to encounter are hostile, aggressive shapeshifters, with a million years of experience. You will need more galactic help this time."

"I have my friends, the Arcturus guides, and I trust Roma to call in the StarSeed Quest if needed. I just have to use my discernment and intuition when it comes to people around me." I wasn't sure if I was consoling my mother or myself at this point.

"It's quite daunting to balance the energy around you. Everything in the Universe is a vibrational match to frequencies emitted by people. Just remember, if someone is compromised and operating from separation duality consciousness, they won't be able to take accountability for their behaviors. They will be vulnerable to attract low vibrational entities. If that happens, Jo, you must face all your emotions with courage," she explained.

I prepared for the lecture that was about to ensue. She was not going to see me for two weeks, so I took deep breaths and provided her with the space to express her feelings and viewpoint.

"As we have learned from the tragic experience with Rey, when compromised people give their power away to external substances or even judgmental gossiping, they attract the darkness. These ancient energies affix to the human ego through the nervous system, allowing the Lizzie hijacking to occur. This is how the Wizard recruits his army. These innocent bystanders become representatives of the Dark Forces to recruit others for global control."

"I am aware how it works, Mom. It's part of my celestial training. Don't worry, I'm not going to put myself or the mission in a compromising situation with alcohol or drugs. If anyone attempts to muzzle my truth, I will alchemize and transmute their energy into light. I will not get caught in the shadowlands of desolation this time. I promise." I embraced my mother, holding her tightly, ending further conversation on this matter.

She had been my rock through this self-discovery, and my heart exploded with love and gratitude for her wisdom and grace.

I couldn't recall if I had packed all the proper essentials for the trip between conversations with my family, texting with Nisha and Daphne, Conrad, and channeling my thoughts to Roma.

I was determined to find her Blade of Truth. I worked on sharpening my intuitive tools, hoping to use my third eye as a honing device. I planned to teleport to the exact location of the sword once I landed on the island.

I was comforted by an intense feeling within me that Gaia was keeping it safe, hidden in her grassy embrace, far from the clutches of the rancid shapeshifters.

As we landed on Tenerife island, the largest and most populated of the Canary Islands, the air was thick with humidity and anticipation. My curly hair frizzed in the dampness instantaneously. I tried to maintain my neutral cool, distancing myself from the excited energy emitted by my hormonal friends.

This was a trip of a lifetime for normal teenagers. If my previous, unenlightened version had attended this excursion seven months ago, I would also have been consumed with the possibilities of romantic endeavors and hard-core partying.

However, I needed to prioritize my mission above everything else. It was essential for me to build my psychic powers with a stronger, lucid foundation.

Even Conrad was giddy with the prospect of consummating our relationship. Unfortunately, I did not share his enthusiasm or desire.

Lately, I was feeling emotionally disconnected from my boyfriend. Perhaps I'd been too distracted by my task or Roma. She was literally always in my mind. The connection with her felt so different, ethereal, and boundless. My every thought was absorbed by her essence as she nourished my strength, wisdom, and Soul.

"Earth to Jo, did you hear Alicia's question?" Nisha asked, annoyed by my lack of focus on the conversation.

"Sorry, Nish, I spaced out. Which question?" I said with a sheepish grin.

"I was just telling Nisha that once we return from our trip, we should organize a Youth Climate Coalition. We really need to act and educate our school about the blazing environmental issues. I propose we strike once a month to get the older generation's attention that change is imminent," Alicia said with passion.

"I didn't realize you felt so strongly about our planet, Alicia. Have you engaged in other climate protests?" Finally, a topic that piqued my interest.

Alicia's calm demeanor and gentle loving aura didn't fit the stereotypical activist traits. She was quite charming, with coarse dark curly hair tied up in a high ponytail. Her glow brightened as she continued to project her passion. No wonder Nisha was enraptured by this beautiful Soul.

"It's so important to inspire our youth with accurate information so we can engage in respectful and peaceful dialogue about the effects of climate change." Alicia paused briefly, as Theo stared at her intensely with irritation.

They were sitting together next to Nisha and Daphne. He didn't seem as passionate on this subject matter. I felt so much empathy for Theo, it was inexplicable. There was a wave of underlying anger, a deeply rooted rage that I instantly recognized. His energy was remarkably similar to Rey's. *May they rest in paradise.*

"There is power in the masses, don't you agree Jo?" Alicia continued, unaffected by Theo.

"This is the only way the school is going to acknowledge our collective voice. We can start small, making changes within our district, neighborhood, then communities. We need to see action. This will only happen if we, the young consumers, raise our voices about alternative environmental methods that could still provide the materialistic lifestyle that we are all accustomed to living," she said ardently.

"Sounds really interesting, Alicia. Nisha, Daphne, and I have had this conversation many times. Perhaps we can take some time during our stay on the islands to come up with a viable plan that our school Principal will approve." I was committed to mobilizing our youth to act. However, I had to save Roma first, and then our planet.

"I'm totally in, guys, but can we just take a couple of days to enjoy our spring break?" Daphne chimed in, blushing innocently.

"Yes, yes, Daph, don't worry. We'll get plenty of beach time," Nisha said, comforting our sweet friend.

"Not just that, Nish. I can't wait to visit one of the highest volcanoes in the world. I read that Teide is Spain's tallest peak, with its two ecosystems. This will be the best trip ever!" Daphne squealed in excitement.

If she only knew that we were also venturing to find the Lost City of Atlantis, the most probable site of Roma's captivity.

"Alicia has some lofty ideas, Jo. Wait until you see her list!" Nisha chuckled at Daphne, totally enchanted by her new crush, gushing like a lovesick puppy.

Alicia continued with her dreams about activism. "There are so many emerging factors; it can get quite overwhelming."

"We are witnessing the effects of climate change every single day, massive environmental disasters all over the world that we simply can't ignore any longer! Mother Earth needs our help, and we must take action that will benefit our entire ecosystem."

The more I listened to Alicia, the more I realized that the vibrational frequency she was emitting had a similar tone and pitch as Roma's. I pondered whether she belonged to the StarSeed Quest.

I had to find out, so I focused my efforts on communicating with Alicia telepathically, but she was not receiving my clairvoyant signal.

Perhaps I could sneak away and find some alone time with Alicia for further exploration once we arrived at the resort. I could use my galactic compass to teleport quietly...wait, why couldn't I find my cosmic pendant? I always kept it in the pocket of my favorite hoodie. I feverishly checked my backpack, my heart pounding a mile a minute.

Breathe, Jo, just breathe.

"What's up Jo? Everything okay?" Nisha asked, perplexed by my reaction.

"Huh? Yup, I just realized that I forgot an extremely important item at home. I can't believe I didn't pack my lucky charm." The look of despair in my eyes was enough for both Nisha and Daphne to understand my cryptic reply. Without the cosmic crystals encased in the compass, I wouldn't be able to time-travel through portals.

How the heck was I going to save Roma without the help of the Council, magic, or my teleportation device?

Breathe, center, align, calm. All is well. This is just a test of my ingenuity and resilience. I would find a way without the celestial shortcuts. No big deal. I had to save Roma from the Lizzie Wizard as a human with plasma light wings.

Sure, I got this.

"Here you go, Jo. The list is long but take a look when you have a moment. I think we should prioritize the top five issues like toxins, climate change, energy, water, and biodiversity." Alicia handed me the well-researched, five-page document. I was quite impressed that she had given this extensive thought.

"But there's also air pollution, waste management, and ozone depletion. Gosh, I don't know where we can start, but as long as we begin to make changes...anyway, Nisha has my handles. DM me in a group chat, and we can continue this conversation after everyone has settled in." Alicia glanced at Nisha, giving her a little wink. They were definitely going to see each other before our group date.

As my heart settled back to normalcy, I couldn't help but feel the warmth radiating through my center every time I observed Nisha's behavior. There was an aura of tranquility yet excitement in her energy that I had not seen in a long time.

I allowed myself to momentarily get immersed in their innocent laughter, draping their energy around me like a cozy blanket as we departed the stifling airport with all our belongings. Their fervent chatter filled the surrounding space with exhilaration.

Conrad was attached to my hip, dragging his suitcase while chattering in anticipation of the great adventures to come. The noise of numerous wheels grating the concrete pavement pierced through my heightened senses. My intuition was broadened and fine-tuned to everything around me, on guard and high alert.

I set my practice to work, spanning out my energy in a radius around us. My quest to find strange, inhuman auras pulled me away from the group conversations.

"Jo! Look at this awesome view!" I turned towards Conrad, zooming back into the reality of human existence. My galactic thoughts were interrupted by the conversations finally breaking through my physical sense.

Conrad exhibited a look of amazement on his face. I followed his gaze to discover the lush green grassy hills surrounded by the captivating azure oceanic presence, engulfing the airport's infrastructure.

"I cannot wait to jump into the ocean for a refreshing swim! Wait till you see my dope bikini!" I heard Nisha exclaim with gusto. "It's total fire!"

Daphne trailed back to line her steps with mine.

"Jo, I feel a little insecure and overwhelmed with anxiety all of a sudden," she whispered, breathing heavily.

"What's wrong, Daph?" I asked, gently cupping her hand.

"The swimsuits. I don't want to look hideous in front of everyone." Her energy permeated my auric field. She was running low on confidence.

"I guess I'm still feeling vulnerable. I know it's in the past, but the mean girls in our school have damaged my self-esteem. The way they would assess me every morning, examining my entire body for flaws so they could judge me, to enable the delusional beliefs of their hierarchical superiority," she said, her lips pursed, swallowing the sadness of her ordeal.

I consoled her. "It's all right, Daph. Take deep, slow breaths. It's important to acknowledge and honor your feelings. Those girls can't harm you and don't have any power over you. Only you do. Keep focusing on your breath and remember the practice of self-love with every inhale." I reminded her of her affirmations to lower her stress hormones.

"Concentrate on your heartbeat. Now pay attention to my voice and receive with an open heart," I directed with certainty. "You are beautiful, powerful, worthy, exceptional, and whole. You are loved beyond measure and are here for a reason. You matter, and your happiness matters," I recited as a gentle reminder.

"I'm so grateful to have you in my life, Daph. You are such a brilliant light. Your beauty shines from within you. You have the kindest and most compassionate heart!" I continued to reiterate the truth, hoping to boost her confidence. I bathed her in my Light energy to calm her rolling emotions.

"But I'm still overweight, and swimsuits don't look good on people like me." She continued to negate my healing frequency.

Daphne had struggled with her self-image most of her adolescence. I held space for her to allow the emotions to the surface without negating her feelings. I showered her with warmth, understanding and compassion.

"Daphne, beauty standards are man-made atrocities. Perhaps you wish to ask yourself if you want to allow external forces to influence your worthiness with their toxic attitudes," I asked.

"Do you want to continue operating from this state of disempowerment? Or do you want to embrace your gift of life and radiate the beauty of your Soul?" My instincts guided my honest words.

"No, you're right, Jo. Why should I allow those girls to take my joy away? I am strong, I am courageous, I am beautiful, I am powerful," Daphne said.

"Exactly, don't ever forget that! Only you can control how you think and feel about yourself. Always choose your sovereignty, my beautiful friend. Take back your power. It's your birthright."

I reiterated how the expansive force of love-consciousness manifested internally through our state of being unified from within. Our thoughts governed our emotions, feelings, and actions. The way we acted reflected our heart and mind coherence. Our freedom to choose our actions signified our sovereignty of the self. And freedom was the external manifestation of our true divine essence, the path to self-love, self-mastery, balance, harmony, and internal peace.

The healing energy of my Light took effect. The chaotic conflict within her aura reduced back to a peaceful hue. She smiled and gave me the warmest embrace.

"Can we take this love fest to the resort, please? We don't want to miss the bus!" Nisha interrupted, grinning widely.

We walked behind Theo and Alicia, who didn't seem as excited to be on the island. Their reserved personalities rendered them even more alluring. I sensed a change in their auras, and intrigue boosted through me. My light probed their energies, and I intuitively got pulled toward Alicia's essence as we boarded the oversized bus.

"Jo, have you landed yet? I can feel you getting closer." I jolted upright instantly in my seat as Roma interjected my thoughts.

"Yes, we're on our way to the resort on Tenerife Island. How do I find you, Roma?"

"I think Ciakar is holding me on a remote private mansion, located in the smallest of the seven Canary Islands. There's massive plant life, vegetation, and wildlife here. His compound is well-hidden from satellite

imagery. Not to mention that it's also home to the endangered species of the giant lizard," she explained.

"Seriously, are you making that up Roma?" I giggled to myself. Was the Wizard that predictable?

"There is nothing funny about this mission, Jo! I didn't mention this before, but Ciakar is using this large compound for human trafficking. This is exactly what the Lizzies did on Lemuria, enslaving the young and innocent. We must not let history repeat itself. Stay focused, use your discernment, and find my blade quickly!"

Before I had a chance to respond, I felt the disconnection. We were cut off abruptly as I dealt with the shocking information. The echo within my energetic vortex wavered downward, trying to process Roma's agitated statement. I recited a silent prayer for her protection as well as our own.

I surrender with grace and flow into a deeper vibrational alignment of the loving and intelligent Universe. I breathe in love and release old fears.

I came back from the trenches of telepathic energy exchange and opened my eyes to the present surroundings. As I exhaled the released energy, I quietly placed my head on the massive glass window, observing the gorgeous scenery. I continued to exercise my psychic skills during the picturesque bus ride.

Could this truly be part of my Ascension mission? The Council was testing my trust.

Breathe, Jo. All is well. I closed my eyes for a moment, realigning my centers.

The next morning, I was deeply thankful to have my best friends with me to confide in. With last night's lack of sleep, I wasn't certain if I was able to handle Roma's shocking revelation and process its potency on my own.

After we defeated the Lord of Darkness and converted the sleepwalkers back to their human teenage selves, my friends had become quite immune to my Celestial shares.

"What the heck does she mean, Jo? A human trafficking operation? On this beautiful, peaceful island?" Flynn echoed my disbelief. With eyes wide open, he could barely consume his burger and fries.

"I just don't understand how you will be able to find Roma, never mind save her from these nasty shapeshifters, Jo. I will help you, of course, but we need cosmic muscle that none of us can provide," Zax stated. His main concern was always my safety. I loved his genuine warmth and gentleness.

"All right, guys, let's regroup before Ms. Rolland shows up with our boring itineraries," Nisha stated.

"I did some research online and human trafficking is a multi-billion-dollar operation. How can this be happening in our society?" she said in disdain. "It's a modern-day form of slavery and a pervasive assault on the victim's fundamental human rights. Who are these consumers? Don't they know what they are enabling?" Nisha exclaimed in a hushed voice.

"From what I understand, Nish, the Lizzie duality consciousness is seizing people's collective thought patterns. These are humans who have been operating in judgment, blame, hatred, and fear," I relayed my teachings.

"The fourth-dimensional astral realm has been hijacked by Lizzie pirates, through corruption, addictions to porn, sugar, drugs, and alcohol. They extract our energy with sinister thought patterns, thrusting us to act under their influences so they can feast on our negative charge." I quietly observed their reactions.

"So, much like the bullies in our school that were turned into sleepwalkers?" Daphne asked.

"Yes, but this is on a collective level. Not individual, so the Lizzie assault on humanity is much more powerful. We know that the Dark Forces are operating the archaic structures on our planet, using mind control to keep us stuck in a state of fear. This frequency is linked to our life force energy." I articulated the download as best as I could.

"So, how are we going to save a bunch of people we don't even know, who may be held captive?" Zax asked. He made a valid point.

"I honestly don't know yet, Zax. But once the darkness has a bounty on the collective mindsets, they will keep them under their control through enslavement. The people that have been detained against their will are dealing with unprocessed and unhealed traumas that create blind spots in their consciousness. They project their hurt on to others through demonic smoke, which is part of their fourth-dimensional reality. We are currently residing in a state of limbo, straddling duality separation and unity consciousness," I continued to explain.

"English, please. What exactly does that mean, Jo? We are not Roma." Nisha smirked sarcastically.

"Basically, there is a global awakening happening on a massive scale. Humans are caught in this tug of war between the Light and Dark Galactic Forces. We are currently passing the bridge, which is a place of purgatory for humans to re-evaluate their lives," I elaborated.

"People who choose to sanitize and purify their Souls through inner work and healing by addressing and processing their emotions will pass through this energetic overpass." I provided as much information as I was able to share.

"Our planet is shifting to a much more inclusive and integrated reality, a dimension of neutrality and harmony. No more competitive stories or playing the game of judgment, division, or shame. It's a simulation of heaven on Earth, refracting from the prism of ethereal existence. It's the next phase for humanity's evolution," I declared with a smile.

"Honestly, I didn't understand most of what you said. But, if I hadn't witnessed the multi-dimensionality of the black hole myself two months ago, I would think you have lost your marbles," Zax retorted in amazement.

Nisha took charge of the conversation. "Bottom line…make sure you are diligent in the practices Jo taught us. Don't be lazy bums on this trip. Take time to meditate in the morning and at night, set your intentions, practice gratitude for the little things. Make sure you're always aware of your emotions and reactions."

"And for goodness' sake, stop being so afraid! Didn't we learn anything from the last time? Fear just causes us to judge ourselves and feel unworthy, which blocks us from expanding our heart-energy field. We are here to embody our higher selves." Nisha said quite eloquently.

"But what happens to those who don't awaken and continue to hurt other people?" Daphne asked in a quivering voice, avoiding eye contact with Nisha.

"Well, as Mother Earth advances and elevates into a new reality, the fragmented Souls that are tethered to the dark structures of our planet will phase out and eventually disintegrate on an energetic level," I warned, fully cognizant of the potency held by my words.

"That's the Lizzie agenda. They are determined to siphon human fear energy to trap us, hold us captive, to recruit, and enslave mankind in this dimensional purgatory." I took a deep breath, defusing the trepidation around me.

"This is how they plan on defeating the Galactic Council of Creation and the sacred Light System. They have done this before, with Lemuria. We can't allow them to succeed with the destruction of planet Earth as well."

As we sat in silence at the resort, surrounded by opulent green palm trees, we continued to process the information with our hearts wide open.

I couldn't help but observe the beauty and magic that surrounded us, which fueled my hope. The tropical island was full of wonder, with lush foliage of Gaia. I could only imagine the paradise that awaited us on the other side of this energetic overpass.

"Jo, I'm working every day to beat my urges and cravings for alcohol and weed. I don't want this addiction to beat me, or to be left behind," Flynn said quietly. The despair emanating from his Soul broke my heart.

"No, Flynn, you will never be left behind! Your heart radiates with purity and the goodness of humanity, my sweet friend. You are incredibly courageous and aware of the challenges that face you every morning." I tried to find the right words to console his worries.

"We are all born with a free will to select the reality we want to manifest. As we navigate the human experience, we become flawed, make mistakes. But every day, when you wake up, you have an opportunity to choose your sobriety and freedom from these external influences, Flynn. You are doing the hard work to unshackle yourself from previous constraints. And remember, it's okay to slip up occasionally as you process your emotions and heal." I said, reiterating his courage and strength to persevere.

"I'm taking accountability for my past behavior, and I'm choosing my abstinence and all the people I love. I mean it this time." Flynn gently held Zax, and heightened energy of profound affection surrounded the group.

"I love that, Flynn. Thank you for speaking your truth. I can sense the energy fields within your auric field oscillating upward, expanding your consciousness as you attract and hold additional light within your system." I made eye contact with my best friends, hoping my words resonated with each of them.

"I guess humanity cannot continue to operate within this false, inorganic, carbon-based matrix of duality," Nisha chimed in, on point, breaking the awkwardness.

"Exactly. I have learned that from a higher perspective, this contrast of duality and darkness is needed to trigger the collective awakening and our remembrance of humanity's truth. When we focus on how external energies perceive us or what others think, we are compromised. We give our power away to others, operating from a space of deficiency and restrictions." I felt the vibrational shift as my friends absorbed the celestial light codes.

"We can't begin to cultivate our superpowers if we continue to internalize or attract the information that doesn't belong to us. It's important to remain impartial and clear. No more drama caused from trauma; you feel me?" I winked at Flynn, trying to lighten up the mood.

"Listen, guys, I know this is a difficult concept to grasp. We've been through so much together. Every pretend story we have told ourselves from a state of victimhood in the past has shaped and fueled our own reckoning. We have started appreciating ourselves and I'm so proud of all of you! You are a powerful, beautiful divine beings. There is no one like you in this entire Universe. Remember how much you are loved, and your value is infinite." I didn't want to sound too preachy, but it was important for them to understand the veracity of the situation.

"Yup, I have superhuman abilities that I haven't exposed yet, so watch out!" Daphne joked. We all laughed as she taunted Zax, pretending to lift his gigantic six-foot muscular stature off the ground. The captain of the football team seemed mortified by the possibility.

I continued to share my knowledge with my friends. "In all seriousness, the Council has communicated that the light codes have been activated on Earth, and everyone must choose, eventually. If we conduct ourselves from our heart space of love, acceptance, kindness, and respect for each other's sovereignty, we will all succeed with this massive ascension."

"Jo, you're lucky to understand your purpose at such a young age. But we're still trying to figure it out. It's not as easy for us mere mortals," Zax said.

"I understand Zax. We all have our unique journeys to discover in this life. But we did not incarnate on this planet just to survive. We are all on Earth in this specific timeline to shift and transform the distorted matrix of programs adopted by our collective psyche. The more we hone our awareness, strengthen our wills, and become empowered through our self-realization, the more we liberate ourselves from the dominant vibrations," I added.

I fully acknowledged that the system we inherited was built-in darkness, oppressing humanity within the density of the illusive veil. As a civilization, we blindly followed the rules and did the bidding of organizations that continued to perpetuate the low entities of the Dark Forces.

"Please, trust me on this, okay?" I grabbed Flynn's hand and placed it near my heart. The surge of energy overwhelmed me as tears streamed down my cheeks involuntarily.

Zax extended his long muscular arms and gave us both a bear hug, squeezing the tension out of our bodies. We all let out a sigh of relief, laughing at the outpouring of emotions.

Just as I gathered myself, Ms. Rolland appeared with her underlings, Pierre and Lavender. They followed her like lost puppies, and I found their behavior quite peculiar. I had never seen teenagers with so much obedience.

She dictated the instructions to the five parent volunteers who were accompanying our groups as chaperones. I felt a pang of regret not accepting my mother's offer. I could have used her help and powerful energy boost at this moment.

As Ms. Rolland addressed our group in her orderly demeanor, a thought popped into my mind. Roma mentioned how the Arcturus focused their energy on amplifying their connection and bond with humans. They were working with us, spearheading this ascension journey for our planet through psychic warfare.

All I had to do was call on their specific energy light codes. As I understood it, the Arcturus were like cosmic personal instructors that helped magnify our desires. They enabled us to attract higher octaves of consciousness bandwidth.

Just like Roma, they were the custodians of planet Earth, holding space for the experience we were meant to have for the sake of Universal expansion. We were all guided and protected while they respected our free will to choose our respective journeys.

"Okay, so, group two will be coming with me to visit the Biosphere Reserve in Valverde. If you have done your homework, then you should recognize it as the capital of El Hierro Island. If your name is on the list, please come prepared for a day in the sun and meet me at nine o'clock sharp tomorrow morning at the front of the resort," Ms. Rolland dictated while she handed out sheets of paper.

"We will be traveling by a high-speed powerboat, so please do not be late."

It appeared that my friends and I were going to spend the day with Ms. Rolland. At least Nisha would be happy exploring the island with Alicia and Theo.

What a serendipitous occurrence. This was exactly where I needed to be if I was going to find Roma. Was this guidance from the Council? For some reason, it felt peculiar.

"Oh my God, we're all together under group two! Isn't that awesome, Jo?" Daphne squealed in delight.

"Yes, that's amazing, Daph. Oh, Conrad is also in our group, that should be fun." As I glanced up from the itinerary, I caught his loving gaze across from me.

Conrad continued to smile at me sheepishly, giving me a quick wink. He was such a sweetheart and an amazing boyfriend...for someone else.

Somehow, my feelings for this incredible boy had changed overnight. I still loved him but as a treasured friend. I no longer felt the pull of the romantic attachments of my teenage crush. Perhaps, I was emotionally maturing as I defused my human Light Body with harmony.

I was not looking forward to breaking this news to him. It would be incredibly uncomfortable to tell him the truth, especially on this trip. I never intended on hurting his feelings. Everything inside of me wanted to shrink away from that situation, to avoid and resist the unpleasant feeling.

Keep focused Jo. Everything will work out as it's meant to be.

For now, I needed to tap into the etheric energy forces that surrounded me for guidance. I concentrated on the Arcturus invocation within my mind, transmitted from the Council. We desperately needed all the help we could get.

I call on all the galactic guardians to help me locate the Blade of Truth. Please, assist me with your loving support, with mercy, grace, and protection through my ascension mission. I accept this opportunity to elevate to a higher vibrational reality. May the Light Beings who sustain the anchoring of love through the overpass illuminate the Crystalline Light upon this planet, for the greatest good of all. May we be empowered and invited to do so now. Through my own free will, so it shall be.

❖ ❖ ❖

"I know you think that you've got it all, by making other people feel small. Makes you think you're unable to fall. And when you do, who you gonna call?"—Superstar by Lauryn Hill

CHAPTER 6
CRYSTALS OF ATLANTIS

"Meditation is the dissolution of thoughts in eternal awareness or pure consciousness without objectification, knowing without thinking, merging finitude in infinity."
—VOLTAIRE

Alicia

Alicia woke up at the crack of dawn, feeling nauseous and discombobulated. She hadn't slept well in anticipation of Ms. Rolland's water excursion. She loved the idea of spending the day with Nisha, discovering the Biosphere Reserve together. Yet Alicia felt an apprehension she couldn't describe.

The nervousness in the pit of her stomach was foreign. Alicia convinced herself that it had to be the two-hour boat ride on the open waters. In all honesty, she would have preferred to remain on the mainland.

Theo understood her anxiety, but he kept wallowing in self-pity. He was bitter about the prospect of revealing his secret. He couldn't very well hide his prosthetic leg on a beach. Alicia never understood why he cared so much about other people's opinions.

The fact that they had both survived a dreadful water accident when they were barely out of diapers was a phenomenal story. However, Alicia was empathetic and compassionate toward her brother.

After all, it was Theo who had lost his leg in the shark attack while they were stranded in the open waters of Hawaii with their father, who had drowned trying to save them.

Their mother enrolled both of them in therapy for years to deal with the trauma of that fatal day. The doctors tried to save Theo's limb from the knee down, but gangrene had set in after a few days.

It was such a dreadful and difficult time for her brother, with all the rehabilitation and pain management at such a young age. Theo was a warrior, a hero in her mind, overcoming so many obstacles while forging forward with his self-identity.

As Alicia prepared her backpack for the tiny island, she peeked out the window toward the dark indigo ocean. She thought that a walk on the beach to catch the sunrise would help settle her stomach.

She checked her cell phone to make sure that it was fully charged and decided to send Theo a quick text to inform him of her plans.

Alicia needed all her strength for this confidential rescue mission. She'd been summoned by the Custodian of the Galaxy for the StarSeed Quest.

Theo was not aware of his sister's celestial identity. Alicia couldn't confide in him about her mission in his altered state. His ego-mind was too programmed with outdated belief systems to see the truth. He still had lots of work to do internally, to process his past trauma.

Alicia knew that her brother's wounds and shadows controlled his every move, operating from a space of anger and blame. His relationship with their stepfather had been strained as they grew older. Theo held him accountable for replacing their father quickly, and he had never forgiven the past.

She tried to explain to him about his state of mind and perception. It was his negative self-chatter and disparaging thoughts that stimulated his inflamed nervous system. From Alicia's perspective, the human ego was not an enemy but the servant to each person's ideology and viewpoint.

If Theo continued to believe that the world was against him and everyone around him was the enemy, then his ego would anchor him to that reality, creating a narrative from that conviction for each encountered experience.

Alicia's brother had been living with these insecurities for years, triggering his ego to take on the protector mode. So, every experience had become a battle for Theo, a threat that would hurt the fragile and vulnerable child that hid behind the shield of misery.

She had to go through her own healing journey as she faced the past traumas and released the patterns that did not support her wellbeing. It was a difficult task, but Alicia had been guided by her intuition toward her higher self. It was her constant companion as she walked the path of life, and Alicia was determined to continue sharing only positive and empowering stories with her inner self.

As she checked the window again before putting on her cap, Alicia noticed a male figure standing on the cobblestone pathway, just before the entrance to the sandy beach. He waved at her in acknowledgment. Much to her surprise, the person motioning her resembled Theo.

Alicia thought it was quite unusual for her brother to be awake before sunrise. She delighted in the prospect of having his company while she settled her nerves.

She grabbed her cell phone and water bottle before heading out. The agitation in her stomach seemed to escalate. Alicia couldn't shake off the reverberation that a catastrophic event was about to ensue.

❖ ❖ ❖

Jo

"Good morning, sunshine. How did you sleep?" Conrad greeted me with a warm smile. We only had forty minutes to eat breakfast, and I was famished. I hoped the rest of the group was already seated at the buffet, so we had time to collaborate before meeting Ms. Rolland for our day trip.

"Hey, Conrad. I slept well, thanks. Daph snores like a trucker, but Nisha and I survived our first night." I laughed nervously, trying hard to postpone our serious talk.

"That's not true. Don't listen to her, Conrad!" Daphne interrupted my tease.

"Did you guys pack extra water bottles? Don't let Alicia catch you with that plastic stuff, Conrad. That's horrible for the environment," Nisha warned.

"What's up Nish, why so cranky?" I asked. I loved her witty sarcasm, but I sensed her rising anxiety.

"Alicia was supposed to meet me outside her room thirty minutes ago. I can't find her anywhere, and she's not answering her freaking phone," Nisha explained. Her voice rose with concern.

"Did you text Theo?" I asked nervously. "Maybe they're together getting ready for the boat ride."

My internal alarm went off, as my heart pounded loudly in my ears. I could feel the eerie chill waterfalling up my spine. Darkness had found us. My ears started to pop with high pitched ringing. The sinister low vibrational frequencies revealed their presence, waiting to stir fear and anxiety.

Theo emerged into the dining area, limping with a frustrated expression. "Have you guys seen my sister? She sent me a text at five in the morning that she couldn't sleep. Apparently, she went for a walk on the beach to calm her nerves. What the heck was she thinking?"

"That was over three hours ago, Theo. Where is she now? She's not answering her phone," Nisha screamed.

"Let's go find Ms. Rolland. Perhaps she has seen Alicia. There has to be an explanation." I tried to console them both, but my unsteady voice betrayed me.

Ms. Rolland didn't seem too concerned with Theo's inquiry, but she proceeded to act out of obligation. She contacted every volunteer parent that accompanied each of the groups. None of them had any interaction with Alicia. They checked with her roommate, who had been asleep until seven-thirty in the morning. She hadn't heard Alicia leave the room.

Tension mounted as we split up to retrace Alicia's steps. Nisha and I followed the path to the beach with Theo. We stopped a local fisherman who had spotted a young girl resembling Alicia's description, getting into a speed boat with a young male. That was over three hours ago.

"All right, everyone, from what I have gathered, it seems that Alicia has decided to take a ride to the island without us." Ms. Rolland appeared agitated. Her eyes shifted frantically every time she spoke.

"This is totally unacceptable and against school protocol. I will have words with her when we get to El Hierro. Please, gather all your belongings and let's get on the bus. We don't want to miss our boat."

"This is bullshit. Alicia would never leave without me. Especially on a boat alone. She was determined to face her fears, but this does not sound like her," Theo shouted.

"I understand you're worried about your sister, young man, but watch the way you speak to me. We will find Alicia, and you can ask her yourself." Ms. Rolland dismissed Theo's outburst, determined to keep her schedule.

I was caught off guard by Ms. Rolland's indifferent reaction, so I shut off the exterior world and focused my clairvoyant abilities to contact Roma.

"*Roma, can you hear me? We have a situation. One of our classmates is missing. I need your help.*" I reached out telepathically, but there was radio silence.

I could feel myself losing control; utter devastation rippled through me. *Breathe, Jo. All is well. Don't allow anything to rock your center or your alignment. Stay neutral emotionally, balanced, calm, and open for the light transmission.* An upgrade to my human DNA was imminent.

As I centered my breath, I mentally focused on my affirmations until my center within my vortex was aligned.

I weave a potent layer of light and protection around me and my friends, that holds me in a space of grace and fortifies my energy fields.

We traveled to the marina in silence. I withdrew from my environment, grounding myself with meditation, hovering above my physical body, observing from a bird's eye perspective.

Ms. Rolland remained cold, distant, without any empathy or compassion for Theo's sister. There was no doubt that she had been compromised, perhaps even hijacked by the Lizzie duality consciousness.

Use your discernment, Jo. Trust your instincts. Don't allow the negative energetic charge to infect your thoughts with panic and worst-case scenarios.

The light illuminated the shadows all around the Earth plane as I tuned into the higher realms in my mind's eye. The veil of density exposed the dark cloak protecting the island. We had approached the fourth-dimensional purgatory that Roma had warned me about. I continued to breathe through it, absorbing the intensity as I slowly integrated the shadow aspects of humanity.

Remain calm and centered. Don't dim your inner light by reacting to fear-based emotions when you are triggered. It's just another opportunity to ascend.

As I meditated and affirmed my power, I realized that I had activated the Stargate ascension through the Universal Law of Oneness. When the Council catalyzed my awakening to perceive the multi-dimensional realities, my DNA was biologically upgraded to receive transmissions and downloads to comprehend the science behind these laws.

Perhaps I was destined to travel this path before I could initiate the fifth-dimensional unity consciousness realm from within as the planet and humanity evolved.

After all, the Arcturus and the Custodian Groups oversaw the re-integration of the Earth hologram, restoring its energetic architecture.

They protected the sovereign rights of all beings to be knowers of the unified Source.

I imagined the geometric Stargate with my pineal gland, called the Merkabah. I visualized its powerful vortex of energy wave continuum. It contained twelve pyramidal triangles that connected into multiple dimensions within the universal time-space matrix. My celestial lessons had taught me that this vortex was an organic manifestation of Universal Creation, made up of the twelve-tree grid hologram.

Within this tree grid, there were twelve planetary gates, open to the Galactic Stargates through portals. The main entries were sealed off by the Custodian Founder Races due to acute destruction and domination by negative Lizzie forces.

Roma had indicated that many of the StarSeeds had agreed to incarnate on Earth during this specific Ascension cycle, to help refurbish the planetary grid lines and initiate the Stargates.

It was interesting to understand the intelligence and anatomy of planet Earth. There were many energetic constructs and dimensional layers within the Earth's auric body, that contained the entire collective consciousness of the planet.

I found out that this system transmitted an energetic spectrum of frequencies, oscillating from higher to lower dimensions, to reach matter and circulate them through the planetary grid network.

I realized that this stage of my ascension journey was to embody more layers of light within my physical body. When this spectrum of energy changed the intelligence awareness through time and space, it shifted my consciousness from one reality to another.

In excitement, I opened my mouth to share this discovery with Nisha and then clamped it shut. There were too many people around me to disclose the information safely.

I glanced at my friends, hoping that the experience we were about to go through would be gentle on them. Through the gradual exposure of light code activations, our planet was evolving into future timelines. This energetic shift was going to compel every person to adapt to the incremental impacts of the upgraded energies.

Each one of us would be presented with the choice to participate in this evolution process, by focusing internally on our heart's desire. The goal was to understand our authentic, true selves behind the masks and conditioned personalities.

Suddenly, the codes flooded my mind, expanding my knowledge further. I witnessed multiple timelines within the holographic Harmonic Universal structures concerning our existence.

I understood that in our third-dimensional physical reality, there were six timelines. We would be exposed to alternate spheres and potential outcomes during this rare movement through the etheric octaves.

I hadn't expected to experience this timeline shift. Ever since the demise of Atlantis, the Lizzies harvested human negative emotional frequencies. They manipulated the future direction of mankind by artificially generating deceptive timelines through mind control methods that shaped anti-human value systems.

When the dark forces controlled the mind and actions of the physical body, they had also cultivated the Soul for their collection.

This galactic, psychic warfare had created fear and trauma in the masses since the beginning of time. Religious dogma, sexual distortion, violence, and gender issues were the most mind-controlled and influenced belief systems that enslaved humanity.

My celestial downloads provided the knowledge on how mind control manipulated the human consciousness as I thought about the innocent victims captured on the island.

My heart sank, realizing that the low-frequency electromagnetic waves signaled the brain to lock on to an external indicator and began to mirror its response. The carrier wave was designed to create distress that triggered emotional pain. This modified the brain chemistry, plunging the human's consciousness into lower, negative states and confused perceptions.

It dawned on me that when a human was mentally and emotionally compromised, they were more vulnerable to the Lizzie manipulation. When governed by fear, they were no longer in charge of their sovereignty. The conditioning and programming infected those exposed through large events of gatherings, executing these triggers in the quantum field.

When their emotions and actions contradicted each other, it prevented them to distinguish between truth and falsehood, reality, and illusory fantasy. This state of confusion arose when they detached from their emotional compass, the guidance system for their life path.

I had finally made the connection. The most predominant mind control arsenal used by the Dark Forces since the beginning of time was the dissemination of the sexual misery program. This was designed to relegate shame and guilt into the lowest forms of human distortion. These harvested sexual energies all fed back into the same artificial grid matrix.

I swallowed hard at this realization, feeling the dryness in the back of my throat. I gazed at Conrad, hoping that he couldn't sense my body's electrical charge with the onslaught of data.

Humanity had unwillingly participated in this sinister scheme facilitated by the Dark Forces. Sadly, this was even more evident in our society. The technology to reach the masses was perpetuated through electromagnetic pulses of artificial systems. The information was shared by networks to confuse populations with false data, corruption, manipulation, and meaningless external drama.

When we focused our attention on a series of false sound and light images, it shaped our brain activity, our beliefs, and eventually our reality. I couldn't imagine the amount of energy we willingly donated through our smartphones.

I felt overwhelmed by this onslaught of information. But deep in my heart, I continued to project feelings of gratitude. I had learned to connect with my inner spirit through the daily practice of empathy, compassion, and forgiveness. And this was the precise remedy that defused mind control tactics to overcome this menacing attack perpetrated by the Dark Forces.

I had hoped that the Higher Light Beings would guide our collective mission into a favorable future timeline that would liberate Gaia and all beings from this purgatory.

I sensed the Arcturus energy circulating the spirals of Source light transmissions through the grid system. These intergalactic plasma waves had accelerated, reaching my core field, leading me through my sixth sense.

As a result, I was more aware of the hypersensitive particles that gathered all around us but were unseen by the human eye. The shadows had emerged into my awareness, greeting us with their malevolent gloom.

The Santa Cruz marina, situated at the edge of the city in Tenerife, boasted a variety of nautical activities. As one of the most popular marinas on the island, it featured impressive tourist attractions. I noticed the lively market square near the golden sandy beaches and gleaming turquoise waters.

A strong gust of wind blew as a warning when we boarded the luxurious Tropicana vessel. The clouds in the sky gathered like phantoms as if they were preparing for a spectacle. I was glad that I had brought my favorite hoodie. The chill in the air prompted my spine with icy resonance, refusing to leave my Light Body.

I watched Nisha, Daphne, Zax, Flynn, Conrad, Theo, and the rest of the group board in excitement, in awe of the fancy vessel. With the love in my heart, I felt a sense of tranquility that oddly washed over me. I was alarmed by the stillness within.

"This is super cool! Don't you think, Jo?" Conrad asked, eyes wide with wonder. He proceeded to sit next to me, ensuring his warmth touched some part of my body. I looked for Nisha and Daphne, who had already taken their seats across from us. Zax and Flynn tried to distract Theo with busy talk as I caught some of their conversations. I was impressed with Zax's nautical knowledge and safety measures. Flynn shared his stories of working as a lifeguard with Theo, assuring him of his swimming capabilities.

My friends had the most beautiful hearts, empathetic and caring, diverting Theo's mind until we found Alicia. I gazed over at Nisha, who seemed to be lost in her own world, locking eyes. *Don't get consumed by the negativity, Nish. That's it, keep my gaze, stay with me. You're not alone.*

I could feel the intrusive thought patterns percolating around our vibrational resonance like a cloud of thick smog, waiting to consume our minds. Our self-talk, what we tell ourselves in the dark, was the most important and sometimes damaging weapon. Often, we reacted blindly, from the space of the mind, thinking of worst-case scenarios, causing ourselves anxiety and fear.

This form of conditioned behavior was slowing down our evolutionary process as a race. We learned to act from our fight or flight response, not trusting the greater plan orchestrated by our Higher Self. It propelled us into an alternate direction, which prolonged our collective ascension.

I had learned to trust the Divine intelligence that worked through my heart-center for my highest good. As I observed our collective patterns, I realized that most people functioned like a dam in the river, getting in the way and intercepting the Universal plan to complete our transformation.

As I considered my friends on this journey, I realized that I didn't want them to experience the unwanted layovers in this existence of life. We were all worthy of the direct flight, in first-class to paradise.

I discovered that taking the difficult path of feeling and transmuting our stuck emotions could be a difficult process. Especially if fervently charged events from our past wounds were still haunting our daily lives.

It occurred to me that my past traumatic emotions created by my subconscious mind had festered in my body, forming discomfort and breakdowns. Especially the negative charge of shame and guilt that chewed its way into my emotional body after Rey's overdose on our last school trip.

The stored experiences negatively impacted my thoughts and choices, releasing damaging energies around my heart center. If this had continued, it would have reduced my ability to provide and receive love. Was this the reason why I was resisting Conrad's affections? I inhaled love for my inner child and exhaled forgiveness.

I forgive myself and expunge the toxic energy from my auric fields. I release any attachments to the narrative that held my emotions hostage as I acknowledge my lack of control over Rey's fate.

With this awareness, I envisioned myself severing ties to the anchor that kept me tethered to the lower realms. I wondered if most of the human collective had this shroud of dense, insidious energy stored around their hearts, which created a form of protection from heartbreak, hurt, and pain—the cause of our suffering and illness.

After all, human emotion was another powerful invisible force, just like gravity, radiation, and electromagnetism. It shaped our humanity through negative electrical charges of feeling the illusive, dualistic framework of fear, which perpetuated anger, hate, ignorance, and judgment. These stuck emotions were the real undetected epidemic that impacted our race and planet.

As I pondered humanity's shadow aspects, a quote that I had read from Mark Twain entered my awareness: "Truth is stranger than fiction, but it is because fiction is obliged to stick to possibilities; the truth is not."

This profound insight impacted me significantly as my body tingled with electric currents. Every human emotion had its unique vibrational rate of recurrence, which affected every other being on a mental, emotional, and physical level. I understood that now more than ever. Each of us had a great responsibility to process and heal our lodged anguish and stress deposited within our energetic fields to evolve.

This transformation would accelerate our DNA, re-coding, and re-configuring our physical cells for the new reality emerging in human evolution.

"Listen, Jo, you've been a bit distant since we arrived on the island. Is everything okay with you?" Conrad interrupted my thoughts. I just didn't have the strength to voice my true feelings for him in the middle of a rescue mission.

"Just a bit jet lagged, I think. I will feel better once we find Alicia," I replied reluctantly.

At that moment, my throat engorged with an energetic blockage. I had difficulty swallowing my inauthentic response. I recognized that I was not going to be able to keep my true feelings from him any longer. Not if I was genuinely operating from my heart space. This was a test, a chance to choose my next path through my conscious behaviors and actions.

Truth, integrity, honor, compassion. This was the vibrational wavelength of my Ascending Angel existence. These lessons were an opportunity for me to find my voice no matter the difficulty, operating from the pureness of love.

"It's really strange how Alicia just disappeared this morning. If that happened to you Jo, I would be beside myself. Promise me you'll stay close so I can protect you." Conrad gazed into my eyes. His heart was so genuine and full.

It dawned on me that when I chose to bypass my true feelings, no matter the situation, I disconnected from my sacred heart space. It led to my imbalance, dismay, and discord within my vibratory fields. And I couldn't save Alicia and Roma without my full energetic alignment and armor.

I took deep cleansing breaths, expanding my abdomen, calming, and aligning my center. I found the courage I needed to ride the emotional currents that ebbed and flowed. I chose to rise above the limitations of my self chatter and observed from my Higher Self. It enabled my celestial guidance to defrost my perspective, much like a windshield, removing the conflicted emotions that had blinded me.

Operating from a state of denial was circumventing what needed to be felt for my Soul's integration. This was not the right relationship for me, my Soul's echo. With this acknowledgment, I refused to make all the unwarranted pit stops along the way toward my ascension.

I swallowed hard, searching for my courageous voice. "Listen, Conrad, I care for you so deeply. I don't want to mislead you in any way. You are the best boyfriend, and I feel so lucky to have experienced our relationship." I spoke from my open, vulnerable heart, surrendering all fear and control.

"Thank you for loving me. I just think that we should continue caring for each other as best friends. I'm so sorry to dump this on you, but I'm just not in the headspace for any romantic entanglements right now. I hope you can understand." My heart pummeled while I watched his facial expressions. The last thing I wanted was to hurt him, but my honesty was the kindest deed that would release him from any misperceptions.

"Oh, I see," he responded calmly, looking away as he momentarily diverted his attention on the ocean waves crashing into the shoreline.

"You don't have to worry about me, Conrad. I don't think Ms. Rolland will allow any one of us to wander off. I'm sure she's freaking out under that cool exterior." I smiled, trying to break the awkward silence.

Before Conrad had a chance to respond, the captain of the twenty-two-foot bowrider began to welcome us on his beautiful, extravagant craft. He instructed us to remove the life jackets stored under the long seating area. We were encouraged to buckle into the colorful vests as part of the marine safety protocol.

The wind caressed my face, nourishing my soul with every gust. I gently reached for Conrad's hand, my energy flowing into his being. I loved the goodness of his heart, his wholeness and kindness. He squeezed my hand in acknowledgment as we sat silently, lost in our emotional deluge.

"Jo, my energy fields are diminishing. I may not have much time left."

Roma's words alerted my sensations. *"Finally, I've been trying to connect with you, Roma. Are you alright?"*

"The Wizard has captured a few of my StarSeeds, holding them hostage. The Fark Forces are growing in power, feasting on the density," she telepathically replied.

"I have called on the Arcturus Light force assistance to help us with our mission. How will they appear?" I asked, hoping for celestial tips.

"They are here, Jo, incarnated in human form, activated with light code transmissions. The Arcturus are the Keepers of the Akashic Records. They work closely with all the ascended masters and are quite versed in every Soul's imprint since creation. As Guardians, they process the reincarnation of each being in between the quantum timelines," Roma explained.

"*Do they possess celestial powers on Earth? Since I don't have my galactic compass, I'm not able to travel through the dimensional portals, Roma. We need the strength of the Light Force for this rescue mission.*" I tried not to emphasize our limitations, but I was operating without direction, on a moment-to-moment basis.

"*Yes, many of the incarnated StarSeeds know that they are not of this world, once activated. They are beings connected with the Pleiadean civilization and other star races of this galaxy. This Quest will re-unite the warriors who have fought the great galactic war against the Lizzies from their beloved planet, Avalon. They are here to save Gaia, as a cohesive force. Trust and embrace the process, Jo.*"

I continued to take deep breaths as the boat rocked back and forth with velocity. Shadows grew darker within the clouds, producing an ominous feel, and a veil of blackness hovered above us. The boat ride to El Hierro island was approximately two hours. With the increased wind intensity, the waves seemed to be crashing against us, delaying our voyage.

"*The Galactic Council has deployed a major offensive in the sub-lunar space against these nefarious beings that are holding Gaia hostage. The Light Forces will emerge triumphant from this final galactic war against these dark Draco entities. The clearing will provide Mother Earth and humanity magnificent liberty, joy, and grace across the entire collective mind. Don't lose hope, no matter what obstacles appear in your reality as the divergence unfolds,*" Roma continued.

I noticed my friends' demeanors, as they sat quietly, fighting the imminent seasickness. Ms. Rolland had not moved from the front of the boat, perched high on the bow. I accidentally made eye contact with her son, Pierre, as he sneered with a vile gleam in his eye, his tongue flicking in and out of the corner of his thin mouth.

"*Oh my God, Roma, I think we have a shapeshifter on the boat with us! One of the students' eyes changed in front of me. Is this possible?*" I inquired, holding on to my neutral state.

"*I'm not surprised, Jo. We are all surrounded by Lizzies posing as humans on the Earth plane. They can metamorphose from one physical form into another in this fourth-dimensional reality. They brought these powers with them from Draco. You are encroaching on dangerous territory. Keep a watchful eye for other shapeshifters among you.*"

As Roma guided me telepathically, I gathered my intuitive powers. I focused my pineal gland as a beacon, reading every person's energy on the vessel. Everyone, including the captain, emanated warm hues of love-consciousness. Everyone except for Ms. Rolland, Pierre, and Lavender.

"*There was something strange with our history teacher and her teenage children from the very beginning. I was not able to read their auric fields. I guess now I know why.*" I confided the shocking revelation with Roma.

"Jo, what's happening? Why are the waters so rough suddenly? I'm going to puke if the storm gets any worse!" Daphne broke the silence, looking pale.

"Here, take some of my anti-nausea chewable, Daph. Maybe it will help," Nisha interrupted, distributing her medication with the rest of the group.

"Thanks for sharing, Nisha. Let's all just concentrate on taking deep breaths. Don't pay attention to the water movement, look ahead in front of you. That may help with nausea," I said.

Halfway into our journey, the captain announced that we should all remain seated.

"Please buckle your lifejackets as we make our way through the eye of the storm. Hold on-to your seats!" he warned.

The waves began to crash against us, soaking our clothes with the coolness of the Atlantic water. Everyone screamed. I sensed the dense vibrations of fear gripping my classmates' hearts.

I diverted my attention and energy, projecting calmness with my light. At that moment, we were dragged into the illusory reality of dread and panic. This duality matrix kept assembling the energy of the collective mind. But I remained grounded within my heart, integrating my Light Body and higher self. It allowed me to maintain my balance and clarity.

Every experience that we encounter is an opportunity for potential growth and ascension. The Council had downloaded the information, firmly encoding my being. I believed passionately that the Divine Light would prevail through any storm, tapping into the cosmic timeline of various probabilities.

After all, I had discovered through my celestial training that time was linear. All versions took place within the quantum field, tapping into the golden framework grids of the Universal Time Matrix.

It occurred to me that there were five mass levels in the cosmic template. Each of them held three density points, a spectrum of trinity frequencies that manifested blueprints of the collective perception and expression.

The first density level within the Harmonic Universe network held aspects and layers of physical matter of planet Earth and the human light body. Through evolution, the first three dimensions of consciousness existed in this timeline.

As the planet evolved into the second level, it was infused with interactive beams to propel Gaia from the fourth to fifth-dimensional timelines, as she shifted and progressed through the sacred gateway. The funnel-shaped lattice of light positioned Gaia on a pathway within the multiverse as part of her ascension and transmutation process.

I couldn't believe what was happening under the surface, unbeknownst to the human eye. The new matrix of fabric reality was allowing us to rise in our ethereal awareness while we encompassed our physical bodies. The rainbow lines pulsated, awakening the sacred codes, energetically stimulating our human circuitry.

We were entering the Lemurian timeline on our physical planet, birthed in our collective hearts. This realm acted as a custodian of the great dream of manifesting our paradise, Heaven on Earth once again.

How was I supposed to explain this phenomenon to anyone? This reality was a simulation and as such, it was important to comprehend the rules of the game. The dynamics that humans needed to observe were the basic understanding of polarity and duality.

Much like playing a video game, the rules were quite simple. All things on our Earth plane had their opposites. We always had a choice between the two largest undercurrents that governed and created our present moment experiences. Light and Dark. Love and fear. Helpfulness and greediness. Service to others and service to self.

As sentient beings incarnated in this present moment's existence, we were presented with a choice. It was up to us to determine our reality based on our actions. I affirmed this knowledge with every ounce of my being.

I will always choose love, until my very last breath.

As I infiltrated everyone's aura, I transmuted their low vibrational emotions. I held this pattern, forming a white plasma light around the vessel. I became a conduit for the Council and all Celestial manifestation as they channeled pure consciousness energy through me. I focused on the rate of contraction and expansion, oscillating through everyone's energy fields, increasing our collective vibration.

I held space for our unfolding, while the angry waters continued their assault, rejecting our presence. All my senses had become ultra-sensitive to the Ocean's parasitical disease. The demonic high-pitched frequency emanating from the Black Crystals hidden below the surface pierced my eardrums.

"Roma, the ocean is fighting us. What's happening with Gaia right now?" I asked in desperation.

"You are now entering the purgatory turbulence, where Atlantis once existed. The Lizzies are harnessing and misusing the karmic powers of nature created from the catastrophic demise of the Atlantis vitality orb," Roma explained.

"Before the deterioration of Atlanteans, the civilization reached a moral and spiritual existence, operating with cruelty, torture, coercion, and corruption. Violence ensued with the discovery of the Black Crystals, brought over by the Lizzies from the Draco galaxy. The greed and hunger for power destroyed society and their advanced technology. Only scattered mountain peaks remain as the great islands crumbled into the sea. The souls have been imprisoned in this vortex, transcending all Universal laws of time and space."

"I'm not sure I can protect our boat from the energetic pull of these Black Crystals, Roma," I cried.

"Don't resist, Jo. Surrender to your path. I won't be able to guide you further, but I'm looking forward to seeing you on the other side. May

you rise with blessings of the Goddess Gaia," Roma delivered her final message.

Our clairvoyant connection had dropped. Roma and her guidance were gone from my psychic wavelength.

With hyper-focus, I gazed inward to my soul's remembrance. An alternate universe appeared, projecting a movie screen in my mind's eye. I emerged as a Lemurian Being of Light with wings, connected deeply to the energies of Gaia. I possessed a crystal sphere, guarding the airways and Light portals of future timelines. I surrendered to this feeling of nourishment and tranquility, remembering the paradise that once existed.

For a split second, I felt the power of this sacred space in my human form, the connection to the absolute radiance of the Source energy. I carried the key that unlocked the experience I desired. But which portal in the great beyond was I supposed to choose to embody?

The stark chill onslaught of the Atlantic Ocean brought me back to my present reality. Each encounter with the seawater resembled an angry lash of a salty whip. Nisha consoled Daphne, Zax and Flynn held each other, and Conrad shielded me from getting drenched.

The coolness of the wind sent shivers throughout my wet physical body. As Conrad hugged me tightly for body warmth, I zoned out somewhere in the ethers. With feelings of gratitude and everlasting devotion for my friends, I visualized the sphere of plasma light, which glittered with the brilliance of a thousand diamonds, around the vessel. It embraced everyone with loving protection, and I understood that I was never truly alone.

Calling on the Angels, I continued to affirm by revitalizing, safeguarding, trusting, and accepting the experience with compassion as I prayed for all our Souls.

The salt water stung my eyes, burning my lungs as I gasped for air. I calmed my thundering heart with every valuable breath, hugging the turquoise waters.

My energy radiated throughout the vastness of the enraged ocean, infiltrating it with the shimmering promise of the Light on its watery surface. I floated above the midnight depths of despair, my skin shriveled with salt flakes, and released my panic.

I let go of old narratives and layers of fear, holding space for unconditional love to flow. I trust in the guidance and wisdom of my higher heart by honoring all expressions of Source. I give thanks for every breath and each moment, as this physical experience is a gift. And so, it is.

I have been here before. But this time, it was not a dream.

❖ ❖ ❖

"What you give is just what you get. I know it hasn't hit you yet. Now I don't mean to get you upset, but every cause has an effect."—Superstar by Lauryn Hill

CHAPTER 7

SHIPWRECKED

*"We can never obtain peace in the outer world
until we make peace with ourselves."*

— DALAI LAMA

Ms. Rolland

The powerful twelve-foot waves of the Atlantic Ocean overwhelmed the medium-sized vessel. The boat capsized, stranding all its inhabitants on a thick, shrubby shoreline.

Ms. Rolland sensed that they had entered the safety of the Atlantic hologram, shedding her human form. She slithered onto the sand with her two Lizzie warriors masquerading as her human children, Pierre and Lavender. She took inventory of the humans, with a realization that Jo and her friends were missing.

The Wizard would be furious. She felt Ciakar's evil presence; his power was mounting on this fourth-dimensional realm. The surge reminded Ms. Rolland of their last human conquest, the sinking and downward spiral of Poseida, Arian, and Oz.

After the first flooding, the island of Poseida governed by the masculine species developed a hierarchical system of corruption and division.

They built the Temple of Knowledge and Regeneration, located on geodesic grids, within proximity of electromagnetic energies that spiraled through the Earth core.

These temples housed the Arcturus crystalline gems, required to fuel Poseida's advanced technology. These grid crystals were triangulated and connected through gold-copper pipes, under a spherical dome. Magnificent architecture existed within these domes, using sacred geometry that amplified the light force field.

Ciakar infiltrated the aristocracy by shapeshifting into one of their giant forms, convincing the higher political groups to develop artificial genetically engineered mutants to serve their masters. The Wizard used mind control and hijacked the leaders' thoughts. He gained access to the Arcturus crystal technology that was housed in dimensional locks.

When he penetrated the energy of peace with the Draco Black Crystal infernal vapor, the dimensional locks imploded with a thermal flicker, exceeding its antigravity bolster. This caused a colossal nuclear explosion, devastating all of Atlantis and weakening the Atlantean plate on planet Earth.

Ciakar had ruled in this realm since the demise, between massive clouds of black smoke that veiled the sun. The wave of earthquakes and tsunamis was triggered by the Wizard whenever Ciakar time-traveled from this portal into another dimensional reality, transcending time and space.

The Galactic War ensued above the Earth Plane as Gaia spiraled in between, fighting for her survival. Ciakar planned on obliterating the StarSeed Quest so that the balance between the Light and Dark would shift in his favor, finally enslaving Mother Earth into the fourth dimension.

When the ethereal crossing to the fifth dimension was shattered, the Lizzie agenda would be fully realized, eradicating all freedom of choice from every sentient being.

Ms. Rolland searched for Jo and her friends using her peripheral senses. Somehow, they had managed to sneak away into the dense shrubbery while she shapeshifted from her human form. Ms. Rolland's mind projected the violence and death of the feeble, intolerable ascending angel as she relished the taste of her impending victory.

But she wouldn't dare defy Ciakar's wishes. He would vaporize her in an instant with the power of the Black Crystal crown, perched securely on his head. Her time would come. Ms. Rolland had her own self-serving agenda and destiny to fulfil.

❖ ❖ ❖

Zax

His whole world flashed before his eyes as the ocean threatened to consume their boat with ferocity. Zax held onto Flynn for dear life through the savage waves pounding their anger into their soaked and chilled bodies.

In those moments, remorse and regret filled his mind as he replayed his life's narrative. Zax reflected on all the wasted moments of his past, squandered with feelings of anger, insecurities, and shame. The sinister thoughts infiltrated his being, plummeting him back into victimhood patterns, which he associated with quite well.

Before coming out and pouring his true feelings for his best friend, Flynn, Zax had the temperament of a wild bull. A minor aggravation would set him off immediately. He chose to blame it on his upbringing;

after all, it was his father who had ingrained the rage within him physically.

The rigid authoritarian background of his childhood fostered a deep sense of fear in Zax from an early age. His father's excessive demands created feelings of incompetence and hopelessness, which perpetuated into his youth.

Zax completely shut down his emotions as he tried to measure up to the perfection ideology of his childhood environment. Ultimately, it led to a level of mistrust of his own identity, muzzling his truth, which developed into intense anger issues from unresolved childhood pain, lack of safety, and an inability to love himself.

With Jo's help, he had become more aware when feelings of anger ignited within his core with a fiery intensity. The sense would surge through his veins in an intoxicating way, often leading him into physical outbursts.

Growing up, Zax was taught to suppress his fury in unhealthy, defective ways. It was so dreaded and condemned in his family that he was driven to channel it in playing football or other competitive sports.

His unnatural behavior resulted in a corrosive emotion, tainting any type of connection with himself or others. During their chats, Jo had explained it to him as an inner fragmentation initiated by a traumatic shock to his mind and body.

Before Zax was able to acknowledge his real feelings for Flynn, he had suppressed his emotions, numbing his vital essence. It eventually resulted in his unhappiness until he began to courageously explore more wholesome alternatives for understanding his truth.

After all, anger was a life force energy within Zax, manifesting his reality in the rawest way possible when provoked. He was beginning to learn new tools and practices to harness this energy and alchemize it into a positive attribute that instilled his persona power.

With this maturity, Zax was able to reflect on his past. Instead of understanding the conditions of his parents' background from their perspective, it was easier for Zax to unload his burdens of unworthiness. He was too afraid to face his truth, so he blamed everyone around him for his sorrow and insecurities.

His father continued to operate from his state of habituation, perpetuating the cycles of attachment, expectations, and dependencies. He came from a proud, traditional African American family, fighting for acknowledgment, equity, and control.

Zax had two older brothers, in whose footsteps he was expected to follow, whether he liked it or not. Brad and Jamie both graduated as their respective team's star players and won scholarships to prestigious universities.

Nothing less was expected of Zax. His father was strict due to his upbringing, growing up in an environment plagued by racism.

Even as an accomplished professional, his father still struggled for legitimacy in his career based on his ancestral history. He was constantly proving himself in his patriarchal law firm dominated by the rich male perspective. Every day, he fought for his inherent rights, substantiating his belonging in the upper-middle-class society.

As Zax reflected on his childhood, he realized that his father demanded the same level of idealized achievement from his boys. He felt sadness in his heart, thinking about the difficult path that his father had to tread to provide his children with better life opportunities.

This melancholy broke through the barriers he'd built up around his heart, initiating feelings of empathy and understanding for his parents.

Zax spent his young life struggling with his emotional and psychological well-being, living with anxiety and with the pressures his parents placed on him.

He decided to change his mindset of playing the blame game with his father. Instead of compromising his values and giving up his inherent power, Zax vowed to collaborate with his father with reverence and healthy communication, to improve their father-son relationship in a wholesome manner.

He was extremely grateful that his love for Flynn had liberated him from his state of discontent. He felt more vulnerable and open to experience joy and peace within himself.

As he weathered the storm, Zax decided that he was not going to allow his future to be taken away from him. Not by the catastrophic ocean waves, nor by the volcanic eruptions of his emotional density.

Once they survived the harrowing voyage, Zax was determined to improve his relationship with his family, with compassion and forgiveness.

He was prepared to fight the malevolent forces that were attempting to devour his Soul and the love of his life with all his strength and human abilities.

❖ ❖ ❖

"I'm freaking soaked, and I smell like sushi!" Daphne complained.

"Shh, lower your voice! We don't want to alert Ms. Rolland to our whereabouts," I whispered back, grateful to have my friends with me.

We endured the ferocious storm, barely getting our sea legs underneath us for our escape.

Flynn demonstrated incredible resilience, pulling people onto the shore.

"Do you even know where we are, Jo?" Nisha asked.

"I think we're actually on El Hierro Island. I feel closer to Roma's magnetic pull, but we must find her blade before we look for Alicia. Let's keep moving." I led with a sense of confidence as I surrendered to the energy of the Arcturus. They were guiding me with a gentle push toward the obscured blade of truth.

As we forged our way through the plush wetlands of the island, I received a thought from my higher self. It was a piece of intuitive advice that sprouted within my mind's eye in this precise timeline. There was a pull to mentally recite the Soul contract revocation for additional energetic protection as we navigated the dense astral plane.

I was grateful to be armed with this previous download from the Council. They were always with me with their wisdom, assisting me in recalling my powers from external forces.

I call all spiritual contracts that exist for the revocation of the divine feminine and Goddess Gaia within my past, present, and future existence, in all dimensions.

At this exact, ever-present, co-creating moment, I summon all DNA lineage ancestors to establish a unified spiritual court of equity so I may find remedy and resolve with all contracts that have inserted fine print during the pre-birth and birth process.

I call forth the proper spiritual court of equity to hear my decree of contract removal.

I revoke all spiritual contracts with earth-based cultures, belief systems, and industries that dominate and control the divine feminine power in our world and create an energetic imbalance that affects every man, woman, and child on the planet.

I hereby revoke contracts of all cultural belief systems that place the feminine in a position of inequality. These include the projections of unequal pay, the inability for a woman to earn a living or receive an education of her choosing.

I do not consent to all social systems that have been put in place to oppress females, make a woman feel like she is too sensitive, emotional, or out of control in an effort of gaslighting a woman's Soul, to make her feel like she is unstable or insignificant.

I hereby revoke all contracts of cultural belief systems where female children are murdered at birth, sexually mutilated, sold off into a billion-dollar child pornography industry, or trafficked as sex slaves.

I declare that I am now clean from these programs of distortion, and I return to the Source of innocence as a divine feminine sovereign being.

I hereby revoke all spiritual contracts with the entertainment and advertising industries that have created programs of self-hatred, low self-esteem, self-medication, self-mutilation, and eating disorders.

I hereby declare that I am more than good enough; I am infinite consciousness. I am Goddess embodied. I am a sovereign being, and I hereby reclaim my divine feminine power in this spiritual court of equity. I am connected to the sacred feminine heart space of introspection, retrospection, and reflection.

I call forth all the ancestors to honor my free will and enter it into the Akashic Records for all sentient beings. And so, it is.

❖   ❖   ❖

"I'm so relieved everyone survived the sinking boat, although I feel bad for the captain. That was a beautiful vessel," Zax said, interjecting my energetic transmutation, his arm resting lovingly around Flynn.

"I couldn't find Ms. Rolland and her kids when I did the headcount. You think they're okay Jo?" Flynn asked.

"I'm sorry to break this to you, but unfortunately, Ms. Rolland, Pierre, and Lavender are Lizzie shapeshifters. They slithered back into their original form while we escaped the shipwreck," I replied. I couldn't shield them any longer from what was about to occur on this island. Roma had made that abundantly clear.

"What the heck are you talking about, Jo? Did you knock your head on a rock or something?" Theo burst out laughing. He was not aware of my ethereal ascension mission or the Angel Academy.

I sensed his repressed anger brewing below the surface. I turned to face him, holding out my hand in a welcoming gesture.

Conrad immediately jumped to my defense. "Okay, calm down, Theo. Jo's just trying to help, there's no reason to lash out at her."

Even after our breakup, he still demonstrated his loving heart and devotion. I truly hoped he knew how special he was to me. He personified this new paradigm of love consciousness, always operating from his heart center with kindness and compassion.

Conrad himself was shifting and rising in front of my eyes, on the same level as the Ascending Masters and Angels. His actions and intentions were pure and wholesome. I finally recognized that Conrad's love was the very embodiment of a selfless, limitless, timeless, unconditional existence of the higher realms. He didn't ask or expect anything in return, ever.

I reached out and acknowledged his loving protective outburst as I continued to address Theo's concerns.

"Look, Theo, we don't know each other well but I would like to ask for your trust," I began. "We are in danger here. There are powerful, Dark Forces all around us with a sinister agenda dating back to the beginning of time. There is a galactic battle for world domination going on in front of us, while we all live in a reflective reality within our blind spots. We have been deceived and manipulated by Ms. Rolland since she started working at our school," I explained, breathing deeply, and emitting from the heart.

"Sounds like airy-fairy science fiction to me. What does any of this have to do with my sister, Jo?" Theo questioned.

"Well, as I understand it, Alicia has been activated by the StarSeed Quest to help save an important person that has been captured by this evil Wizard. Her name is Roma. We have been communicating tele-pathically throughout this whole journey," I explained, simultaneously conveying the urgency.

"We don't have too much time to get into the whole story, but it's super important to find the galactic sword that she lost during her capture. It's hidden in these shrubs somewhere," I said while radiating healing pulsations toward his heart center.

If I could soothe the inflammation of his central nervous system, perhaps he would consent to receive the healing energy upgrade.

"Listen, dude, we have all seen what these entities are capable of doing. Just use your instincts and know that we are on the right path. We are seeking the truth, it's up to us to decide and find our own voices. I trust Jo with all my heart. I hope you can too," Zax said.

Theo looked bewildered as he tilted onto his right leg. The pain was written all over his face. "Do you mind if I adjust my leg? It's killing me from the dampness of the saltwater," he muttered.

"Of course, mate! Zax and I will keep watch for slimy intruders." Flynn tapped Theo on the shoulder in support.

"You can lean on me, Theo, if you need balance." Conrad offered his shoulder.

As Theo removed his prosthetic leg, Nisha handed him a small towel she had brought from the resort.

"Does it hurt?" Daphne asked.

"It's not so bad anymore. I only feel the pinch in dampness. The years of rehabilitation have helped me adjust to some degree of normalcy," Theo replied in a hushed voice.

"Honestly, I had no idea. I think you're super brave, Theo." Nisha gave him a supportive wink.

"I don't feel brave, Nisha. I can't believe I didn't protect my sister on this damn trip! After all that we have been through, Alicia has been my rock. She's been by my side, through the dark days of isolation, misery and self-pity," he responded in angst and genuine concern.

"Listen, I'm the last person to say this, Theo, but that little insidious and incredibly destructive voice in your head only exists to disempower and isolate you," Nisha replied. "I have learned the hard way that negative thought forms keep us from realizing our full potential and inner peace."

Nisha was speaking from experience. Her powerful words expelled healing energy that she wasn't even aware of.

"I totally agree, Nish. The darkness creeps into our minds dozens of times within every hour. The more we focus on the negativity, the more we energize them, giving them access to our being," I continued.

"Ya, it's like opening the door to our intelligence and inviting it for a latte and donuts," Daphne chimed in, mimicking the darkness in a sinister voice.

"*Come on in, please, shit all over my internal landscape and mess up my vibratory field. Would you like whipped cream with your mochaccino?*" Nisha chuckled at Daphne's portrayal.

"All kidding aside, I want you to know that we hear you, Theo. And I'm so sorry that you're going through this. It's difficult to see past the narrative and old patterns, but only you have the power and the free will to change your mindset," I explained.

"Yes, we can continue to propagate and dwell on the damaging thoughts, or we can try to do our best to overcome our obstacles." I didn't mince my words. "Do you want to wallow in shame, guilt, and victimhood all your life, or do you want to change the outcome of your perceived reality?"

I asked him point-blank. Unfortunately, we didn't have the luxury of time for a long discussion, and I hoped the potency of the words would infiltrate the density within his auric field.

"We have all witnessed what negativity and self-hatred can do to a person. It was too late for our friend Rey, but if you listen to Jo, she can help you shift your debilitating patterns and behaviors," Daphne commented.

"We really don't have time for this right now, guys. Can't you expedite his energy upgrade or something, Jo?" Nisha asked, frustrated.

"I'm already sending you healing energy, Theo, but it's your choice. We all have the free will to decide the path we take in life. If you continuously enable the negative self-chatter in your mind, you become enslaved to them. Once you focus your attention on certain ideas and you boost those impulses through your emotions, you magnetically attract that frequency into your reality," I said, providing a quick summary of the Law of Attraction.

"When you dial into that low-vibrational radio station, you are compromised. You then tap into the collective negative patterns lingering in the ethers. With every emotional reaction of anger, fear, or blame for an extended period, you fuel this dense energy of unworthiness and separation. This is exactly what the Lizzie's want so they can continue to feast on people's misery," I continued, fully aware of our endangerment.

"Well, try being a disabled, transgender person. If you'd spent most of your life as an outsider, bullied, and treated like a freak, you would not be so quick to judge. Being trans belongs to me. This stupid artificial leg does not! And it's my right to express myself anyway I wish," Theo retorted.

"I don't judge you, Theo. None of us do. And I can't pretend to know how you feel. It's just that I have learned so much over the past year. I have expanded and recognized that every experience is an opportunity for growth. The goal is to become the alchemists of our own lives, refusing to be victims of circumstance. Hopefully one day, we can share our stories," I replied with compassion.

"And, if I may be honest, I think you may be assessing yourself negatively, Theo. You are your worst critic. And judgment is one of the lowest vibrational frequencies to emit into the universal quantum field. Let that go, forgive yourself and the past. It's over, done. Accept your life as it is right now. You are here, breathing, alive. What's important is

155

this moment and what actions we decide to take for a better tomorrow," I reiterated, sensing the decrease in his inflammation as I interpreted his aura.

"This is especially important while we're on this island, vulnerable to the Lizzies and the Dark Forces. As I understand it, the spirits of the Atlantis civilization are stuck in this purgatory underworld. Our mission is to help liberate their Souls, so they can be escorted back into the redemption of the sacred Light."

I realized that Theo would not resonate with this information, but it was important for him to understand the potency of his trauma-based emotional responses. We didn't want to provide any more power to the Lizzie mind control agenda, as they would use Theo's compromised vessel as their host.

"Alicia told me what you both went through when you were young, Theo. I admire and respect you. I think you're both incredibly resilient and much more interesting people, to be honest." Nisha smiled, placing her hand on his shoulder.

"Thanks, Nisha. I appreciate that. I'm not sure I can control my feelings, Jo, but I'm willing to try. Sometimes, these emotions explode out of my teeth, and lashing out relieves the pain. At least now I can be more aware when it's happening. I will do anything to save my sister and help you guys as much as I can. You have all been nothing but kind. Thanks for that," Theo admitted.

"You are so strong, Theo, more than you know. Thank you for helping us on this mission to liberate Roma," I said.

As we continued searching for the sword, the stench of the swamp enveloped my senses. *It's the Lizzies, they're getting close!* I was alerted to the threat ahead.

"Hurry, we are running out of time!" I yelled at Zax and Flynn to follow my lead.

"What does it look like, Jo? Is it like a Ninja sword?" Nisha asked.

"Just look for any shiny object, Nish. It's adorned with powerful plasma blue crystals on the handle. I'm sure it's ethereal in stature," I replied.

Although the dark clouds emitted an ominous and eerie atmosphere, hope propelled us forward in this celestial time capsule provided by the Arcturus. I was so grateful for their guidance and protection.

My sixth sense sharpened to attract the signal emitted from the crystals embedded within the sword. I guided my friends in its general direction, surrounded by Canary palm trees and juniper shrubs.

There was a large overwhelming Dracaena Tree in the distance, past the Lily plants. It oozed dark red sap, like dragon's blood. Roma had alluded to its medicinal and magical properties. My entire being oscillated while I envisioned the mysterious estate hidden under the remote Draco plantation.

As we moved away from the young plants and trees located on the hot and humid shoreline, we encountered a nook that surrounded a graceful umbrella-shaped tree with numerous forked branches. Each branch represented a cluster of long sword-shaped leaves on the end.

Could this be the location of the Custodian's sword? That would be so clever of Gaia, to hide Roma's blade in such plain and obvious sight! My heart palpitated in excitement as we all ran into the opening of the mysterious, sacred tree.

We heard a clinking sound, metal on metal. I turned toward Zax and Flynn for an explanation. They shrugged in wonder at my gaze as Theo reacted in bewilderment. He cleared the long grassy plantation and moved his prosthetic leg from the area. Bright light reflected, illuminating the moss-laden forest surrounding.

"Jo, I think I found it!" Theo exclaimed eagerly.

I immediately followed the reflection emanating from the plush earth and grabbed the large handle of Roma's blade. It was extremely heavy; however, as soon as my energy fused with the crystals, I emerged with the strength and power of a hundred thoroughbreds.

As I unearthed the Blade of Truth from Gaia's hold, all the knowledge of the Akashic Records downloaded into my being in slow motion. Time stood still. The light codes, translucent and glowing with information, hovered all around me. My friends stood frozen with expressions of astonishment and disbelief.

It was incredible how humans had been conditioned and schooled with belief systems that went against our biochemistry. We grew up with a limited understanding that we only possessed five senses. However, our highest intuitive sense went beyond attachment to the physicality of our existence. It was a clear remembrance and knowing that other energies were aspects of the Source vitality, experiencing life through a unique lens and with distinctive perspectives.

This entire reality was engineered with precision that always came back into perfect balance. The light and dark were dependent upon our collective awareness of truth. The higher-dimensional viewpoint resided within an infinite quantum field of intelligence. I had come to realize that this matrix was much like a super database, with codes that brought everything back into the equilibrium of infinite probabilities.

My pineal gland crystallized like a magnet, attracting all the light codes of information. I witnessed the beginning of time, the Angels of Lemuria, and the darkness of Atlantis.

These dark entities existed in human form, contorting our choices. From the beginning of time, all human behavior that deliberately harmed or violated another being's free will without consent nourished the malevolent darkness.

We have evolved into a race with fragmented Souls reincarnating into this false reality, resulting in today's divisive, traumatized community. Without realizing it, we continued to perpetuate this separation, fear-based unconsciousness of the old limiting paradigm. It had to stop. It was time to break the cycle of fear, shame, deceit, rivalry, manipulation, and disempowerment.

I recognized that this shift would require a purification through a cleansing of the mass's collective initiation. We needed to take accountability for our actions, to integrate our thoughts and emotions with our spirits. By doing so, we would relinquish all external control and claim back our inherent sovereignty and power.

As I became invigorated with this powerful code activation, my ethereal wings illuminated the physical realm. I soared above the ground and enclosed my beloved friends with celestial protection. Without much difficulty, I lifted the Blade of Truth and formed a circle of white light around my Soul tribe.

I activated the Akashic imprints, raising the capacity of compassion on the planet. The old energy had been transformed, converted with new intention and purpose, born out of the purity of love.

While honoring the Goddess of Gaia, I noticed the green slithery tails of the gigantic Lizzie assassins within my expanded vision.

I gasped at their gargantuan, formidable presence. Instinctively, I pointed the blade toward the Dracaena Tree, creating a spiral between two saplings struck by lightning. The energy of the blade combined with the circular motion opened an etheric gateway between the worlds.

Just as we entered the portal within our protective bubble to escape the assassins, I quickly tapped into Ms. Rolland's thoughts.

Her motives were soberingly clear.

Devour everyone. Secure the blade and capture the Ascending Angel as an offering for Ciakar.

❖   ❖   ❖

"I know that you don't wanna hear my opinion, but there come many paths and you must choose one. And if you don't change then the rain soon come. You might win some, but you just lost one."—Lost Ones by Lauryn Hill

CHAPTER 8

ROMA'S SHADOWS

"In a conflict between the heart and the brain, follow your heart."
— SWAMI VIVEKANANDA

Roma

R oma was unable to feel her arms. They dangled her in chains as she suspended from the arched ceiling of the mid-century estate to be taunted and belittled. The architectural design that featured exposed beams and floor-to-ceiling glass within the atrium created a pleasant atmosphere for the elite guests.

She was certain the host would never allow the wealthy visitors to view the torture chamber hidden behind the glass walls of the great room, doubling as mirrors. After weeks of questioning and torment, Roma dug into her energetic reserves. Her human vessel would diminish rapidly without water and food.

She had fought many battles in the parallel universes of Earth's timelines on her beloved Lemuria. Roma's people were manipulated and exploited with endless wars, deprivation, ignorance, and deception. After the onslaught of attacks by the Lizzie forces, the Lemurians lost their interstellar awareness, their magical abilities, and their self-confidence.

The society diminished as it was no longer regarded as the guiding light and wisdom of peaceful divinity they once proliferated. Lemuria became unrecognizable. Everything was replaced by ruthlessness and vulgarity. The civilization was oppressed, censored, and operated from inadequacy-based beliefs.

As a Lemurian descendant, Roma retained all the memories of her past lives and reincarnations stored within the Akashic Records. This was her gift, her quandary when she became an Ascended Master and joined the Galactic Guardianship.

Normally, when a Soul reincarnated on Earth, an energetic cloak of forgetfulness, a partition, was erected within the being's auric spheres. It ensured that all prior memories and experiences of past lives elapsed, separating the operative portion of existence from the Soul's entirety.

Although the essence of Lemuria was ejected from Gaia's template within the current timeline, the spirit of life had been etched into Roma's blueprint. Lemuria's heartbeat still operated the planet's core, manifesting in all the beauty and magic of Mother Earth.

Roma recalled the pureness of the Divine Feminine energy existence when Light Beings lived as humans in peace, harmony, creativity, and affluence. This took her back nearly twenty-six thousand galactic years, to reflect on the golden age of the Empirical Sun.

The Lemurians were the first interplanetary Galactic Beings that dwelled on the physical realms of the magnificent blue planet, governed by Goddess Gaia. They were thought projections that embodied pure love and infinite light of the Divine Source energy, operating as the ascended masters of the Universe in human form.

These Galactic Beings represented one hundred and forty-four Soul groups from the Red Planet, Sirius, and the Pleiades. They all chose to incarnate on Lemuria within the Water Kingdom, Animal Kingdom, and the Plant Kingdom. It was the home of some of the most beautiful, magical species.

Roma's family lineage originated from the Ka-ha-lee bloodline, who were the protectors and keepers of Gaia's natural resources. Her mother and her sister, Avalina, descended from the long line of indigenous dark-skinned enlightened beings who had resided on Lemuria for centuries.

Roma's mother was a mystic healer, a Galactic Shaman, known for her kind, loving, generosity. Since they vibrated at higher frequencies of light, they were able to control the four elements of the planet. She recalled her mother's abilities to transform atomic constructs of the environment while walking on water or transporting herself through the air.

As Roma reminisced about her beloved heaven on Earth, she remembered her Lemurian regal aquatic nine-foot vessel. Her skin was once luminous, changing from blue to green, depending on the two seasonal cycles of the planet. Her oval face captured the large vertical sapphire eyes magnificently, centered along her elongated head.

Her textured skin was scaly, allowing her intake of breath within the atmosphere of the Light-activated planet.

The Lemurians were boundless, magical souls that embodied all the characteristics of the unified Source, co-creating their universes with peaceful harmony. They were a gentle, androgynous society as they didn't identify with the labels of male or female. They operated solely from their heart center.

Roma's existence was free from stress, diseases, or pestilence. They were completely liberated and developed their clairvoyant abilities over thousands of years of societal practice. She loved her family and community with her entire being.

They didn't require land vehicles for transportation. They used astral travel, teleportation, and excelled in telepathy. Roma's entire family feasted off the lavish land, abundant with plants that harbored medicinal properties. The society relied on an organic culture of food consumption through vegetation, in concord with nature and balanced existence.

Lemurians didn't require artificial technology since they preferred to use psychic energies to move objects. Roma recalled that her sister Ava used to love using sonic, crystal energy to emit ultra-high-frequency as a power source to contact other worldly-beings.

As children, Roma and Ava loved to ride with the Unicorns across the magical land, exploring the intelligent creatures that existed within the vastness of Goddess Gaia. The heart-based connections that they formed with their four-legged friends bound their relationships for lifetimes.

Roma cherished the spirits of the Animal Kingdom. On one of their outings during a storm, she found herself in a quarry, submerged within tempestuous lush forests. She had fallen off her unicorn into the gorge surrounded by thunderous waterfalls.

As she tried to unshackle herself from the turbulence, her spirit animal, Pegasus, appeared in front of her, revealing its white, lustrous wings. Roma instantly fell in love with the beautiful, wild, and free mystical creature that embodied the divine essence of protection and sovereignty.

This powerful Light Being had chosen to bond with Roma's eternal spirit, communicating with her telepathically as they liberated her from the valley. Roma recognized the formidable forces that worked in harmony and agreement with all living beings, united by the radiant life force energy.

Pegasus activated Roma for her Galactic mission with sacred blessings. They forged their relationship of purity, friendship, and unbounded love with every interaction, soaring above the oceans and exploring new lands to be harvested.

Roma's bloodline built their sacred kingdom in service of all beings and the Goddess Gaia. They maintained peace and congruence for every citizen, ensuring that no one suffered from hunger or homelessness. There was plenty of nourishment for their communities to co-exist in tranquility and joy. However, Gaia's generosity was both her greatest strength and weakness. It made her vulnerable to the powerful, predatory forces that sought to control the beautiful planet with grandeur and affluence.

The Lizzie consciousness from Draco took advantage of Gaia's benevolence. They exploited Roma's pure and angelic home with deception, war, ignorance, corruption, and deprivation.

In defense, Roma entered the High Priesthood, who were the sovereign keepers of Gaia, and pledged her eternal Soul to uphold Lemuria's independence, restoring the traditions of the great Ka-ha-lee.

The Dark Forces firmly planted their dense, contracting presence, rooted in separation, limitation, and fear-based reality. The evolution of the tyrannical doctrine was forcefully adopted as humanity's existence evolved with the fragmentation of Lemurian Souls.

Through her mission, Roma discovered the secret underworld used by the Draco invasion during the great war. These tunnels were dug between her beloved Lemuria and Atlantis. She was part of the Light Warriors Regime, tasked with the destruction of the underground pathways; however, their attempt to seal off the entrances resulted in cataclysmic outcomes.

The Draco Dark Forces commissioned an army of the Ciakar Lizzies to erupt Earth's core with a powerful explosive arsenal. The destruction

rendered the tunnels unstable, causing devastating earthquakes, volcanoes, floods, and sinkholes. Millions of humans and innocent magical
creatures were obliterated, including Roma's mother and extended family, forcing the ice age era.

Roma escaped the Lizzies through a portal, jumping into another
timeline, unable to save Pegasus and her sister. The Ciakar species were
driven underground, enslaving the remaining human race for their
self-gratification. Unfortunately, Ava had been captured by the vicious
beasts, never to be seen again. The anguish of this memory still haunted
Roma to this very day.

The emotional trauma of the collective civilization had resulted in
intergenerational wounding over lifetimes. The cycle of violence caused
the darkness to feast on the energy generated by these lower realms of
today's third-dimensional society.

The Wizard had leaped into this parallel timeline to repeat the
sequence of psychic warfare, using the false, illusive matrix of complex
shadow systems. The sinister Lizzie energy crept into the collective unconsciousness like a virus, gripping mindsets and hijacking the murky
thought patterns of humanity's past.

These dark corners of the mind were traumatized aspects of each
being that hid in the shadows. The more humans ignored their suffering, the more they birthed false illusive masks to cover their pain.
This compromised their existence and made them susceptible to the
Lizzie psychic warfare, which was used as a weapon for oppression and
domination.

The ancient tunnel system still existed in the current timeline.
It connected the entire globe, through continents under oceans. The
Lizzies possessed electromagnetic lasers to melt and pulverize rocks and
matter to build underground structures.

Roma was aware of this place, where all the horrific acts of the unnatural, underworld such as human trafficking, rituals, cannibalism, medical experiments, and human cloning existed.

Today's technology had also been available during ancient Egypt, introduced by the Lizzies. They had harnessed the power of the black rocks from the Draco galaxy. Since everything in the universe was operated by electrical energy, this current flowed using the vibrational potency of thought forms. The energy sparked human bodies, while each organ operated at a different rate of recurrence.

Roma was successful at decoding some of the universal electrical codes of existence, but not all. She had several thousand lifetimes to understand frequency ranges. For example, Roma had discovered that planet earth vibrated at 7.83 hertz, which symbolized life. The general frequency of the entire human body was also 7.83 hertz (7+8+3 = 18).

Neurons within the brain operated on this electricity and chemistry. A brain cell was remarkably similar to a living storage container with channels that separated its internal environment from the external. When a neuron received a strong input within its structure, it generated an electrical current that acted as wires that conducted energy, which vibrated using water.

The human body was comprised of seventy percent of fluid. Roma had realized that this was more than a coincidence since water pulsated at the frequency of 100 hertz (1+0+0=1), which symbolized the Source of Oneness.

Roma had also discovered that the great Sun operated at the frequency range of 5.9642 gigahertz (5+9+6+4+2=26), the numerical value associated with Divine God Source, which was infinite (2+6=8). This numerology was used to crack the codes of the entire universe and existence, to reveal the secrets and power of life force energy that resided within the sacred Akashic Records. This had been the primary cause of the galactic battle between the Light and Dark.

The Draco Dark Forces were determined to control the archives of existence to gain intergalactic power and dominate the Source of Creation and Light. These cosmic logs contained an archive of multi-dimensional consciousness of every soul since creation. It was the key that provided access to the Prime Creator.

The Lizzies had emerged from the black hole to gain control over these records once again. They required the coveted Lemurian blue crystals that held the Divine Feminine superpower to abolish Gaia's influence.

Merged with the Draco Black Crystals, they would cause a combustion which would illuminate a cosmic path to the sacred spheres of creation that housed the Akashic Records. It would galvanize the Lizzies to control the solar system, the Milky Way galaxy with the billions of stars, and eventually the entire quantum field Universe.

If the Wizard succeeded in obtaining these records, the Lizzies would have the power required to eliminate the Council of Divine Creation with intergalactic plasma waves and demolish the presence of the sacred Light.

Since the Akashic Records contained the sum of the past, present, and future experiences, the Dark Forces would possess the ability to alter the natural progression of existence, becoming the Prime Creator of the Universe, shifting the balance, and propelling all life into darkness.

The Lizzies had excelled in harvesting the power of ideas. They figured out that thought-forms were faster than the speed of light and the speed of sound. They used their advanced technology through mind control and supernatural psychic powers.

They continued to control human behavior with acts of violence, murder, incest, oppression, deceit, manipulations, violations, and greed.

It wasn't too difficult to achieve; after all, most of the population was hypnotized. The human identity was based on a personality, a character, and a belief system that people had adopted.

Upon reincarnation, Roma had agreed to allow the clearing of ancestral lineages, to resolve the wounds and unprocessed pain of all lifetimes before. This was an incredible opportunity for her to further the course of humanity's mastery.

As a human, Roma identified more with states of contraction. This built up the pressure of a spontaneous expansion of her consciousness to clear the cellular memory of the past, to heal and illuminate her shadows. Through the Soul contraction, there was a foreshadowing of greater expansion of morality, equality, inclusion, and respect for all beings.

This remembrance was Roma's greatest contribution to today's civilization. She had finally integrated her disruptive struggles, reaching the deepest level of healing possible within oneself.

In some of her past lives, raising her awareness felt like a spiritual invasion rather than a cosmic rescue mission. If she was triggered by any type of conflict, division, judgment, or anger, it was a trauma response that needed to be healed and cleared.

Roma was able to recall every experience from every past life stored within the Akashic archives. As a Custodian of the Galaxy, she had the freedom to choose to time-travel in any dimension. She chose to quantum leap into this polarized matrix of duality to help Gaia and to shift the entire human collective into the fifth-dimensional realm. Roma was determined to save humanity.

This was a massive undertaking, but Roma was not alone. The entire StarSeed Quest of 144,000 Light Warriors had been activated for this mission. Humans had the power through freedom of choice to catalyze their ascension by exposing the darkness out of the shadows.

Roma was tasked with this operation, knowing that there was a massive galactic change occurring. A cosmic reboot had been permeating and transforming sporadic colonies of planets into the most intentional galactic communities.

She had been given the invitation, intention, and mission as a transformer of reality, without the threat of persecution that she vividly remembered from past lives. This time, Gaia was ready for the shift into higher levels of consciousness, preparing and initiating all her inhabitants.

The Light Warriors worked on accelerating the journey expansion of all beings. The rescue mission was an interruption of the normalcy of the collective conditioning. Oneness was being birthed as chaos cleared the space for new frontiers to be perceived.

Although Roma's captivity seemed dire and hopeless, as she hung from the ceiling of Ciakar's compound, she knew without a shadow of a doubt that there was a bigger plan unfolding with immaculate conception. These lowest moments in existence presented an opportunity to experience the greatest aspects of her heart's pureness.

Roma was determined to transform the planet from a duality battlefield into the heaven on Earth she had always cherished. Her beloved Lemuria would rise again with resonance, harmony, imagination, clarity, and balance. It was Gaia's destiny and intention.

"Wake up, you feeble, pathetic stardust. We're not done with you yet!" The callousness of the wicked shapeshifter snapped her back into stark reality.

"You will give us the codes, now! Your Council and Light force cannot save you here." A female's voice pierced Roma's eardrums.

She opened her eyes, barely able to see through the blurring and swelling. The shapeshifter moved toward her, planning to extract her thoughts through forceful clairvoyance. As she prepared her mind for the psychic warfare, Roma instantly recognized the face of the interrogator.

She was tall and slender, looked prim and proper, with her dark hair slicked back in a tight bun. Her black eyes gleamed with terror, shrouded with shadows, malice, and secrets. Roma was immediately mesmerized by her energy, seeing through her screens of cruelty.

She had aged since the last human encounter lifetimes ago, but the resemblance was uncanny. The pangs of guilt for the golden dreams that had long perished still hovered within Roma's heart.

"Ava...Ava, is that you?" Roma whispered, her heart pounding with elation. The thought of reuniting with her sister in this incarnation ignited her with hope.

"Shut up! You will only speak to me with permission. You are no longer the adorned, mighty Light Warrior. Look at you, swaying like a marionette doll, frail and disenchanted. Well, dance for me, puppet, dance!" Ms. Rolland snickered while she continued her barbaric torture with electric currents.

"If Ciakar is so smart, why doesn't he figure it out himself instead of hiding like a coward on this big orb of mass?" Roma asked, barely able to speak due to the electrocution. "Where is he, Ava? Or are you still doing his dirty work?"

"I will cut your tongue out and feed it to my dogs if you don't shut your mouth. Where did you hide the crystals?" she hissed with disdain.

Roma laughed in her face, further taunting and agitating her oppressor.

"By the power of Ciakar, I order you to give me the keys to your precious existence!" She lashed out again without mercy.

The sting from the throng of electric shocks sent Roma into a state of deep unconsciousness, where she preferred to disappear while she waited for Jo and the Light Beings.

Her inner world was peaceful, safe, and full of magic. From this space, she was able to birth new energy with her pineal gland, new universes. A paradise that her heart yearned, a profound longing.

For Roma, heaven was a dimension of radiant selflessness, Souls helping each other awaken and expand. She knew quite well that it was not meant for a world lost in a loop of trauma responses, with narratives of righteousness and delusion. Only consciousness that demonstrated morality, integrity, and compassion of action would evolve and ascend.

Roma had learned to welcome devastation into her heart, to hold space for harmony, allowing the Light to guide her. She surrendered and embraced her tragedies, her shadows of the past, with unwavering, unconditional integrity. The Light Force energy she harnessed was much more powerful than any dark frequency that resided within her Soul's blueprint.

Once again, with honor and grace, Roma reclaimed her sovereignty by the power of heavenly virtue. She activated her last Arcturus source within her reserves, resolute that Light would always illuminate the Dark to restore the Galactic balance.

Ms. Rolland

Ms. Rolland's Lizzie body bowed down in front of Ciakar, his menacing frame perched atop the stone. The power of the Black Crystal crown magnified his evil aura.

"Where is the Ascending Angel? Show her to me!" Ciakar's murmur penetrated the air.

Ms. Rolland shuddered with dread. The Wizard of Bondage had her gripped by the neck, placing her in a vulnerable position. His energy emanated by the dark crystals, enabled the magnified pulsations of torture and pain, without him moving a muscle.

"My Lord, forgive me. They got away using the Custodian's Blade. Please, Ciakar, give me another chance to make things right." Ms. Rolland pleaded, fearing for her life. She was quite familiar with the Wizard's lack of empathy.

"You let her get away with the sword? Your lack of diligence may jeopardize our entire agenda! How disappointing!" Ciakar's power intensified, grounding her into the cement tunnel.

"I can fix this, my Lord. I can try to track the coordinates of the energy emitted by the blue crystals," Ms. Rolland implored. The sword's power on the astral plane had been unanticipated.

"I need that Blade of Truth to harness the Lemurian power force. Without it, I will not be able to unleash the fatal transgressions of malice needed to normalize this purgatory!" Ciakar hissed. "Once humanity's sins have all been released, it will distract the Light Beings. While they try to save their precious pets, I will have complete access to the Galactic Akashic Records, without any impediments."

The Wizard finally conveyed his evil plans. The destruction of Gaia included the emancipation of the sinister cinders trapped below the volcanic plates that covered the Lost City of Atlantis on Earth.

These forces made up the Dark Army that was originally created by the Founders to assist the Celestial Light in destroying nefarious unconscious cosmic entities.

However, the Draco entities had managed to corrupt and program the Founder's Army to perform their bidding on Earth, on a massive scale. They infiltrated the Atlanteans with arrogant eyes, a deceitful tongue, with hands that spilled innocent blood, a heart filled with hatred and wickedness, with a false propaganda and conflicting accusations.

The Dark Army annihilated the entire civilization, contaminating the Divine Feminine energy to combat the creative force that brought everything into existence within the natural world.

In Lemuria, the Draco Lizzies discovered their innate enemy, who threatened their galactic domination agenda. It was the universal frequency of Divine Feminine that exemplified the foundation of the physical and spiritual existence, the Great Goddess, spiritual mother, and the supreme life-giver.

Lemuria's Goddess Consciousness was a state of awareness that connected to the feminine life force energy of Source. It was the cosmic mother for all creation, a divine vessel for heart and soul wisdom required for natural laws to govern the goodness of humanity.

This container disseminated peaceful, harmonious, and loving frequencies that influenced human behaviors, procreation, and warrior spirits. Over time, the Divine Feminine energy overcame the emotional struggles and upheld justice, equality, morality, and balance.

The Ciakar sought to possess the Goddess energy that alchemized opposing negative frequencies for higher purposes, separating pure matter from the impure. By dominating and controlling the Divine Feminine, the Dark Forces would succeed in obliterating the sentient being, disconnecting it from the unified Source.

As such, the Lizzies distorted the representation of the Divine Feminine through their version of the Dark Army. Ciakar planned to release Lion's sinister ash of pride, to contaminate the planet's farmlands with rotten larvae that would destroy all food consumption. Without the food source, humanity would plunge into global famine.

The Wizard's favorite weapon that easily enveloped humans was the Grizzly's sinister ash of lethargy. Ciakar infiltrated the vulnerable, compromised humans through mind control and released the deadly vapor of impotence that caused immediate depression, internal conflict, lack of control, and feelings of powerlessness.

Once Ciakar further polarized the human race from Source energy, he planned to unleash Fox's sinister ash of greed. The intense and selfish desire entered the humans through their eyes, causing an infection in a form of black bile, engorging itself with its tentacles on humanity's blood for zombification.

The Wizard of Bondage could not afford any mistakes with his plans. His final act on Earth would involve the release of the Dragon's sinister ash of wrath. This fatal transgression took the form of a malevolent mermaid with the head of a cyclops. The explosions and eruptions around Earth would weaken Gaia's resources, grooming her into eternal oppression.

Ciakar released his grip on Ms. Rolland's throat after exerting his punishment for her malfunction.

"Perhaps this will motivate you to follow my exact orders." He raised a hand and a black mist formed in the air in the shape of a spear.

Without hesitation, the Wizard hurled the smoky lance into Pierre's head, completely vaporizing Ms. Rolland's son, without any mercy.

Failure was not an option.

❖ ❖ ❖

"I look at my environment and wonder where the fire went. What happened to everything we used to be?" —The Miseducation of Lauryn Hill by Lauryn Hill

CHAPTER 9

TUNNEL OF ANGUISH

"Re-examine all you have been told. Dismiss what insults your soul."

—WALT WHITMAN

Jo

The sight of Ms. Rolland's Lizzie form temporarily shook me to my very core. It was the most appalling and intimidating spectacle to witness as a human. While I processed her true intentions, I had to reject the nerve-twisting charge that attempted to evade my precious field.

As we time-travelled through the portal into the Wizard's compound, all my senses remained on high alert, preparing the Blade for battle. Resolution slammed into me, and I expanded the span of my inner eye to detect the enemies in our radius.

"Guys, get behind me. I will shield you from any unwelcome surprises with the blade," I called out to my friends, getting ready to fight. The sword's energy coursed through my veins, strengthening my momentum. I fixed myself in an offensive stance to ward off any potential attacks.

"Jo, be careful!" Conrad exclaimed, still worried about my safety.

"We need to make a half-circle around Jo!" Nisha commanded, and everyone jumped into action without hesitation. I sensed their fear. I didn't blame them. This scary reality was something out of a science-fiction movie.

I couldn't deny that the gigantic cold-blooded beings were quite menacing; however, I had no time to dwell on their physical appearance. I altered my friends' inflamed nervous systems with a peaceful healing chant.

Their selfless ongoing support and protection demonstrated how much they cared for my well-being and humanity. Their love radiated with exuberant light, increasing my warrior essence with calm and serenity. I honored and acknowledged their willingness to assist on this mission, even in these dangerous circumstances.

"What do you see, Jo? Keep us posted, I don't want any surprises," Theo remarked, encased in the protective light I had bubbled around him.

"Stay alert. Ms. Rolland may have alarmed the Wizard's guards. They are only after me and Roma's blade." I explained. "Don't be afraid, I'll make sure you're all protected, even if it's the last thing I do." I was determined to keep my friends safe.

"Don't worry about us, Jo! We are here with you through thick and thin!" Daphne said.

My ethereal wings shed light on my friends, bathing them in celestial energy. My code activation helped me formulate a plan, enabling further access to the celestial force embedded in the Blade of Truth.

"If for any reason we encounter life-threatening danger, I will make sure to teleport you out of the compound to safety," I warned my friends, briefing them about my ideas.

"Jo, we can help you distract the guards. Don't send us away too quickly," Zax pleaded as my friends unanimously agreed with his self-less offer.

The salty scent of the sea filled my senses as I inhaled deep, cleansing breaths. There was a calming effect before the foreboding storm. I closed my eyes and centered myself. I aligned my energy, visualizing a column of plasma light circulating through the vortex of my Light Body energy fields with peace and zero-point neutrality.

I acknowledge the Forces of Light, requesting guidance, courage, and determination to reveal deeper truths and deceptions for the highest good. May the love of divine Source protect me and my friends from any forms of harm and lower vibrational potency, no matter the horrific obstacles we might encounter. Help us shed layers of illusory aspects of our lives to better embody our remembrance. May our triggers teach us and guide us toward our healing, integration, and ascension through these experiences.

May we confront our fears and alchemize our emotions, turning anger and feelings of being lost into healthy boundaries as we navigate our path. May we heal the separation, the veil of density between our human existence and divine selves, to help restore the greater union of cohesive consciousness. May we respond to our situations, not from victimhood, but as transformers, as we convert the collective pain into compassion.

Help me retain my inner peace and access all versions of my divine Spirit through the sacred Akashic Records, to fortify my mission in this now moment. And so, it is.

With this affirmation, my pineal gland burst with high-frequency codes as I tuned in to all the information Roma had managed to relay. I tethered my energy to the fourth-dimensional frequency realm to secure the channel for further telepathic communication.

The Lizzie censors popped up on my radar and helped me pin-point our enemies. Surprisingly, there were a handful of guards on the premises. I kept tabs on them as I searched for similar dense energy textures, as well as Alicia's and Roma's auric hues. Before I was able to sharpen and determine their locations, I heard a deep, collective gasp.

I opened my eyes just in time to witness a giant Lizzie rapidly slith-ering toward us. The green scales on its body shimmered in the fading light, emphasizing its strong, powerful thigh muscles with every move-ment. The alligator-looking heinous face stood in contrast with our human frames.

"Jo! Watch out!" Zax yelled, throwing his arms out in front of me.

"Guys, huddle! Together, we can defeat this ugly beast!" Conrad raced behind me and circled his arms around my waist, ready to whip me out of the ensuing attack.

"Stay back! The sword will shield us!" Everything happened in an instant, and I shrugged off his protective hands.

It was my duty to defend them, not the other way around. I raised the Blade of Truth and channeled the Lemurian crystal energy, the sword crackling with light. I slammed the blade into the ground, satis-fied with the gathered power, and the energy exploded in pale blue spar-kles all around us. The intensity of the light blasted the Lizzie creature, sending it into the air and crashing it onto its back.

I utilized the time to focus my third eye on launching a gateway. I connected to the high frequency, sifting through the multiple auras popping up on my radar. One area with several mixed types of energies blipped on my galactic detector, and I didn't waste a moment to visualize the victims held against their will.

Tethering myself to the energies, I raised the Blade into the air and opened another portal. A void appeared in the atmosphere, encircled by high static electric energy.

"Everyone, move! Hurry!" I shouted, holding the portal open long enough for all my friends to make their escape.

Once we were on the other side, I sealed the entryway behind me, and I slammed into the cemented floor with force, gathering myself to explore our surroundings. Rubbing my arm in agony, I found my friends lying on the ground in various positions, their breathing rapid from the narrow escape.

"Well, that sucked. I wasn't expecting to crash face-first into hard cement," Daphne mumbled, breaking the silence.

"That was a close one!" Nisha exclaimed, crawling toward Theo to help him up.

"Is everyone okay?" I asked, ensuring no one had sustained any serious injuries. The sword's crackling energy subsided as I released the dimensional grip on my galactic powers.

"Phew. Jo, are you alright?" Conrad hobbled toward me, his limp on full display.

"Yes, I am fine, thanks. I didn't anticipate the intensity of our narrow escape, as you can tell." I laughed, tapping into everyone's auric field to take their pulse. The energetic chaos subsided as light passed through them, and my strength defused their emotions.

"Where are we now, Jo?" Nisha asked.

We were surrounded by cement walls, with low-bearing, rounded ceilings. It resembled a dark tunnel with a few barrels scattered in corners. The dank smell of human feces permeated the space. I could sense the intensifying frequencies of fear, pain, and suffering.

"I think we are in the underworld of the Wizard's compound." I expanded my awareness and detected multiple hues and their exuberant Lights. I reached out telepathically, hoping Roma would answer.

"*Roma? Can you hear me?*" I tuned into the secure channel.

"*Yes, Jo. Where are you?*" Roma answered immediately. "*I think they're holding me on the main floor.*" Relief washed over me with her confirmation and my heart elevated in anticipation. We were finally close.

"*I am in a dingy underground tunnel with my friends, Roma. I was able to open a portal with your Blade that we located within the island's shrubbery,*" I explained. "*Gaia was protecting it from the Lizzies. That's how we entered the private mansion.*" I relayed the good news, still marveling over Gaia's defense.

"*Thank you for finding it, Jo! I knew the Goddess Gaia would protect my powerful sword from sinister beings,*" Roma said.

"*Make sure you follow the tunnel in the direction of the massive vault. Use the force of the Blade to unlock its entrance. You should be able to find Alicia there with the rest of the detainees. Brace yourselves for what's to come,*" she continued in an ominous tone.

"*I'm not sure how I will be able to free everyone, Roma. How many are enslaved within the compound?*" I asked.

"*There are dozens of innocent beings that have been captured for personal entertainment, Jo,*" Roma explained as I prepared myself.

"*This type of slavery has a huge energetic impact and consequence that creates a serious negative imbalance within all grid timelines of existence, through cause-and-effect karmic retribution. The Lizzies have evolved their weaponry to steal other humans' soul energy. We must stop them from subjugating and causing intentional harm to innocent people. Blood sacrifices and pedophilia are the primary methods by which the elite can delay responsibilities for their actions. Once you free me from my bondage, I will be able to put an end to this wretched bloodline cycle. Just hurry, Jo."*

Roma concluded relaying her instructions as I sensed her deteriorating energy. Her guidance troubled me, but I centered myself and separated the human emotions on the rise around me.

I recalled all the celestial downloads and wisdom from the Council to prepare for this moment. I was ready to overcome any obstacle that stood between me and my mission.

"Okay, guys, we are going back into the compound, through the vault doors at the end of this tunnel," I explained to my friends. "Everyone, please be vigilant. We never know what will pop out of the corners," I warned them, making sure they understood the implications. I was amazed by their continued valor and fortitude to assist with the rescue mission. I continued to pray silently for all our Souls.

"What the heck is this place?" I heard Theo comment behind me as we continued through the tunnels. I hoped we all had the strength to face the horrific acts perpetuated by these sinister entities.

"Jo, I'm getting a bad feeling about this. It's worse than our battle with the Lord of Darkness," Zax said, inching closer to Flynn for comfort.

"I have no idea what's on the other side of the vault, but we need to prepare ourselves. Ciakar is running a human trafficking ring from this tiny island. Once we locate the ones captured against their will, our goal is to help liberate them from the Wizard of Bondage," I replied, preparing them for possible scenarios.

I couldn't fathom the fact that human trafficking had become a modern-day slavery ritual. It was difficult to believe that something so heinous was taking place on the island. *How many of these types of compounds exist around the world? And how many humans have been detained by these Lizzies?*

Roma was right. We could not allow the same fate to occur for the human race as that of the Lyrians.

"I'm freaking out, Jo. My sister is in there! What if something horrific has happened to her?" Theo cried out in disbelief and concern.

"I understand your worry, Theo. Please, try not to focus on the worst-case scenarios. That's what the Lizzies want. You can visualize Alicia in your mind's eye, safe and sound once we remove her from this place. You will be reunited very soon, I promise," I tried to console the poor guy. The whole experience was overwhelming as we rummaged through the pits of hell.

It was our collective responsibility to assist Gaia through this process as she cleared herself of these Dark Forces. They had infiltrated every aspect of our planet with their sinister fleas. The Lizzies polluted and poisoned our food and water to weaken humans and all-natural life for far too long.

No matter the difficulty, we needed to stay strong and resist their mind-control and manipulative energy through this holographic shift. Roma had described their evil agenda clearly. I was confident that we would all be united in our victory as we embraced the powerful Light Force.

Nisha provided further comfort and explanation. "Theo, we all have to be mindful of our thoughts, not allow our emotional reactions to fuel the negative energy, especially now."

"If we're acutely aware of every now moment, we will be able to shift our timelines and reality, with preferable probabilities and outcomes," Nisha said in a soothing voice. She had been listening to me all this time.

"Thanks, Nish, you're absolutely right! Together, with conscious thought, we can collapse the veil of density, pulling our combined energy into higher timelines. We need to be willing to allow whatever outcomes are meant for us, not resist. Once we choose with our visualization, we will transmute the shadows in our path into the light." I continued to relay the knowledge and guidance to my friends.

Everyone needed to understand how the shadows unraveled through the delusion under the veil of density. Fear was powerful and potent, a cunning influence. We had the choice to stand in our understanding of the truth as sentient beings. It was our divine birthright.

"When we pay attention to what emotions we are emitting, we can take responsibility for our actions. This is how we can unravel the false belief systems and constructs that have brought us to this moment. Only empathy, compassion, and love will prevail," I explained.

I realized it was a lot of information for my friends to process. My words were activating their light codes within their DNA structures as I provided healing with every intention. Once we mastered the art form of recognizing events objectively, clearing all judgmental views, we were not easily polarized. It allowed us to receive and attract information from the quantum field that was not distorted.

Throughout my downloads, I had discovered an important lesson. When we were attached to our external circumstances, we allowed others to determine our feelings. This disabled us to become co-creators of our realities with this compromised mindset. Negative emotions that bubbled within us were alerts, signals that informed us we were not in alignment with our higher self.

From the beginning of time, our Soul's sovereignty enabled us to play with our beliefs. It was the ability to bounce around without being governed by anything through attachment because our intention was always pure. We were in service for humanity's highest good, for the ascension of the collective. The unified mindset enabled us to rise against the tyranny and manipulation of these Lizzie forces as they assaulted humanity's existence.

I felt a pang of empathy for Theo. I couldn't imagine the depth of his worry and angst.

"We will find Alicia, no matter what. We won't let anything happen to her, Theo. She is a StarSeed activated and summoned by Roma and, apparently, Mother Earth. She will be able to handle herself." Daphne comforted Theo, locking her arms with his.

I was in awe of my best friends and their compassionate hearts. Even in these dangerous circumstances, they soared above the traumatic events to embody their higher selves.

Theo's chaotic nerves calmed considerably, and he nodded at me in acceptance. His lips pursed while he concentrated on positive outcomes on our walk toward the vault.

"Alicia is an extraordinarily strong person, Theo. I admire her so much for her resilient personality. She will be able to take care of herself, I have no doubts," Nisha chimed in.

I could sense her worry for Alicia, but she exercised the meditation technique I had shared with everyone to align their centers and control their rolling emotions.

"We are a team, and we will fight and defeat this gnarly Wizard. He can join his buddy, the Lord of Darkness, in the black abyss." Flynn chuckled as he slapped Theo on the back in support.

All my friends came together for each other, providing me with contentment and peace. It was quite a feeling to be born into a supporting, loving family. But to also be so blessed with chosen friendships and deep soulful connections fortified my tribe as we experienced our journeys together.

"What will we do when we come face to face with Ciakar? And how will we fight him, Jo?" Daphne questioned, apprehensive of the upcoming battle.

"First, we find Alicia. Then we rescue Roma, that's our priority. She is our guide on this mission and a Custodian of the Galaxy. But if we end up facing him or Ms. Rolland without Roma, then we fight. We fight with all the Forces of Light," I replied, not having a concrete plan.

I still relied on Roma to steer this operation. However, I trusted our intelligent Universe to guide us. I knew in my heart that my strong belief and the Arcturus energy force would protect my friends for whatever outcomes were ahead.

"Hold on. I think we have found it." I walked ahead and placed my hand on the cold, steel door. The aura of misery behind the entrance was unmistakable, and I could feel the anguish of humans trapped on the other side.

"What is it?" Conrad stepped closer to me as he marveled at the engineering of the wall. I activated my ethereal wings with the Blade, illuminating the dark hallway.

"We need to break through this lock. Alicia and others are on the other side. Everyone, step back." As my friends moved away to a safe distance, I activated the Blade of Truth. With one swift movement, the galactic sword erupted through the gigantic concrete lock and chain. I pushed open the heavy metal door until it was only slightly ajar.

"Ready?" I whispered, initiating the protective light shield around them as we entered the underworld.

A strong stench charred our physical senses as dozens of terrified eyes reflected at us through the darkness. Their misery slammed into my field as I absorbed their agony. I took an involuntary step back. Their collective energy overwhelmed me for a moment, but I remained grounded and vigilant, erecting my protective boundaries. The sight of so many people tied up in this inhuman place was the most heartbreaking event I had ever witnessed.

"Oh, my God…" Nisha whispered, taking a step forward toward the front of the large, cold room. She lit the lantern situated by the door, illuminating the horrors of this reality.

They were so young, girls and boys, from every corner of the world. They cowered away in fear of our presence, their faces frightened by the prospect of further torment. Their hands were tied in front of them, restricting their movements.

"It's okay, we won't harm you," I whispered gently, raising both of my hands up in the air. My friends gasped in disbelief, overwhelmed by the poor conditions and surroundings.

Tears streamed down Daphne's face as she entered behind me, her hands also raised in a cautionary manner. None of us could have possibly prepared for this atrocity.

"We are here to help you. Don't be alarmed. Does anyone speak English?" Zax asked in a consoling voice.

I stepped forward and filled them with my light. It required a significant amount of celestial energy to infuse the inflammation of their nervous systems. Their fear slowly subsided at my quest as their auras echoed a slightly muted aroma of terror.

"Let's go untie them. Hurry, before anyone finds us." Flynn broke the silence, and everyone hopped into action, making their way around the room to free dozens of people with their tiny camping knives.

Meanwhile, I took the pulse of our environment, locating the next spot that glowed with human auras within the compound. I found another area as I empathically connected to their frequencies of heartache and despair within my radar.

"Alicia, are you in here? Has anyone seen my sister, Alicia?" Theo asked, hoping for some direction.

No one spoke a word. I realized that they were too paralyzed with fear. I continued to focus on their inflamed nervous systems, infusing them with my healing energy.

"No," a quiet, feeble voice answered.

"There's no Alicia here."

"Hi, my name is Conrad. We are here to help you. What's your name?" He approached the brave Soul, making initial contact with a frail dark-haired girl that had found her voice. Her large brown eyes blinked widely with panic. She had an exotic look, beautiful, elegant, and demure.

"They call me number 369," she answered softly.

"Do you remember your real name, your family?" Conrad continued his questioning. The young girl shook her head solemnly, unable to respond further. Her traumatic response to her captivity had blocked her memory.

I continued to evaluate the surroundings, feeling my friends' emotions as they struggled to process this moment.

"Listen, guys, this experience will be disturbing for us all. Let's put up our boundaries, try to breathe through our emotionally charged reactions and remain calm. We must neutralize our energy, so we are not spreading their collective fear. Remember, we are here to free any person held against their will," I quickly said to combat their imbalance.

No matter how much I tried, I was unable to prepare my friends or myself for the shocking situation.

"How do you propose we do that, Jo? We can't get out of this hell hole without getting caught ourselves. What if the Wizard has enslaved hundreds of people?" Zax voiced his concern.

"We're here to help your mission any way we can, Jo. Just let us know what you need," Daphne interjected, punching his arm. Zax winced at the sudden reminder, calming himself.

"Thanks, Daph, and I hear you, Zax. You're quite right, but we have to trust the Light Forces guiding us at this moment," I replied sincerely. It was my truth.

"Everyone looks so petrified in here. I hope we can gain their trust," Flynn added with unease.

"All I know is that we are the catalysts that will facilitate their internal healing, on a massive level. Just like we have done with our traumas from our trip to Spain." I had noticed a similar pattern when we helped liberate the sleepwalkers.

"Each one of us has a unique journey to counteract the shadow aspects of our experience. It helps if we think of ourselves as super-computers. Through healing, we create more space and light, allowing ourselves the ability to open additional browsers within our quantum mind. So, our past experiences don't crowd the space anymore, making it simpler to filter through the accumulated files. We can then decide to integrate what's already processed or delete what no longer serves us." I glanced at Nisha, who had been unusually quiet.

"Ya, ya, we get it, Jo. We are un-identifying from our human roles and narratives of the past that we associated with. We understand that we are not the ideas and beliefs we were raised with. I think we're all working on stabilizing our internal traumas. But what does this have to do with finding Alicia? We need to stop chatting and take action," Nisha yelled in frustration.

"I know, Nish. I'm just relaying and infusing these light codes into everyone's system, so we are prepared for battle. When the light empowers us to connect with empathy, we can gain their trust and rescue the captives that have been traumatized by this purgatory." I understood her annoyance as I reassured myself. I looked around the dark, dingy space, and I detected dozens of other chambers within the vaulted compound.

"I can help guide you to the other sections if you wish." The young girl known as 369 approached me with her slim hand, blank eyes, and quiet demeanor.

"It's quite dark, and the others know me. Maybe they can help locate your friend, Alicia," she continued. I noticed her youthful essence, thinking she was not much younger than me.

"Thank you, that is truly kind of you. How long have you been on this island?" I asked with caution.

"I can't really remember, but I know that I am the only surviving member of my family from Rwanda. I recall being homeless when some tourists approached me and offered me a housekeeping job. The next thing I know, I'm sold into slavery and brought here. I was eight years old," she explained.

My breath caught as my heart sank against my ribs with every word, tapping into her devastation. I continued to establish invisible boundaries around my center field for my protection. The Lizzie unconsciousness relied on our energy leaks, extracting our vital force fields like blood-thirsty vampires. I had to remain balanced and neutral, without assessing or reacting to the captive's experience.

I understood that only the higher echelon Draconian entities possessed the power to syphon a human Soul's emotional or psychic energy. The Lizzies could hijack our thoughts, but they had not yet harnessed the skills to prey on our collective Souls.

The thought frightened me as the momentary doubt disrupted my thoughts, diverting my attention to a negative outcome.

Is this the intention of the Dark Forces, using fear-based propaganda?

I dismissed the pessimistic thought out of my system, rejecting the malware. I wouldn't allow it to fester into my mind any longer. If this was an experience that was meant for my ascension journey, I would deal with it as required.

After all, some humans also preyed on others due to their unresolved pain and suffering. They drained the un-suspecting being with their attachment, co-dependent behaviors, leaving them chronically fatigued, depressed, and irritable. Developing healthy boundaries around these energy suckers was an important defense system for our protection.

They latched onto our subconscious guilt and sorrow like leeches, manipulating us through emotional blackmail. The dysfunctional learned behavior of this type of predator most likely originated from their low self-esteem and severe abuse during childhood.

As I learned about the importance of shadow work in this trauma-based, third-dimensional existence, I understood that these types of problems occurred from a lack of nurturing, love, validation, and support as children.

From my experience dealing with the sleepwalkers, I knew most of these human energy vampires emitted frequencies of unworthiness. Their despicable treatment of others was merely a reflection of how they viewed themselves. They projected their insecurities and reinforced their inflamed egos by belittling others, making them feel ashamed and pathetic. They searched and extracted these emotions from those around them as they drowned in their own perpetuated torments.

In such situations, it was important for us to remain vigilant in protecting our own precious, energetic spheres. I tried to always remind myself that true self-worth dwelled within.

With this knowledge, I had gained much empathy and awareness of the pain these individuals projected when we dealt with the bullies at school. I learned to dispel the hurtful comments and never responded from a defensive space. The best way to shield and nurture our energies around such beings was to maintain a balanced and aligned essence.

It was evident that the lessons I was to integrate through this stage of the Ascending Angel Academy were to understand the truth of why people reacted from the state of limitations and deficiency. It temporarily relieved them of their uncomfortable feelings that they had not processed or healed.

To master my mystic, I had to learn not to be triggered by external forces. It was how I would outgrow my program and attachment to my past emotional reactions of gossip, blame, or victimhood.

At this moment, I began transcending the animalistic tendencies of survival encoded within my DNA through the limited lens of my conditioned mind. My challenge was to remove all judgment and blame against others, no matter the gravity of their unconscious behaviors.

I discovered that the integration of the unified Source blueprint necessitated the harmonization of all twelve cosmic spheres and energy fields. Over time, the human heart center field split as our souls fragmented from our eternal selves. My mission was to unite those separated aspects, paving our path back into our crystalline wholeness of infinite love consciousness.

Emboldened by this reminder, I inhaled the desolation of my surroundings, and recognized how difficult this lesson was going to be. I paused to self-regulate, waiting for my body chemicals to settle down before I continued with the mission.

We followed the young girl known as 369 through a gloomy tunnel into another area filled with humans. I could hear my friends focusing on their breath-work. The human odor that emanated from the rooms continued to overwhelm our senses. An unpleasant sensation hit my stomach as nausea assaulted my body with every breath.

"This is number 136, he's been here longer than me. After his father died, he was forced to live with his grandmother in Cambodia. She didn't approve of his gender preferences, so she sold him to a brothel. He tried to escape, but he was captured, beaten, and brought to the island." The young girl introduced us to a few more victims. Most were so youthful, in their early teens, trafficked for sexual exploitation.

They were all ensnared and captured by force, coercion, or deception. They scraped by, trying to survive in the darkness, merely to witness another day of horror.

"Our friend 57 has twelve siblings and was sold by her family to a wealthy man who owned young, blonde girls as his property. This is 159; she thought she found a way out of Romania with a modeling job offer. When she went for the interview, she was drugged and abducted, then disappeared from her family without a trace. They destroyed her passport and identity. She's been here for a while as well." The stories persisted as we met more of the captives.

While we continued to search for Alicia throughout the tunnels, I received a telepathic message from Roma.

"Jo, this compound is just one of many hidden on private islands and mansions around the world. There are millions held in captivity, moved from location to location in this billion-dollar human trafficking trade. The value of human life has diminished, replaced with greed and materialistic gain from this lucrative criminal behavior. The Wizard is perpetuating this darkness, satiating the demanding inhuman appetite for lust and gluttony," Roma explained quickly, sensing my anguish.

"What's the plan, Roma? How do we save everyone?" I asked, keeping my anxiety at bay.

"Just find Alicia and get me down from my captivity. The rest will occur quite quickly. Don't allow yourself to absorb the pain and suffering all around you, Jo. Use your training and discernment, observe from your higher self, without judgement. This is how you propel yourself from this web of density." Roma stopped emitting her signal. She was getting weaker by the moment.

The petrified energies of the victims' suffering lingered around us like thick gray smoke. The mortifying trauma endured on a massive scale, imprinted in this dimension, cementing their grasp into Gaia's roots.

My mission sharpened my understanding and I experienced sudden clarity—we were here to displace the collective frequencies that had been stuck within the planetary grid. The greatest service to humanity was to integrate these dark shadows with compassion, empathy, and mercy. Our planet's environmental demise was a manifestation of humanity's collective anguish that we could no longer ignore.

We were experiencing this timeline to light the torch for mankind's future with examples of love, generosity, and caring for one another. This was the new paradigm shift of our collective perception.

The light would eventually release the excessive distress signals that were lodged within the vibratory fields of the captives. These blockages would be transmuted within their collective wounds, liberating their consciousness from the purgatory generated by the wicked Wizard of Bondage.

❖   ❖   ❖

"I hear so many cries for help, searching outside of themselves. Now I know that His strength is within me."—The Miseducation of Lauryn Hill by Lauryn Hill

CHAPTER 10
THE STARGATE

"A life of reaction is a life of slavery, intellectually and spiritually. One must fight for a life of action, not reaction."

—RITA MAE BROWN

Jo

T heo looked crestfallen at the discovery that Alicia was not among the captives. He paled at the sight of the captured humans in their fragile state of mind and bodies.

All of us took a moment to process the unfamiliar emotions of our current environment. We were in disbelief, with ashen complexions after taking stock of the crowded room. The enslaved victims waited in despair as they were being prepared for human trafficking. I could sense the energies within my friends switch rapidly from trepidation to anger at the horrific discoveries.

"Theo, we will find Alicia. We are getting closer to the StarSeeds," I comforted him, trying to provide a semblance of emotional support.

"They better not have done anything to Alicia. We need to destroy these bastards, Jo! I can't tolerate the sight of this anymore." Nisha shook with fury. I filled her with my healing Light to calm her inflammation as best as I could.

I understood the rage. I tried to process it while containing its explosive bite, knowing that this experience was a lesson. A message for me to find the strength and bravery within as I neutralized my emotive reactions.

"Guys, stay focused. I know this is horrific, but we must remain calm and impartial to save Alicia and Roma," I said, reminding them of the importance of maintaining their energies so they wouldn't become compromised in the purgatory.

I gazed down the dark corridor and sensed that the captives had incorporated my healing Light. The least I could do in the moment was to take away some of their pain and provide them with hope.

"Alicia…what she must be going through right now!" Theo's lowered tone exasperated his worry, his eyes fixated on the captives.

"Theo, let's not jump to conclusions, okay? We must be brave and trust in your sister's strength. We need to keep moving forward." Daphne inched closer to his drooping frame, holding him by his shoulder for support.

I appreciated the sincere efforts of my friends in helping me and supporting each other through the harshest circumstances.

"Jo, what's the next move?" Conrad asked, waiting for my direction.

I took a deep breath and centered myself, my inner eye spanning out toward the entrance of the compound. I felt several spots of heightened emotions at the end of the tunnel.

There was a specific charge of energy in another chamber, where the StarSeeds were detained. I addressed the crowd that had formed following our every step. I lifted the Blade above my head in a swift move and activated more light. I was able to see dozens of faces huddled in the darkness of the long dingy corridor.

"Everyone, we will need you to remain in the tunnel for a bit longer. Don't worry, we are here to release you from this place, so please remain calm until we come back to retrieve you. I promise we're not leaving you behind." I expanded my healing Light and calming forces with my hands to cloak the suffering humans like a warm embrace.

I tried something new using the Blade of Truth. Cupping my hands in front of me, I concentrated my cosmic power to form an irregular sphere of luminosity. I continued chanting the centering statement in my head as energy began to spark in the air between my hands.

"Oh, my God, Jo! That is so cool!" Zax's voice reached my ears amidst my concentration, and my lips quirked up in a smile at the incredible results.

"I never knew you had these magical powers! What the heck!" Flynn exclaimed. All my friends surrounded me in intrigue and wonderment.

"I AM the light that I AM, I AM the light that I AM." My own words filled my being as the ball grew, floating in the air. My energy expanded with every second, strengthening my pineal gland. I intended to leave this floating orb with the captives, to radiate the energy of optimism.

"We have a personal light bulb with us now. No need to waste worldly energy, guys!" Daphne joked, and everyone managed to chuckle. I could feel the sense of intrigue from the captive humans, their eyes focused on the spherical glow.

I moved my hands upwards, and the Light adjusted with me, bathing everything around us in soft, golden illumination.

I floated the sphere above the long tunnel of anguish, shedding the frequency of Light over every corner, exposing the shadows of humans and critters enslaved in darkness.

"Thank you for being here with us, it feels nice to have someone care for our well-being." A person toward the back of the corridor sobbed with relief. My healing Light amplified as I managed to transmute some of their pain. The Council had entrusted me with liberating these beautiful Souls, and I was willing to go to absolute lengths to ensure our success.

"We are leaving now, but I assure you that we will be back soon. Do not be afraid! Focus on the orb of light until we return," I reassured the masses.

"Okay, guys, let's go find Alicia and Roma." I guided my friends up a narrow staircase, toward an opening.

"Just keep an eye out for the Wizard's security guards. They are humans, guarding the complex from intruders." I raised the sword to ignite its powers. The blue crystal gleamed as I soaked it with my vitality, expanding the camouflaging energy amplified by the sword. My senses heightened further as I concentrated on building a mental tether between the StarSeeds and our location.

"Jo, what happens if we encounter the guards? They will be armed. Do you plan to open another portal?" Flynn inquired, grabbing my attention. He raised a valid point, and my friends began to offer their thoughts before I could answer.

"I don't think we need to worry about that, Flynn. Jo is a strong Light Warrior, and I trust her completely." Conrad replied in my support.

"Jo can definitely crush them with the Blade," Nisha interjected.

"I don't think Jo will kill anyone, even if they are partnered with Ciakar," Daphne said. She was right; I had no intention on harming another human. Not if I could help it.

"These humans who work for the Wizard are compromised and have been seized by Ciakar. Just like the sleepwalkers, their thoughts have been programmed through mind-control technology. Their brains have been polluted by nano-bites, assimilating with artificial energy. That's the reason humans fall prey to low vibrational beings like Ciakar. They strike when humans are weak, vulnerable, and have their guard down. Set your boundaries because an eruptive mind perpetuates the low-density pulsations, fueling the Wizard's powers. We have the ability to disarm their weaponry and reverse the sinister programs through our internal ascension," I continued to preach as we discovered an opening on the second level of the large basement.

"What about the people dealing with trauma? How do we help them manage their emotions?" Conrad questioned, getting nods from the rest of the group.

"We can help by clearing Earth of the pollution and toxicity that has penetrated the planet's core. Our weakness only amplifies the density within this reality, the dimensional purgatory that we're trying to cross over. Every negative thought, emotion, behavior, and action diminishes Gaia's power," I articulated in my limited human capacity.

"Alicia is a StarSeed, Jo. How did she fall prey to Ciakar? Didn't she have the same activation as you did?" Theo's voice pierced my auric field. I could sense his light force spiraling down the vortex of his energetic spheres. It was imperative to keep his emotions balanced and aligned without blame or judgment.

"That, I do not know, Theo. Alicia has been initiated recently, and she could have been dealing with an unprocessed trauma during her capture," I replied truthfully. "In my first phase of the Angel Academy, I found it equally difficult to manage my emotions as a Light Being. Everything was deeply overwhelming." I said, hoping it would help Theo feel less anxious about our current predicament.

201

We made our way in silence through another set of hallways, as my ethereal wings illuminated our path. My radar picked up the strong StarSeed energy.

"We are close. Get ready." I instructed my friends as we encountered a tall iron galvanized door with two padlocks. Suddenly, erratic energy slammed into me like a wall of concrete. I paused and took a step back. The alarm penetrating through the doors was strong.

I raised the Blade of Truth and signaled to my friends to keep moving. I pierced both deadbolts with the sword to break them open. They fell to the ground with a loud clang. Before I knew it, Theo passed me by and pushed open the door.

Inside, we found six StarSeeds affixed to the wall in rusted iron chains, seemingly unconscious. As we approached each person, I realized they had been immobilized with toxic drugs.

Theo spotted Alicia toward the back of the room. She was not moving. I focused my Light on all their physical bodies, extracting the drugs from their veins with my hands. I pooled my core with the Arcturus cosmic energy to strengthen my powers. The removal began to take form as we witnessed their movements in their captivity.

Each StarSeed began to gain consciousness. Alicia moved her fingers, clearly in a daze. Her eyes met Theo's. Her brother hovered over her with worry, and her expression morphed into one of confusion as well as relief.

"Theo…is it really you?" she questioned in a raspy tone as she struggled to pick herself up from the stone floor.

"Yes, of course it's me. Are you okay, sis? Did they hurt you?" Theo's frantic voice exhibited relief, tears flooding his face.

After a brief embrace, he helped Alicia sit up. Nisha could barely contain herself as she jumped in to assist Theo. Alicia wobbled to her feet but quickly stabilized. I felt her using her energy to rejuvenate herself, and I was relieved to see that she retained immense control over her galactic powers.

"I am all right. Oh, God, Theo, I am so sorry. I don't know what happened, I wanted to clear my head on the beach and saw you waiting for me. When I reached the waterfront, I was knocked out cold and brought here," Alicia explained, breathing heavily as she found her words.

She had been tricked into thinking the Lizzie shapeshifter was Theo. Her concern and worry for her brother had always been her weakness, making her vulnerable to Ciakar's insidious energy.

"Alicia, thank goodness you're okay. We don't have much time. We must rescue Roma; her light force is diminishing with every minute. Are you able to restore the rest of the StarSeeds?" I asked, fully aware that she needed a reprieve from her guilt.

"Yes, I haven't been here long so I'm much stronger than the rest of them. Thank you for finding me." Alicia's heartfelt gratitude emitted a frequency code that infused the StarSeeds with the vital galactic force, activating their powers.

I joined forces with her, providing healing and strength as the StarSeeds awakened from their constrained slumber. As we all began to help each other, I invoked an invisible shield of light around them as well, safeguarding them from external threats.

"Stay close, everyone. I have activated the armor to protect us. We cannot risk our safety. Just know that we are now invisible to the guards and all Lizzie shapeshifters on the complex." Alicia smiled, impressed by the powers of the galactic sword.

As we reached the main floor of the massive complex, laden with marble and gold trimmings, we passed the guards tasked with securing the entrance into the tunnels. We entered the great room that boasted high ceilings and expansive windows. The sunlight beamed through the Draconian Garo tree branches, barely infiltrating the compound. I noticed the opposite wall of the great hall, decorated with three-dimensional mirrors.

"Roma, can you see us through the two-way mirror?" I reached out to her telepathically. She didn't reply. I sensed that she was conserving her energy.

I used the Blade of Truth to detect her exuberant light. It pulled me toward the mirrored wall. I found and activated the hidden compartment with the blue crystal encasing the handle of Roma's sword.

The panel slowly slid open, exposing another dark chamber filled with whips and leather-bound artifacts. We all gasped in shock as we discovered a thin, tall figure hanging from the vaulted ceilings, in chains. The sword pulled me towards the suspended body. It was Roma.

The blood rushed through my veins as my heart thundered against my rib cage, pounding in a jagged rhythm. Dampening my lower lip with my tongue and teeth, I felt woozy, unstable. Her bruised condition momentarily horrified me, but I controlled my reaction, searching for inner strength.

I noticed the dark blood that trickled down her temples and wrists as the chains dug deep into her flesh. Her human form had been brutalized with burns and cuts. She was unconscious from the torture, and I could sense the toxic drugs that coursed through her veins.

I was finally in the presence of the enigmatic and powerful Roma who had resided comfortably within the crevices of my mind over the past few weeks. We had forged a deep soulful connection that felt like I had known her over many lifetimes.

I rushed toward her while maintaining the invisible bubble of protection around my friends. Alicia guarded the door as I reached Roma and unshackled her with the sword.

My knees wobbled as I inspected her beautiful face with the thick, dark lashes that draped her elegant, almond-shaped eyes.

As my heart erupted with unfiltered and limitless, potent love for this incredible Light Being, my energy imbued the entire room, bursting into a million shards of ethereal light.

All my Ascending Angel Academy training and downloads from the Council flashed in front of my eyes, suspending the space-time continuum. My rise through the Hall of Learning and integration was marked by this very moment.

My pulsating pineal gland projected my experiences through my third eye gateway. It emulated a movie theater, exposing the screen through the curtain of amnesia. It revealed the dramatic scripts occurring through the planet's electromagnetic templates into the divergence.

I witnessed the initiation of the trauma-based third-dimensional, unconscious matrix that oscillated at a lower speed within the quantum field.

It was difficult to ascertain that we helped form this existence based on the agreements we had made through bloodlines and controlling structures over past lifetimes.

Ancestors, parents, society, and institutions had passed down this energy—absorbing, imprinting, and perpetuating the same generational patterns in every child until the cycle was finally broken.

These programs were installed and embedded into our systems. It had been difficult for humans to evolve into a higher state of frequency due to conformity and lack of shrewdness. These disseminating mind-control realities were survival-oriented, unintentionally allowing entities to feast on our stress hormones.

I finally comprehended the simple truth of every Soul's existence on Earth. Our journey was internal, personal, and secluded. When our external reality was in a vibrational accord with our inner vortex of frequency, we purged the dense energies housed in our systems from birth.

As I came back to the present moment awareness of linear time, it dawned on me that Roma had been preserving her human form by quantum leaping her spirit back to her home-based frequency, Lemuria.

I cuddled Roma's frail body into my arms, carefully laying her on the floor. My warm touch sparked the heat between us, igniting our soul connection. I drew in a shallow breath, confused by the sweaty palms and feelings of jitteriness in the pit of my stomach.

I gently brushed the hair away from her face as I trailed my finger down her neckline, feeling for a pulse. It was weak and scattered. I continued to focus on moving my hand down to her chest, watching for the rise and fall of the swell of her breasts.

Come on, Roma, come back to me! In a final attempt, I decided to place the Blade of Truth into her hand. The contact immediately spurred an electrical charge with her human vessel as we witnessed a miracle.

Within seconds, Roma's wounds began to heal, her body regaining the strength and vitality of her ethereal essence. A Light Warrior, the Custodian of the Galaxy.

In complete awe, respect, and humility, I watched her slender limbs twitch as she opened her stunning crystal sapphire eyes to gaze into mine. Our energetic connection sent a bolt of electricity through my entire Soul.

With a ruckus of sensations, we blended blue codes of unification, upgrading my entire body. I could feel the change in my DNA as my eyes mirrored the same oceanic crystalline orbs. This merge reflected our Souls' bond for infinity, revealing the sacred union of existence within the higher-dimensional realms of Lemuria.

Roma smiled at me with a warm embrace, as if we had known each other for eternity. My cheeks warmed as I fully acknowledged her magnificent presence.

"You did it, Jo. Took you long enough," she teased, lifting herself with all the might of a powerful warrior.

I was astounded by the force she exuberated in just a few seconds. She had been tortured and malnourished for weeks but still managed to heal herself instantaneously. What an incredible ability to self-regulate oneself with all the intelligence of cosmic capacity.

Roma's resolve enriched my determination, and I knew in my heart that the Light would always prevail. Before I could find my voice to speak to her for the first time without clairvoyance, Alicia interrupted our exchange.

"Roma, a large Lizzie is slithering toward us. Take cover!" she yelled as she positioned herself in a fighting stance at the entrance of the door.

"They can't see us through the invisible shield, Alicia. But Roma is still too vulnerable to engage in battle. Everyone, just remain quiet!" I quickly moved Alicia out of the way in time to observe Lavender enter the room. She had shapeshifted into her human form, totally unaware of our presence as she addressed Roma.

"So, I see you managed to break free, you pathetic stardust. Let's see how you escape from my superior Lizzie powers!" Lavender immediately morphed back into her original grotesque shape. She glared at Roma, who was holding her position calmly, with her hands behind her back.

As Lavender lunged toward her with her gargantuan, green, cold-blooded force, Roma rapidly raised her Blade of Truth and plunged its pure cosmic power into her center. In what seemed like slow motion, the Lizzie dismantled and evaporated in the dust of black, eerie smoke.

"Alicia, Jo! Let's combine our Light Force energy to form the Cosmic Stargate. We can use this gateway to evacuate the StarSeeds and all humans held captive in this compound." Roma mobilized as she explained the plan to form a triangle.

The geometric pattern represented the synergy between the collective mind, body, and spirit as we detoxified and cleansed the physical space around us. The major influx of cosmic Mother-Source divine light amplified the integration of past ancestral lessons and experiences.

It was incredible to think that Gaia herself was a crystalline Stargate bridge between several planetary structures. The goddess was the anchor point within the Universe, transmitting higher levels of energy as the embodied consciousness of an ancient constellation.

As we took our positions, the blueprint for another layer of cosmic holographic reality was downloaded through crystal generators within Gaia, becoming more visible within the quantum field. The rainbow bridge expanded its sacred geometric patterns, reflecting dimensional spheres of creation with her template.

During our brief interaction, Roma and I exchanged sacred key codes stored within our human blueprints from the Galactic activations.

Solar light infusion launched the stargate portal, spanning into multi-dimensional realities.

"Nisha, once you leap into this wormhole, it will lead you back into the tunnels to guide all the captives away from the island and the Wizard of Bondage," I instructed my friends for their escape. The last thing I wanted was to separate from them, but it was the best course of action to ensure their safety.

"I'm not leaving Alicia behind," Theo insisted.

"I'll be all right, Theo. I promise! We don't want to find ourselves compromised by exposing you to the Wizard. We are StarSeeds and this Quest is our mission. I love you, brother. Trust me." Alicia gave Theo a quick hug, but he refused to release her from his embrace.

"You can help us by escorting all the innocent victims out of this compound. Perhaps you can contact their families to relay their whereabouts. I'm sure they will be relieved to discover that they are safe. Please, don't argue, guys. We don't have much time!" I pleaded for Theo's trust as he slowly released his sister.

"Don't worry, Theo, I will stay to help Jo and Alicia. You guys go ahead," Conrad asserted against my better judgment.

"All right, but I better see you guys back on the main island, or I will kick your angelic asses. I will not miss this hell-hole, that's for sure," Nisha said. I smiled at my incredible friends with profound gratitude. My heart overflowed with feelings of admiration and love as we separated for the first time.

We began clearing the dense etheric layers around Gaia holding conditioned thought forms and astral ticks of our collective shadows, unprocessed trauma, and rage. The old grids destabilized, and the timelines split emerged through the cracks.

As we held the frequencies of the Stargate, plasma diamond waves streamed into the compound, attuning Gaia with higher gamma vibrational rates of light. We watched our loved ones evacuate the captives away from the dense Draco overpass, into an elevated realm of the love consciousness timeline.

Just as the last person cleared the portal over the ethereal bridge, our high frequency bandwidth holding the cosmic gateway abruptly disconnected. An alarming, high pitched sound wave pierced our celestial senses.

"What's happening, Roma?" I asked, perplexed by the sudden events.

"It's Ciakar. He has breached our sacred Light!" Roma exclaimed, putting her sword down. A siren blasted through the compound at an alarming volume. I moved close to Conrad to provide protection. He stared at me in bewilderment, conveying his nervousness about our safety.

The abrupt onslaught of blackness stripped us of our radiant life force, leaving Roma, Alicia, and myself powerless against the Wizard and his forces of darkness.

❖ ❖ ❖

"You're just too good to be true, can't take my eyes off of you. You'd be like heaven to touch, I wanna hold you so much. At long last love has arrived, and I thank God I'm alive."— Can't Take My Eyes of You by Lauryn Hill

CHAPTER 11

COSMIC REBOOT

*"If you wish to know the divine, feel the wind on
your face and the warm sun on your back."*

—EIDO TAI SHIMANO ROSHI

Ciakar

"**L**ord Ciakar, the intruders have infiltrated the compound
and have liberated the StarSeeds!" A Lizzie shapeshifter
informed the Wizard of Bondage. Ciakar perched above
his throne, gorging on flesh and bone.

"Initiate the lockdown immediately!" he commanded. Within seconds, he galvanized the power of the black stones embedded in his
crown to enforce the Draco energy field around the complex. The lower
frequency jammed all organic energetic radio waves that connected to
the Galactic Light.

The lockdown automatically diminished the capabilities of any
cosmic being who dared to infiltrate the fourth-dimensional plane.
Smirking to himself, Ciakar visualized all the ancient methods of consuming the irritating Light Warriors that continued to interrupt his
plans.

His powers had grown immensely in this timeline and he could taste the victory over Gaia. The humans were compromised, chaos ensued all over Earth as they destroyed each other and their precious planet. Their DNA was marked for alteration with chemical arsenal infiltration. Their inherent higher sensory perceptions were successfully calcified.

Ciakar was determined to be victorious in his agenda to change human neurological functionality on behalf of the Dark Forces. He would use the Draco remote-targeting AI technology through mind-control, using electromagnetic waves to harass and terrorize their victims.

This method to reverse and confuse the human brain signals had proven effective with the Atlantis society. Ciakar particularly enjoyed its potent resources that conditioned the compromised human to create and feel pain, while initiating their pleasure centers.

He knew quite well that the cycle between agony and joy escalated into deviant behaviors and harmful addictions in humans. This flagrant attack was a big part of the Lizzie agenda for domination. They planned to penetrate the human nervous system through neural pathways, using their egos as a firewall to prevent light code activations. This successful tactic had worked for the Draco Dark Forces over many timelines, as they proficiently adapted its execution.

Ciakar smirked at the thought of another imminent conquest. The Wizard of Bondage was determined to obliterate the sacred Akashic Records and the precious Light System once and for all.

The metal doorways within the complex fused shut, melting all openings, windows, and exits. The electrical energy fizzled out, and the dense surroundings were completely immersed in darkness.

Jo

I grabbed Conrad's hand in the pitch black without wasting one precious second. My heart pounded with anticipation, expecting for something menacing to strike.

"Ciakar is using the Black Stones from Draco to bind our powers. My blade is ineffective without the plasma light source," Roma informed us. I tried to channel my galactic powers, but my energy refused to comply.

"Is there any way to tap into the Arcturus power source? They have been guiding us this whole time," I inquired, trying to establish the gravity of our situation, as Alicia continued to guard the entrance of the room.

"The Black Stone mutes our celestial abilities, which affects time travel or teleportation through portals. That puts us in a bind, but we will face Ciakar and put an end to his tyranny once and for all," Roma reassured, determined.

Conrad removed his phone from his pocket and turned on the light. "We don't have data coverage, but my batteries haven't died yet," he stated, providing us guidance in the darkness.

"We need to get outside to harness the Light and Gaia's power source," Alicia claimed. "I have an idea, but I will need your help." We followed her out of the great room, sensing the danger all around us.

"Be prepared for any unresolved human shadows to emerge in this purgatory," Roma warned. "It's important to acknowledge whatever arises. They are just human aspects of your past inner experiences and lessons that have been disowned, rejected, and repressed. They will come to the surface to test your bravery, heightened by the sinister energies around us, so don't feed them with your fear," she whispered.

213

Her message resonated with me profusely as this was the basis of my emotional body's ascent lesson. During my initiation phase, I went through a series of shadow work as I processed my ancestral bloodline curse, triggered by a traumatic grief response to Rey's death.

It personified everything that I refused to acknowledge within myself. I learned that, when I experienced suffering that was difficult to deal with, I quarantined the pain within my subconscious mind in avoidance. The dense emotion weighed me down like an anchor, preventing my energetic vortex from spiraling upward into higher octaves.

With the activations of the Council's downloads and light codes, I had finally found the courage to face my repressive dark feelings. I had discovered an energetic hack that guided me through the process without attaching judgment or a narrative to those emotions.

I had to take the time to feel the pain and heartbreaking loss, making the conscious choice to release its potency. I'm not sure if I completely discharged the attachment to guilt and playing the blame game. But I acknowledged its significance, mending my heart while the energy flowed through me.

This was done by visualizing an anchor within the deep oceans as I released the heaviness of the density, cutting its cords from my vessel. This purged my old patterns and liberated my essence as I embodied my journey with honor and grace. Without this clearing and healing mechanism, the grief continued to perpetuate the traumatic cycles of unconsciousness.

As I reflected on this lesson, my gut triggered a warning. Without taking the time to investigate my intuitive realm, I focused my attention on Alicia. She led us back to the entrance of the dungeons where the captives were held.

The tunnels were evacuated, so only the guards and Lizzie's remained. I was on high alert for Ms. Rolland, fully expecting her to attack at any moment and exert revenge for Lavender.

There was a window adjacent to the fake door leading to the tunnels. A single string of vine protruded from the surface through the encased opening.

Alicia finally divulged her plan. "Roma, I need you to use your Custodian strength and power to physically activate my pineal gland. Don't worry about causing my forehead damage. I have been practicing my shapeshifting abilities while in confinement, but I don't have an external plasma source."

"Alicia, I don't think you need to sacrifice yourself for the Quest. That's not what the Council has in mind for our ascension," I replied, horrified at the prospect of Roma hurting her.

"Jo, you need to trust me on this. During my captivity, I had to face the hidden aspects of my human mind. I had to break down completely to realize that I needed to acknowledge my childhood trauma," Alicia reassured. "I have honored its existence and integrated the lessons within my celestial awareness. Since my activation, I am now able to shapeshift into nature and can link to the Garoe Tree, as my heart is connected to Mother Earth," she explained, stunning us with her magical revelation.

"What is significant about that tree, Alicia?" Roma asked with curiosity.

"This Garoe Tree outside of the estate was once a life source for the island inhabitants. According to the legend, the Tree was struck down by a cosmic light source. The combined energy of the tree and Gaia made it possible for the islanders to channel water through it. It was kept as a huge secret during that period, since pirates used to invade the islands for treasure. This island was kept safe because of the perceived lack of freshwater resources. I can call on Gaia for help and channel the tree's energy," Alicia explained, clearly educated on the island's history.

I thought the plan was genius, and I finally felt a surge of optimism regarding our escape. Once she was safely outside of the compound, Alicia would be free to direct celestial assistance, unrestricted by the power of the Black Crystal.

"Excellent idea! It's worth a try, Alicia. Take this crystal from Lemuria and initiate the StarSeed Quest signal for backup." Roma quickly removed a small hidden gem resembling a sapphire from the back of her molar.

"Be safe, Alicia. See you on the outside." I embraced her briefly, connecting to her heart center during our energy exchange. I was so inspired by her bravery and resilience. Her dedication to our mission was beyond limitless.

"Guys, I hear them coming!" Conrad yelled as our hearts all united. Roma grabbed the handle of her Blade of Truth and forcefully stamped its Merkabah emblem into Alicia's forehead, right between her eyebrows.

Within seconds, Alicia shrank down into a microcosm and merged with the single vine, creating another branch. Using its roots, she escaped to the other side of the dark confinement, shapeshifting as an extension to the magical Garoe tree.

"Form a triangle, back-to-back, now!" Roma yelled. We heard the icy creak as the hinges screeched opening the massive wooden doors, to reveal the menacing threat. The Lizzie chaos fell upon us with the might of the Draco force.

Roma fought with all her strength, taking out the human guards sent by Ms. Rolland. Only a few more remained, but we were still powerless against the malevolent entities.

I breathed through my heart center and tapped into my inner light as I prayed for the Souls of the humans that perished by Roma's sword. I completely surrendered to my unwavering belief in humanity's integrity.

"Jo. Align to your sacred neutral space. I can feel your heightened emotions. Do not forget, you need to maintain your cool through the trickiest of situations. This is the divine plan, unfolding with immaculate perception. Remember the Source of your energy, Light Warrior," Roma echoed telepathically, reading my thoughts.

"Sorry, Roma, I just panicked a little. I didn't expect the death of the guards. I am grateful that we were able to free my friends and the captives. I just wish Conrad was with them." I took deep breaths as the frequency of worry and regret percolated into my awareness.

We were cosmic beings, and regardless of the obstacles placed in our path, we were guided by a higher presence. Roma was right. With this awareness, I reminded myself of my mantra, realigning my center.

I tapped into my remembrance and acknowledged that the external environment had a big impact on my auric field. If any shadows still dwelled within my internal vortex, I would be triggered.

I recalled the codes and guidance provided by the Council. As I catalyzed my ascension process, I focused on the vibrational tone that I wished to align with.

I am a Light Being entrusted with a cosmic mission, and no hiccup in our plan will derail us from the quest of saving Gaia and the humans from these dark entities.

I reaffirmed my intentions of the Light. The Lizzies had conquered other galaxies, but we were the expression of the greatest force in the Universe—Love.

I acknowledged that this foundational truth beat the hearts of all beings, through the energy of the Prime Creator, the Source, and compassionate light.

I AM STRONG, I AM POWERFUL, I AM FREE. We will defeat these horrendous monsters and liberate the planet from enslavement!

As Roma fought through the remaining guards, Ms. Rolland emerged in front of us in her Lizzie form. Her menacing appearance sent shivers down my spine. We finally stood face to face with our nemesis. In a matter of seconds, she attacked with her electric powers of destruction.

Without hesitation, Conrad lunged in front of my body, shielding me from her force that emanated from the Black Crystal. She intended on annihilating my human vessel. In an instant, the Lizzie bolt struck Conrad in the chest, as he dove in front of my body, to protect me from the vile assault.

Within a nanosecond, my entire reality and state of being imploded, triggering the remaining trauma-based cinders trapped within the cracks of my heart.

No! This can't be happening again! Please, don't take Conrad away from me. I have already lost Rey! I shrieked in the echo of silent disarray, forbidding my voice to escape the void of utter devastation within the purgatory.

Multiple explosions of light shattered within my pineal gland, propelling me into a state of oblivion. My mind completely shut down, disassociating from my lessons, downloads, and celestial teachings. It was an internal power outage as the grim blackness ensued within my essence.

I heaved in despair, reacting emotionally from a state of desolation and loss. Holding Conrad in my arms, I embraced his limp body as regret filled my core. Fighting the urge to fully withdraw from life, I sulked with the heaviness of my broken heart.

Tears of anguish flooded my face as I sobbed into Conrad's warm chest. I listened for his beautiful beating heart, but I only found the resonance of stillness. I whispered blessings and prayers for his Soul, kissing his forehead with my wetness.

Regret and guilt engulfed me immediately. *Why didn't I tell him how much I appreciated his friendship, his kindness, his unconditional love while I had the chance?* This was my fault; I risked his life on Earth.

Within that moment, I spiraled back down into the energetic vortex of the limiting, divisive, and trauma-based realm, exposing my vulnerabilities.

As Roma continued to fight for our survival, the devastation and victimhood thoughts populated and infected my mind, loading it with unworthiness, shame, anger, and blame.

"Jo, this is your cosmic initiation, remember who you are! Get up and reclaim your power now, Light Warrior!" Roma yelled at me. But it was too late.

"Look at what you have done! This is your fault! You are a selfish, arrogant human. You are not worthy of anyone's love. You deserve to burn in hell!" The sinister thought-forms breached my celestial boundaries as Ciakar hijacked my mind through telepathy.

"Jo, you are a sentient Light Being. Hold on to your truth and don't fall for the illusion. Choose wisely!" With a final attempt, Roma's words infringed through Ciakar's dark web as a physical blow to my head rendered me unconscious.

❖ ❖ ❖

Roma

"We meet again, Roma." Ms. Rolland shapeshifted back into her human form, spewing venom.

"Ava, I know it's you. You don't have to do this, sister." Roma calmly appealed to the goodness of her human form. "I can help you transform back into the Light. Don't you want to get back home to our beloved Lemuria?" Roma faced her lost sister, reflecting on memories from another world.

"You speak of a time that no longer exists, Roma. You romanticize that timeline, forgetting the wreckage and obliteration," Ms. Rolland responded, positioned in a fighting stance.

"This time it's different, Ava. Modern humans are enlightened, interdimensional beings. They have worked hard to transform the generational darkness of Atlantis and have infused Gaia's grids with a multitude of healing light codes. The human DNA is undergoing a massive upgrade with waves of plasma light that have permeated the planet in this timeline. Can you feel the pulsating galactic energy of the central sun? It's aiding humanity to shift into higher consciousness. There are hundreds and thousands of StarSeeds that have been activated to navigate the rainbow bridge gateway to the fifth dimension. Just choose the Light, and come home with me, sister." Roma appealed to a memory of her cherished sibling.

"You think I care about the despicable humans or your perception of home?" Ms. Rolland yelled. "True power remains with the Dark Forces of Draco. I have emerged from the original lineage of the Ciakar race, and I am destined for greatness. I will continue to devour your humans and demolish your precious Light. Just like with Lemuria, you don't stand a chance saving Gaia." She continued to relay her venom of hatred.

"I'm so sorry about Lemuria, Ava. I regret leaving you behind," Roma said, trying to tap into some semblance of light within her sister as she inched closer to her human form.

"You left me to perish in the pits of hell for your ludicrous cause. The pain and suffering I endured follow me into every timeline. But don't worry, sister. You will know my grief quite well." Surprisingly, Ms. Rolland lunged toward Roma before shapeshifting back into her Lizzie form.

With a swift and precise movement, Roma plunged her Blade of Truth into Ms. Rolland's human heart, twisting the sacred sword through the flesh until the blue crystals on the handle infused her organs. Instantaneously, it evaporated the beating Lizzie heart into ash and brimstone.

With deep breaths, Roma recounted the Akashic invocations of past life bloodline contracts and agreements.

"I cut the emotional cords that bind our blood through the timelines. Your programmed Lizzie actions don't have any karmic power over me. I forgive you, sister. Lemurian Light and Goddess Gaia forgive you. I set your Soul free from darkness and cinders of evil," Roma whispered as human tears of heartbreak trickled down her face.

Joyful childhood memories of their shared experience on Lemuria flashed in front of her eyes as she released the guilt within her human system.

"Please, flourish in peace and harmony. Let your Soul unfold into purity and wholeness for I AM liberated from guilt and sorrow! By the power of Ka-ha-lee, I set you free from bondage." For the first time in centuries, Roma was able to immerse herself in real emotions through her warrior heart expansion.

Embracing her feelings fully as she cleared the energetic discord through the broken fragments of her heart, Roma felt grateful to be alive, fueling her resilience to fight for the Galactic Light Force.

❖ ❖ ❖

My mind was transfixed, unable to think straight. The sensations of grief heightened within my heart center, shattering into a million crystalline pieces. I was still trying to process Conrad's death, but my thoughts were hijacked and controlled by the Wizard.

The momentary imbalance in my emotional vortex weakened my defenses, opening a path for Ciakar's repulsive bondage to infiltrate my essence.

However, the light codes already embedded in my Light Body shielded the Wizard's dark energy from consuming my Soul. They propelled me into another realm of non-existence for safety and protection.

I was floating, lost between the worlds. The familiar pull of dread took hold of me once again. Looming archetypal shadows lingered on the edge of my mind, crushing me beneath the sorrow.

I couldn't help feeling the weariness that emerged over me like thick smog. I could barely see the glow of light—the weight of heavy stones compressed my chest, depleting me of my breath. I clawed my way back, one inch at a time, grasping at straws made of smoke and ash.

I was falling deep into the abyss of darkness as the sinister hooks continued to drag me further into their pit of misery. This dreamscape was different, unlike anything I had encountered in the past.

I saw my mom's face in a cloudy mist, calling to me, ushering me into a black backdrop teeming with cosmic stars. She kept trying to convey an important message, but I couldn't hear her.

I focused my awareness on her frequency. The warmth of her love embraced me with a mesh of light and halted my plummeting further into the gorge.

Feelings of security, freedom, and unrestricted devotion infused my Soul as she cradled me in her arms, our hearts beating in harmony. This was my heaven, my peace, and tranquility. I never wanted to leave this serenity.

"Jo, don't be afraid. Everything will be okay." I heard Roma's gentle voice pierce through my safety net with thought transference.

"What you are experiencing right now, the feelings of bliss, are the exact sensation of euphoria that we are trying to manifest on Earth. We are ascending our collective consciousness into our physical bodies, so you never have to leave this reality," she continued, while I retreated within the safety net of my cosmic womb.

"Remember, this Matrix that we are living in is a holographic reality composed of props. It's a simulation projected by an extraordinary powerful processor that has controlled our consciousness for eons through electric pulses. The only thing that's real is the presence of self." Roma invaded my bubble as I floated in silent defiance.

"It's important for you to understand the multiple layers of denser frequencies that are simultaneously clearing from the grids above Earth as new light code activations are anchoring the template," she continued relentlessly.

"Please, Roma, just let me drift into eternity in peace," I finally responded.

"*You are shedding constructs of the old paradigm, identities and characters of the past that have assimilated into denser reality frameworks. This is triggering old wounds and fears within you that no longer require space within the new gateway of the quantum field for all humanity. Don't forget, disassociation and detachment from your authentic self is just a protective mechanism from many timelines. Don't allow the old programs of unconsciousness to dim your inner glow by falling for comfortable patterns and old habits,*" Roma pleaded.

"*I tried, Roma. I practiced self-love to anchor my Soul in alignment with Gaia. The pain I feel is too intense for me to process and to embody the Light,*" I responded honestly.

"*These template upgrades to your Light Body are the final activation of code sequences that have been dormant within your system from past lifetimes. Surrender to the higher heart expansion gold waves that are permeating your core with cosmic activation keys. These are needed layers of linear cognitive processing patterns required for clearing all your automatic traumatic reactions. As you override your thought patterns from your heart center, you will rebalance your system through hyper-stimulus waves, allowing these fractal light ripples to stream into the electromagnetic data fields. Your throat, heart and solar plexus gateways will recalibrate to a faster bandwidth, causing a huge planetary upgrade.*" Roma revealed the ascension lesson.

"*You can't resist your inner Light, Jo. Creative intelligence is permeating your entire system through these triggers. This is how the light enters the cracks of your human heart. It's the sacred fire of redemption. It's up to you to alchemize it or continue denying it,*" she persisted relentlessly.

"*Ultimately, it's your choice to make if you wish to hide and retreat from your destiny, Jo. I don't blame you or judge you, as I've been in a similar situation before. No matter what you choose, my beauty, Gaia and the world will evolve with or without you, into the light, or remain within the trajectory of the darkness timeline.*" Roma's words pierced through my heart with resonance.

Everyone I loved was counting on me. Everyone but Conrad. He was now with Rey, hovering blissfully in the cosmos. I genuinely wanted to be there with them. Perhaps one day, we would all unite, chuckling at our shared experience.

I was at the precipice of a cosmic shift, a reboot, triggered by emotional turmoil and wounds that were resurfacing to be released. It was the splitting of two worlds—the physical fear-based reality and the multi-dimensional spiritual world that was unfathomable to the un-awakened human mind.

The physical reality that we dwelled in was completely restrictive and incredibly limiting. It held us back, trapped, and stagnant in our experiences, repeating the same cycles. It prevented us from integrating our spirits to truly embody our Higher Selves. I was battling the visceral restraints of my human vessel.

With Conrad's passing, I was experiencing another Dark Night of the Soul but on a cosmic level. I was replaying the same heightened narrative response to the trauma experienced by Rey's accidental overdose. It was like someone hit the restart button, a pause, an opportunity to clear the wounding that I was avoiding and bypassing, stemming from loss.

I underestimated Conrad's adoration. Without hesitation or reluctance, he had sacrificed his life for me. *For me.*

How could I allow the purity of his actions and devotion to be wasted with my self-pity and victimhood patterns? It was the most honorable and selfless act that anyone had demonstrated in my human reality.

His unbounded behavior surpassed the third-dimensional matrix. It stemmed from a higher realm where there was no reliance upon any form of reciprocation. The true meaning of purity, an unadulterated, wholesome love that I had only experienced from my family.

This was not a myth or a fantasy. Somehow, I got lost in our delusional society, totally forgetting what my mother had preached all her life. The Universal powerful force of love was more potent than gravity itself.

Our society had been taught to respond with attachment in its place. True love was replaced with conditions, dependencies on behaviors, expectations, guilt, and self-gratification.

Conrad's actions were genuine, driven by purpose and intention to spare my life, to fulfill my celestial objectives in contentment and peace.

With this realization, my heart burst with feelings of gratitude and appreciation for his beautiful essence, his magnetic Soul that radiated his self-love and knowing. His actions tore down the impediments surrounding my heart center and infiltrated my core with beams of invigoration and hope.

They healed my lingering scars burdened by others before me. In the flush of his light, I found my strength and bravery to accept his sacrifice with an open, thankful, and humble heart.

Through his mastery, Conrad reminded me that only pure love had the power to liberate us from bondage, to integrate our physical blueprint with our intuitive divinity. The lesson here was to let go of the ancestral encoded states of karma perpetuating drama that was no longer part of my narrative.

I was unconsciously holding on to my karma's vibrational discord, diverting me from my sovereign power and purpose to achieve my celestial trajectory.

Although I understood this subjectively, I needed to acknowledge that my reaction was an automatic response, a crutch, holding on-to familiarity. This attachment was part of my energetic entanglement, unhealed shadow aspects, and limiting beliefs that no longer served or provided value for my inner peace and evolution.

It was an utter spiritual disconnection and emptiness separating me from my Higher Self and Source energy. I had been in this state before, consumed by intense human emotional storms of hopelessness, and melancholy.

This spiritual depression was an opportunity for me to purge my human vessel of all fear-based programs and pre-conceived judgment. It was the ultimate purification of my Soul, replenishing my essence back into divine totality.

I needed to stop giving my power away to external forces and events. It was time for my Soul, Spirit, and my human temple to integrate and co-create my existence through a unified lens.

With this galactic shift, there was a great deal of plasma Light entering the Earth plane, exposing the collective to face our inner demons.

This golden Light illuminated every dark corner of my mind that was resisting to transmute itself. It mirrored parallel worlds experiencing this great purge, echoing our civilization's reality. The frequency was modified within every human on Earth, sending out colossal planetary change throughout all creation.

It was incredible to think that this massive cosmic reboot was affecting every Soul reincarnated on this planet in the shape of a physical form while it still existed in those higher realms.

I needed to be more objective as I exceeded my human ego-based emotions and trusted the unfolding of the higher intelligence, the divine plan. I respectfully maintained my connection to this dimension while I returned to my human Light Body.

I acknowledged my courage to be completely vulnerable, raw, and open to all aspects of myself, even as I spoke the truth on polarized occasions. With these experiences, my voice, although shaky and tainted with frustration, lit a spark for someone else's darkness.

I had a purpose and a mission to fulfill. The highest honor and service to humanity was to master my evolution. This was the secret to transforming our beloved planet. Each of us held the key, the power to become the change that we all hoped to realize.

I decided to reunite and integrate my Higher Self aspect with my physical vessel and lessons. I imagined myself back in my mother's safety net, where everything was still, quiet, and serene. I felt completely at ease, replenished, and at peace. The silence emitted a powerful, potent transmitter of higher energetic light.

I became a portal into the celestial realms and the Galactic Council. With these loving seeds of light and remembrance, I developed an awareness of my subconscious expansion. Through this integration and deep healing, I had finally found vitality, self-acceptance, and freedom.

I was fluctuating between different vibrational sectors, uprooting energies stuck within the grid templates of the planet. Bringing resolution to these energies, I disembarked from the emotional rollercoaster to liberate myself as well as humanity.

With the conscious observance of all the mortal imprints of the past, I released the belief, transcending the pain points lodged in the collective body of past life traumas.

This transformation enabled me to convert my despair and anger into strength, finding truth, integrity, and compassion for myself. I assumed more responsibility within my being, ready to serve humanity with grace and humility.

This was my vibrational assignment through this mission, becoming a timeline jumper. Facing, integrating, and healing the repressed parts of myself was truly restorative for my Soul.

I now understood the saying "pain is inevitable in this reality; however, suffering is optional." It was up to us to choose to let go of agony with self-love, honoring our own sacred, unique journeys.

This stage of the Ascending Angel Academy had taught me valuable lessons. I released the collective shame and blame game. I was worthy and deserving of acceptance of my inherent wholeness. When I didn't acknowledge my shadows within, I declared a personality of non-existence.

I chose to love all parts of myself, every aspect and experience, morphing into my mastery. I affirmed my sovereignty and aligned my vibratory fields with the quantum I AM Source.

My heart is an infinite surge of unconditional love. I open the gateway to deeper layers of Divine Love energy and release all narratives that inhibit the flow of this powerful force.

As I opened my eyes to the dark chaos that still existed all around my physical vessel, I realized that I was bound. My head pounded, my wrists were tied behind my back, and I could feel the ache on the side of my head forming into a nice goose egg.

The putrid stench permeated my senses, inducing stinging tears to my eyes. Ciakar was here, in this present moment timeline. I couldn't see clearly through the blackness, but I could sense his dense energy, engulfing my ears and nose, as it sucked every bit of oxygen from the perimeter.

I blinked once, twice, adjusting to the darkness. Tiny goosebumps appeared on the back of my neck, announcing Ciakar's evil presence. My heart pounded against my chest in anticipation. My fingers tingled with numbness. I didn't dare move a muscle in my detainment.

"I am not afraid of you, Wizard of Bondage. Show yourself if you dare." I found my voice and asserted my celestial arrival with composure and defiance.

Although his menacing authority was intimidating to my human form, my ethereal being was filled with morbid curiosity. I imagined the incredible experiences and insights he possessed. It was almost like watching a horror movie, wanting to look away when everything inside of you screamed. But the plot successfully hooked you with the suspense and intrigue.

Was it hypocritical to judge the Lizzies for their horrific acts of violence and terror? After all, they were operating from their state of awareness, regardless of source.

From my understanding of the great experiment perpetrated on the star system of Lyra, the Draco beings didn't possess a spirit. They were considered Forces of Darkness, stemming from separative, polarized, duality consciousness.

Was it possible that they embodied the properties of the enigmatic dark matter within the ever-expanding Universe? My mind wandered to this unexplained thought.

I understood that sixty-eight percent of the Cosmos was comprised of dark energy, which was responsible for the accelerated expansion of our Universe. Within this force, twenty-seven percent was dark matter, which only interacted with gravity. That only left five percent, a tiny fraction of the Universe, for Earth, Light, and other planetary star systems.

I had learned that these high concentrations of gravitational field had the attributes to bend light. Perhaps the Lizzies controlled mysterious particles that only existed within dark matter, granting them the power of time travel through portals and black holes?

Regardless of their lineage, they propagated the actions adopted from their environment, originating from the constellation Draco galaxy, containing self-serving malevolent behaviors.

The Lizzies' primary goal for existence was to raid realities and seek conquests through different portals of space and passages of time. They did not follow the Galactic guidelines of Light, allowing civilizations to develop their timelines.

As I sat waiting patiently for my human demise, I felt a twinge of empathy for these entities. They were simply a product of their environment, using whatever level of power was necessary to achieve their purpose of world domination. As such, they operated from a state of negative divergence, consuming all formations of consciousness in their path, much like a metastasizing disease.

Wow, did I just compare them to cancer?

The Draco consciousness existed on various realms of density, of astral planes, and was quite neutral within the Universal Separative Principle. So, if the Lizzies could choose between Light and Darkness depending on their desire, perhaps they were not as inherently evil as we projected them to be.

Are we able to save Gaia and humanity by showing them compassion and forgiveness for all their atrocities?

This ideology still eluded me, even with my Celestial training and activations. It was the greatest colossal quandary, stemming from the beginning of time. Perhaps, it was not my place to question the Galactic

Wars. I needed to observe, learn, and elevate my perception with my path of truth and knowing.

"Jo, I'm right behind you, in the other room," Roma interjected telepathically, jolting me back to the present moment. *"I'm glad you decided to join me, sleeping beauty,"* she teased, putting a smile on my face amid the trepidation and foreboding madness.

"Roma, Ciakar is here, isn't he?" I asked.

"Yes, he's keeping you hostage to bait me out of hiding," she quickly replied.

"Are you all right? I know what happened with Ms. Rolland," I said tentatively. Roma never confided in me about her sister, but I could read her thoughts.

"I'm fine, Jo. I tried to find the slightest bit of light inside of her, but she was consumed by brutality, greed, and power. Her Lemurian Soul was completely compromised. My sister Ava perished a long time ago, in another world," Roma stated without emotion.

"I don't know how you manage to keep your purity and wholeness, Roma. I have lost two of my best friends since starting my ascension journey. I'm not sure I can follow your path and be a Light Warrior through many lifetimes." I exhaled deeply as I marveled over Roma's strength, courage, and incredible resiliency.

"Your destiny is unique, Jo. You don't follow anyone's path but your own. The secret is to be present in every living moment, immersed in the human experience, but not be defined by it," she further explained. Even when we were stuck on a battlefield, she found a teaching opportunity.

"You must clear out the shadows buried underneath the collective patriarchal structures. We have to learn to exist in this world, not ignore

it. *Don't get completely lost in the drama of being human. Balance is key, conscious awareness of every thought, emotion, and action. I know it's difficult to come to terms with Conrad's transformation from physical reality, but that was his destiny, his agreement with the Universe. When tumultuous circumstances like this happen outside of our control, we need to realign ourselves,"* Roma reiterated.

"I have integrated my density and shadows, Roma. There is nothing left to trigger my emotional responses to grief. I am fully operating from a sacred neutral space with an open heart, compassion, integrity, and truth," I replied.

"Good, because we are evolving humanity's consciousness toward unification. The timelines between the duality-reality and heart-centered unity are becoming more apparent with the great shift of Mother Earth," she responded.

"Will this evolution of the collective consciousness save Gaia from extinction?" I asked, hoping our mission would be successful.

"I believe so, but the balance can shift in an instant. It's a choice the human race has to make collectively. For those who refuse to awaken to their truth, their Souls will eventually extinguish from the Akashic Records, much like Ava's," she responded.

"So, the world will split into two parallels? We will continue to co-exist in the third-dimensional physical matrix as well as an evolved Earth?" I asked, perplexed about the state of our future.

"Yes, dualistic constructs are perceptual ways of being. Each Soul is free to choose the timeline and reality they wish to follow. Suffering is a man-made construct that is no longer necessary. This doesn't mean we won't experience pain in our human vessels, but we will be able to make better choices of not prolonging the cycle of that experience," Roma clarified.

"*I understand, Roma. No matter what happens, I can heal, process and work through the most difficult experiences with levity. I get that perception is key. But being human means that I'm flawed and will fall back into old habits,*" I confessed with humility.

"*It's okay to have those emotions, Jo. Honor them, feel them fully. It takes time to integrate your Higher Self with your emotional body. And don't forget, you will continue to be tested on your ascension journey,*" she cautioned. This experience was not over.

"*People who carry the frequency of freedom are highly targeted by those who are still zombified. When you broadcast a catalytic signal of your Higher Self, it reflects a charge in others like a walking magnifier web of distorted unconsciousness. Freedom of thought and expression gives rise to others' limitations within the collective, attacking your vibratory field. And this is okay because you are helping their evolution journey by radiating your truth and light, Jo,*" she said.

"*If we want to manifest heaven on Earth, just like my beloved Lemuria, we must break the shackles of oppression. The 144,000 StarSeeds incarnated in this timeline have overcome major obstacles that kept them trapped in the material physical plane. Never forget, Jo, that Light will always consume shadows in the expansion of all that is.*" Roma concluded her wise and valuable lesson.

I understood that humans were in avoidance of their repressed traumas, denying their light. Their shadow aspect was left unattended, unhealed, and not integrated with their spirit.

These existing regressive energies of childhood sufferings and un-resolved fear comprised the human, as they vacated their emotional Body since they didn't feel safe in their vessel. And when people were dislocated from their wholeness, they acted from a space of separation and divisiveness.

Our planet continued to be engulfed in higher golden light frequencies and activated light codes. Love consciousness would never encroach on another being's free will. Everyone had the right to live their truth with integrity and respect.

I recognized that humanity was on the verge of a massive breakdown before being propelled into the higher realms. The omnipresence of Source Light had permeated every living thing on planet Earth, releasing the hidden shadows. It was part of an organic purification and ascension process for Gaia before the cosmic revolution.

"And by the way, while you were floating in your fluffy cloud, I was able to communicate with Alicia using our dedicated channel," Roma interrupted my thoughts again.

"So, you heard my entire inner monologue?" I asked sheepishly, casually waiting for the gigantic Lizzie to devour my human vessel.

"Yup, our circuitry is tethered for life in this timeline, whether you like it or not. It can only be severed by a cosmic disruption. Now, silence please. I need to use this secure channel." Roma changed her tone, reinforcing the seriousness of the next moments.

"Alicia, are you there?" Roma established a telepathic connection.

"Roma! I made it to the coastline. What should I do next?" Alicia asked as I simultaneously observed my surroundings with my heightened senses.

"Point the sacred indigo gem toward the water, above your pineal gland. Align it with the Merkabah emblem on your forehead and focus your clairvoyance on my frequency. Together, we can activate a light beam emanating from the Lemurian stone." Roma advised Alicia to balance herself during the process.

"*Give me a few seconds. I will let you know once the connection is established.*" I could hear Alicia take a deep breath as she activated the cosmic ray.

"*Okay, Roma, I'm ready.*" Alicia maintained the connection both ways and continued to channel her energy.

As Roma emitted the signal to the Galactic Council, I heard movement within the murky haze of the compound. Faced with the prospect of physical death, I lifted my tear-stained face in defiance. The hair on the back of my neck had erected in full anticipation.

"*Roma, it's time.*"

❖ ❖ ❖

"Your movement's similar to a serpent, tried to play straight, how your whole style bent? Consequence is no coincidence; hypocrites always want to play innocent."—Lost Ones by Lauryn Hill

CHAPTER 12
THE GREAT ESCAPE

"Compassion is the wish for another being to be free from suffering; love is wanting them to have happiness."
—DALAI LAMA

Alicia

The beacon transmitted a surge of light up into space. Alicia shielded her eyes from the brightness emitted by the sacred stone. Within moments, the clouds took shape, resembling invisible spheres of Pleiadean Beam ships. Alicia was aware that the Council often permitted vessels in specific landing places for urgent Galactic missions.

She watched as the Starships cloaked by clouds hovered above her with a buzz that only enlightened beings could recognize. These spacecrafts could shield themselves optically and acoustically by activating a thin layer of the protective screen with specific gravitational fields. They were undetectable by any tracking device and human radar technology.

The crafts that operated in secrecy around Earth belonged to a specific category of small reconnaissance ships with intergalactic capabilities. Others were capable of interplanetary and interdimensional travel.

Alicia noticed the size of the incredible discs, ranging from five to twenty-two meters in diameter. Maintained by Androids, these vessels were equipped with thrust technique, enabling slower travel at velocities below the speed of light in physical realms. She marveled at the prospect of these ships used as a device for hyperdimensional transitions, transporting their crew in a blink of an eye.

As she witnessed the arrival of the magnificent Beam Ships, she received a clairvoyant transmission from a unique frequency source that she didn't recognize.

"Do not be alarmed, dear one. We have been sent by the Council of Creation. Where is the Custodian of the Galaxy?"

Alicia relayed the situation of how Roma and Jo were trapped inside the compound with Ciakar, the Wizard of Bondage. She explained that Roma couldn't access her Galactic powers inside the dense purgatory.

In a matter of minutes, the Beam Ships surrounded the Wizard's complex, preparing blazing lasers to infiltrate the lockdown. Alicia transmitted a telepathic message to Roma and Jo, hopeful for the emancipation of her beloved world.

❖ ❖ ❖

Jo

Ciakar emerged into the great room, revealing his powerful predatory presence.

"Finally, my prophecy will be realized. I've been waiting for this meal a long time. Show yourself, Custodian of the Galaxy!" he hissed, the force of his gigantic Lizzie tail striking every obstacle in his path.

"Who shall I eat first?" His alligator teeth exposed the sharpness of a carnivore.

We were surrounded by the Wizard's remaining Lizzie guards, who had shapeshifted from their human form. There were three of them, waiting for Ciakar's command. I took deep breaths, focusing on neutralizing my heart rate, as my human form baited the darkness out of hiding.

The lockdown was still in place, and we were stuck inside the compound, unable to escape from the foreboding doom. I pretended to be unconscious, showing a lack of vigilance as the Wizard approached my body.

I won't allow Ciakar to enslave my mind.

His energy launched an attack into my being. I focused internally, bringing my emotions into balance. I maintained the equilibrium of the masculine and feminine energies of my ethereal form. My light wings took form, metamorphosing as translucent electricity. It burned the matter that bonded my hands behind my back.

I slowly rose from my captivity, empowered in my wholeness. Using my pineal gland, I activated the energetic magnitude of the island's surroundings. This ignited the plasma waves emitted from the blue oceans, flowing from Gaia. I surrendered to the womb portal of the higher heart, flowing with intuitive wisdom, and exiting the linear timeline.

Clearing the Lemurian and Atlantean dimensional realms within the quantum field, I anchored the vibrational frequencies. The memories were liberated from the fourth-dimensional astral plane matrix, releasing the spirits enslaved in between the worlds.

The integration of my Higher Self manifested my Celestial powers into my human form. I connected to Gaia's crystalline grid architecture, tapping into the Lemurian templates.

I navigated the light codes with my internal guidance system through the density and shadows. I held space for the clearing of outdated imprints stuck within the Atlantean collective web.

Gaia recalibrated from the ancestral purging of the old paradigm, awakening the collective consciousness from generational insomnia, and directed its trajectory into the new cosmic reality.

The electromagnetic shifts expanded the dimensional bandwidth of the planet. New grid structures were anchored to support the activation of plasma light flowing through Gaia's heart center. These holographic upgrades shifted Earth's reality into higher-dimensional resonance, reflecting new octaves of consciousness.

I opened my arms, as I confronted Ciakar, offering myself in totality, illuminating completely with Gaia's power source. My actions had stunned the Wizard. He didn't anticipate the shards of light, projecting from my third eye. They momentarily blinded him, as Roma emerged out of hiding and lunged at his Lizzie form with her mighty Galactic force.

I watched in awe as Roma battled the Wizard with her Blade of Truth. She dodged Ciakar's black tendrils, masterfully maneuvering with her sword, her lithe body in full Warrior mode.

"Oh, you wish to play, stardust. Have you not learned from our last encounter? You will never defeat me!" Ciakar roared, unleashing his Lizzies onto Roma.

"Get behind me, Jo!" Roma yelled as I moved out of her way.

Roma fought with the Lizzies, one at a time, fueled by superhuman speed. The clanging of metal on metal caused a high-pitched sound, reverberating throughout the compound. She managed to trap her sword between two of the Lizzie black daggers. With expanded velocity, she backflipped out of the entanglement and rolled across the marble floor in a distorted combat dance of lethal moves.

The Lizzies were slow to recover from the blinding speed. Roma plunged her blade into the first guard's heart. She quickly withdrew her galactic sword and somersaulted above the second guard, severing the Lizzie's head.

Ciakar was undaunted by Roma's warrior abilities. He thrust his enormous tail, pummeling Roma in the chest. The force catapulted her to the other side of the great room as she tried to maintain control of her blade.

The unease within increased as my mind kept visualizing the worst-case scenario, but I flicked it out of my awareness before it rooted its ugly claws. I observed helplessly as Roma dodged Ciakar's consistent electric attacks, one after another.

Unfortunately, Roma missed a step from her combat ballet and fell to the floor, releasing her grasp of the Blade of Truth. A tremor coursed from my sacral up to my spine. I fixated my celestial energy toward Roma's blade.

Ciakar sneered at her tumble, firing black jolting flares toward Roma. I screamed in warning, but my voice didn't cooperate with me. Horror rumbled through me as I watched Roma get engulfed by the Lizzie's menacing smoke.

The Wizard grinned at me with malice as he paused to momentarily feast on his own guard's carcass, fueling his power. The dark blood stained the entire white marble floor as the battleground became a gruesome combat zone.

A shadow appeared within the periphery of my physical vision. The last remaining Lizzie guard shapeshifted into his human form and snuck up behind me, blasting me into the cold, sticky floor, and pinned me down with his body weight.

"Did you think we have forgotten about you, Ascending Angel?" he whispered in my ear with his foul breath. "I'm about to eat your wings for a snack, you pathetic little cosmic waste."

The ravaged mutter drew my gaze upward. Blood oozed from his gums as he flashed his incisors, aiming to feast on my flesh.

"Roma, Jo, take cover! Galactic help has arrived, and they are coming for you." I received Alicia's telepathic warning as I tried to ward off my assailant.

A precipitous siren blared through the compound, stopping everyone in their tracks. I stared in silence underneath the guard's oppressive force.

Ciakar glared, confused, as the walls around the complex began to melt. Sunshine filtered in, flooding everything with light, followed by the eruption of the Galactic Plasma beams.

The sudden surge of illumination pierced through my eyelids as I shut them tight to protect myself from the brightness. Every corner and shadow of the great room was fully exposed, revealing the carnage.

Roma used the distraction and jumped at the opportunity to grab her sword, bouncing back on her feet. She raised the Blade of Truth into the oncoming beam of Celestial light, absorbing its cosmic powers into the blue, crystal-laden handle.

Within seconds, Roma transformed in front of my eyes into her majestic Lemurian form. Her spell-binding beauty was breathtaking, but it was her confidence that exuded all the brilliance of a fully embodied, robust, enigmatic Goddess.

She was determined to defend Gaia and humanity from the Wizard's diabolical influence. Her intensity and resolve to battle Ciakar's Dark Forces on Earth were irrefutable. Roma would not allow innocent Souls within the physical or astral realms to be devoured again by this sinister entity.

Roma's celestial presence finally revealed the secret of the StarSeed Quest with her transformation on the physical plane, as required for the battle. The radiant life force energy liberated Gaia's hidden world, buried beneath her vast oceans, emerging as the blatant truth.

The Draco forces utilized the secret of time, the most deceitful and elusive knowledge of humanity's history. This was suppressed by the Lizzies, agents of darkness, disclosing Ciakar's authority and self-serving agenda to infect the underworld and Gaia's alkaline water source, using contaminated microbes released by pilfered thought tremors.

I noticed the exuberant look of triumph on Roma's face as she grinned at Ciakar in a threatening manner. As the protector of Mother Earth, she was fully empowered with her galactic superpowers to transform into elements of air, and the ability to resist burns in fire.

Roma swept down on my oppressor like a giant bird of prey. Her wings fully unmasked, the Custodian of the Galaxy snapped the guard's neck before he had a chance to shapeshift.

"Oh, are you hungry, great and powerful Wizard?" she said as I escaped into a corner. Roma cut out the Lizzie's heart and heaved it at Ciakar.

"Here, snack on this!" she yelled, her azure eyes flaming with lightning bolts.

I was overwhelmed by Roma's newfound strength and resilience, witnessing her for the first time in all her glory. Her confidence infused me with optimism.

"You will not escape me this time, Ciakar." Roma pitched, getting back into her fighting stance.

I observed how the hypnotic cinders around me blossomed into angry orange flames. There were several beam ships, hovering in the air, above the emblazoned compound. Celestial light beams projected in every direction. Joy coursed through me as I absorbed the cosmic energy with every fiber of my Light Body.

Roma's Blade of Truth was illuminated with boisterous radiance, the blue crystals shining brighter than ever. For a split second, she turned her attention to me, and we locked eyes. She fully acknowledged my visceral form with pride. Her intense sapphire spheres pierced through my Soul as we connected energetically.

Her powerful transcendent impact catalyzed a transformation through my being, showering me with a surge of love and bliss. It was the symbol of her greatest eternal gift. I felt complete and unharmed, like no piece was missing from my spirit.

I focused on the warmth of her affection as I kindled a flash back memory of our sacred union, in another timeline. An unusual sense of déjà vu fluttered over me as if this familiar moment in time had already taken place, in another world.

Roma's healing energy infused my physical form, unblocking every spinning wheel in my energetic vortex, returning to me my strength and physical power. I concentrated on my center and balanced my erratic emotions. My wings flapped with my movements as I levitated in the air with the rhythmic reflections of my illuminated surroundings.

Ciakar attacked Roma with vengeance, gleaming with the black crystals perched on his crown. "Hand over the sword, Custodian," he threatened, penetrating her auric field with his toxicity.

Roma thwarted his assault and glared back in defiance; her light shield fully erected in preparation for the biggest battle of her existence.

"You should reconsider, Ciakar. The Pleiadeans have arrived on the physical Earth plane. You are not strong enough to fight the Galactic Light Force in this realm, and there's nowhere for you to escape this time," Roma asserted, raising her Blade above her in a warrior stance.

I cupped my hands in front of me, attempting to form electric light globes to distract Ciakar. I hoped to divert his attention with the shocks, providing Roma the advantage.

"Jo, stay out of this. This is my mission, and the Wizard is my responsibility," Roma instructed. Her eyes remained glued to every movement Ciakar made.

"Really noble of you, Custodian. Do you think you can stop me from incinerating your pitiful ascending angel over there?" Ciakar smirked, drawing more power from the Black Crystals.

"This is between you and me, Ciakar, and no one else. Let's finish this battle once and for all. A fight between my Blade of Truth and your stolen Black Crystals." Roma advanced toward his gruesome presence.

"Stolen crystals? I consider them rightfully mine, earned with every battle and triumph. Who are you to declare war on my crown, you pompous bundle of bones?" Ciakar warned.

"Your precious Light doesn't govern the dark energy of the Universe. You and your treasured planet are nothing but a drop in this cosmic pool." Ciakar glared at Roma with fury.

"Your days are numbered, Ciakar," said Roma. "The Celestial Light has debugged your unreliable, disruptive, and dysfunctional operating system within the matrix. The Galactic Light Force has defeated the Draco entities. You are on your own, without any backup, and I will not allow you to poison Gaia's resources any longer!" Roma yelled, lunging toward the Wizard in the air.

Ciakar blasted his electric stings, barely missing his target. Roma countered the attack with her sword, firing beams from her own Blade's crystals.

As I observed this great battle, I tried to communicate with Alicia telepathically. The temperature inside the melting compound was rising to a dangerous level.

"*Alicia? Can you hear me?*" Concentrating on my psychic powers, I focused on helping Roma by hurtling moving objects within the great room with my mind.

I watched helplessly as Roma bent on her knee, slashing at Ciakar's immense Lizzie form with her sword. He dodged the attack with his tail. The Wizard used the long silver candle holders on the mantle as weapons. He twisted them with his mind and successfully catapulted the sharp objects at Roma's head.

Urgency raided through me as I activated my telekinesis energy force. I focused my mind on the bookshelf, propelling the large structure toward Ciakar. It temporarily halted him from gaining an advantage over Roma.

Nervousness surged through my veins at the prospect of Roma's demise. I harnessed its energy and formed powerful electricity between my hands. I took a deep breath and channeled the Arcturus force, using my Light Body as a conduit.

"Jo? It looks like the compound is on fire! What's happening in there?" Alicia's voice filtered through my head.

"Alicia, are you able to connect and channel the Beam Ships?" I asked, sharpening my plan. *"We need your StarSeed power source to help Roma defeat Ciakar."*

The Wizard's extra-terrestrial mass and strength outmatched Roma's stature. However, she persisted with retribution.

"You are not strong enough, Custodian. Surrender now, and I may consider you for breeding my future generations. You can serve me for the rest of your days, just like Ava." Ciakar laughed, unleashing his sinister thought-forms to incite guilt within Roma.

"Never! I will never back down, even if I have to destroy myself in the process. You are a menace and have wreaked evil havoc throughout the Universe for your self-serving gains. It stops now!" Roma bellowed.

This moment in time was bigger than any of us. I knew Roma would never give up the battle, even if it meant sacrificing her life. She was an incredible force, a fierce guardian and protector of the Light.

"Hang in there, Jo. You are strong. You can get through this." Alicia boosted my confidence from a distance.

As I prepared to receive the Galactic energy source that was going to generate enough power to vanquish the Black Stones into the Black Hole, I positioned myself within the apex of Roma's Blade.

Alicia communicated her location, ensuring a perfect Stargate triangle emanating from our auric fields. I expanded my energy toward Roma, infusing all sources of Light filtering through the air, and I felt the Arcturus frequencies within my orbit.

I opened my pineal gland to receive the upgrades and transmissions. The information of Galactic data trickled through my energy centers. There was a new presence of another Light Being, forging through the telepathic channel.

"Jo, it's me, Conrad!" His vibrational imprint shocked me to my core. Stunned, I focused on maintaining the connection.

"Conrad? How are you talking to me right now? Oh, my God! I am so sorry I was not able to save you!" Grief tried to creep back into my heart, but I maintained my neutral emotions.

"I am an Arcturus Light Being, Jo. I volunteered for the StarSeed Quest, specifically to protect you on this mission on Earth," Conrad stated calmly.

"We are generating enough power Source to equip you and the Custodian with plasma energy. Alicia and I are in position, based on your location within the compound," he explained.

I was beyond elated at this revelation. I observed the figure of a celestial being descending from the Beam Ship toward Alicia's physical location.

Conrad's ethereal form was exuberantly beautiful. His wings glowed with iridescent light, and my heart opened up with joy and gratitude.

All of this was occurring simultaneously as the great battle continued with the clash of the opposing forces. Roma dove toward Ciakar with immense cosmic power. The ripple effect coupled with my telekinesis ability forced the Black Stone Crown off the Wizard's gargantuan scaly head.

Within a flash, Roma crushed the Black Stones into a dozen pieces. The plasma light from the Blade of Truth unleashed high-energy radiation, disturbing the gravitational vortex around the compound.

Alicia, Conrad, and I released our Light Force Energy in that precise moment with immense strength, forming a perfect trinity with Roma's Blade. The supernova explosion inverted the iron atoms that had been infused into the density of the compound.

We opened a black hole within the Universal vortex that magnetized and pulled the Black Stones into interstellar space. The powerful gamma plasma rays burst the mass, devouring the dense evil smoke, propelling it into another dimension, far away from the sacred Light.

I continued to anchor the high-vibrational frequencies from the crown circuitry matrix into the heart-centered field. As my ethereal form integrated the golden light codes within my physical body, enhanced blue rays activated the next wave of pure Source energy.

Thus began the transmutation process of the density surrounding the Island, dismantling the artificial fear-based programs of oppression.

"Roma! The veil has been lifted. Gaia is finally able to transcend the astral realm into the fifth dimension!" I found my voice as I relayed our victory with confidence. My entire being tingled with joy while we assisted our beloved Mother Earth and humanity into the new paradigm.

Roma smiled at me, acknowledging our collective triumph for a fleeting moment. Our hearts united, triggering an explosive force field. Without warning, Ciakar swooped down on Roma. She raised her Blade in one final lunge, striking into his abdomen.

The Wizard collapsed back in shock, and just as Roma was about to puncture his heart, Ciakar initiated a new portal with a remaining tiny piece of the Black Crystal, into a different dimension and timeline. Within seconds, he leaped through the gateway. Using his momentum and massive Lizzie tail, he forcefully pulled Roma into the portal with him, both disappearing in front of my eyes within milliseconds.

I watched in dismay and disbelief as the events unfolded in slow motion. Deafening silence streamed through me for a brief moment before I unleashed a piercing scream of high octaves, disintegrating all the windows and mirrors within the estate.

"Roma!" I floated toward the disappearing portal as it vanished into thin air. I collapsed onto my knees with devastation. The ground beneath me began to quiver with tremors as the planet integrated the dynamic events and shifted timelines.

The celestial plasma light within me invoked the White Light redemption, transmitting its power into the Earth core.

Alicia managed to drag me out of the blaze before the entire estate collapsed into molten ash. The compound erupted in smoldering flames, disintegrating all evidence of the illusive estate in the Canary Islands, where darkness reigned on innocent Souls.

I was shocked at the outcome. The curtains had fallen; the Universe and the Council had spoken. The density of the veil remained intact within Gaia. I had never imagined this ending unfolding—leaving the island without Roma.

I inhaled deeply, taking a pulse of my internal state, and questioning all of my actions. *Did I make the right choices to solidify the best reality within the Higher realms? Is this the physical potential of my future existence?* I reimagined all of my movements, searching for alternate timeline possibilities.

Roma. Roma. My heart dropped. Her essence was completely gone from my field. The silence and emptiness felt daunting, cutting my energy cord from her magnetic Soul. I took deep breaths, encoding the quantum messages of the Arcturus and the Council.

I slowly realized the duplicitous impediment that had been fogging up my lens of perception. I was developing a reliance on her vitality.

The trepidation I felt letting go of Roma were due to the last piece of attachment and co-dependency that had remained in my physical form. It was a delusion that was connected to another potential positive future outcome.

In the moment, I declared my complete surrender to Universal intelligence. I no longer desired to be the blockage in the process of my manifestation.

I did my best. I found courage and bravery along the way as I released my uncertainties and trusted the process. I believed in my inherent power to co-create my existence within a harmonious and blissful timeline.

The lesson was abundantly clear. When I observed my past through the channel of time, I enlightened newly formed aspects of myself, connected to my awareness. All of these versions created light ripples within the future reality.

As I finally came to my senses in my human vessel, fully submerged in my heartbreak, I noticed the catastrophic events that had begun to take place. Somewhere nearby, volcanoes erupted in multiple locations, between the layers of dimensions and timelines.

Roma's Blade of Truth had finally disrupted the oppression of Lizzies' purgatory, releasing its stronghold over Gaia. The remaining underground tunnels of anguish were destroyed, damaging the fourth-dimensional pathways and existence of the astral realm.

Balance was temporarily restored on planet Earth as the Sacred Light prevailed throughout the Galaxy, consuming the shades of gloom. Humanity's future evolution was temporarily halted, as Gaia immersed herself into the embryonic cosmic cleanse within the cerulean healing waters.

❖　❖　❖

"Deep in my heart the answer it was in me. And I made up my mind to define my own destiny." — The Miseducation of Lauryn Hill by Lauryn Hill

CHAPTER 13

GOLDEN REFLECTIONS

"Your own Self-Realization is the greatest
service you can render the world."

— RAMANA MAHARSHI

Jo

I gazed up at the heavens and admired the vast night sky, illustrated with brilliant stars within the grand design. The beauty and magic humbled my perspective of the intelligent reality, framed by the specters of the moon.

My heart yearned for a better world that awaited all of humanity, filled with hope and compassion. I dreamed of a possibility where a new utopian existence would emerge, aligned emotionally and in harmony. A New Earth where telepathy, levitation, astral travel, and telekinesis were as prevalent as breathing.

I inhaled deeply and acknowledged the moment that would be transcribed into a memory, etched into the archives of space, between the cosmos and parallel timelines.

Crickets performed in the background, coordinating the nocturnal beings that heralded the night. I embraced each minute with an open and loving heart as tranquility tantalized each of my senses.

I recognized that my physical body was operating from an upgraded, newer version of me, straddling dimensions. Everything I witnessed through this lens of hyperreality blended the worlds of human existence and celestial realms. I existed in an intertwined dimension, with no clear discrepancy between where one ends and the other begins.

"So, what's the verdict, Jo? Are you getting new and improved Angel wings, or what?" Nisha teased, sipping on her hot chocolate.

We were all huddled around the wood-burning fireplace in my backyard, reflecting on our experiences on the island. We had catapulted into higher frequencies by jumping multiple timelines. It was primarily due to our collective shift in our human evolution through our unified experience.

My brows rose in uncertainty. It was a new beginning, a clean slate for humanity. The perceptional awareness of this reality within my mind's eye was subtle, but my sentiments had changed. I would never take my safety and security for granted again.

"I won't know until I see the Council, Nish. Honestly, I wouldn't be surprised if they ask for a celestial re-do," I replied, half-joking. "After all, I didn't exactly succeed in recovering Roma." I felt the pangs of regret set into my chest as I surrendered to it fully.

The emotion consumed me, as I blamed myself for my perceived desired outcome. I inhaled deeply and processed the feelings of loss, disappointment, and released them with every exhale, cutting their weighted cords from my energetic vortex.

"You did everything humanly possible, Jo. Roma chose to time-hop through that portal. It was evident how badly she wanted to destroy the underground tunnels," Alicia said, holding Nisha's hand. "She's one bad-ass warrior, I tell you!" They were inseparable since spring break.

"So, how does it work, exactly?" Zax inquired. "Do you have exams or midterms in this Angel Academy? Like, how does the Council grade your progression? Is there a prescribed criterion to graduate, Jo?" He seemed perplexed by the celestial academic standards.

"There's no grading system, Zax. They just review my energetic exchange of every action on Earth and measure my Soul's level of remembrance prescribed by my human experiences and lessons." I answered with as much clarity as possible. In all honesty, I didn't possess much insight into the Council's assessment methods.

"Should we test you before you time-travel back into the cosmos?" Flynn asked, grinning. His smile was so infectious. It was obvious to me that he had gone through a major DNA upgrade through the timeline shift. His aura emanated the warm hues of serenity, inner peace, and joy.

"Flynn, you are a genius! I think we should all ask Jo a series of questions so she can reflect on her lessons," Daphne said, but her smile evaporated quickly. "Unless you don't want to talk about Conrad?" she asked, concerned, reaching me for a hug.

"I have made peace with Conrad's departure from our world, Daph. I'm sure I will see him very soon." I smiled, grateful for the experience to have connected with an Arcturus Light Being in human form.

"Let's make this fun, shall we?" Flynn interrupted. "We'll play spin the bottle, and this time, instead of truth or dare, the person it points to gets to quiz Jo."

"Sounds like fun. I'm in! Come on, Theo, get your butt in the circle with the rest of us," Alicia teased her brother.

Whatever excitement I felt about my graduation from the Angel Academy was tempered by the fact that there was one last stage remaining until my final ascent into mastery. It wasn't clear if I would continue my life attending high school with my friends, as we planned our grade eleven courses.

I missed writing my music and playing the electric piano. Our school band was quite excited about the annual International Music Competition that took place during fall of every year.

Although this crazy path was my mission on Earth, my friends were incredibly sweet and supportive of my ascension journey. I tried to share as much as I could with them without compromising their enlightenment process.

Sometimes, the messages didn't always resonate with them since we vibrated on different frequencies. It was like tuning into multiple radio stations that were forecasting the weather in different languages.

I was curious to know if they were aware enough to articulate the timeline shift from their perception. The human body had never evolved at such an expedited rate before. It allowed us to stand firmly and clearly within the fifth-dimensional love consciousness.

This upgrade to our human vessels would require time for the collective to mourn our older versions that operated within the outdated paradigms. Many people would experience different physical symptoms, causing major disorientation and identity crisis.

Zax took the opportunity to spin the bottle while the rest of us sipped on iced tea, courtesy of my mom. She loved to host my friends, lavishing us with incredible appetizers and desserts.

"All right, looks like you're up Nish," he said, grinning widely.

"Fine, I'll go first. Josephine, what was the primary lesson of your ascension journey?" Nisha asked, mimicking Ms. Rolland's voice.

I laughed at the impersonation, even though the tingle of the experience was still quite fresh, leaving me with a nasty taste in my mouth.

"Well, the main theme of my ascension was to realize that the experiences I encountered on my journey were opportunities to transition from my ego-based perception into my Higher Self," I replied with a nervous giggle. I never liked exams of any kind.

"Every time I chose to see life from a survival viewpoint, I was operating from the space of remorse, which ultimately led to playing the blame game." I chose my words carefully. It was so much easier to articulate these thoughts when I was communicating clairvoyantly in the ethereal realms.

"That's easier said than done, Jo. How do you move out from the blaming life?" Theo asked, with the next spin of the bottle.

"Great question, Theo. I'm still working on it, to be honest. But the one thing I have learned from losing Rey and Conrad is to take time for my grieving process, with self-compassion. No matter how ruthless, or harsh the world is, we must be gentle with ourselves, without judgment," I answered truthfully.

"These types of obstacles are actually opportunities for growth and expansion of our Soul that requires no criticism, punishment, or disapproval. The journey ultimately is about self-love," I replied, acknowledging my Higher Self for aiding me in overcoming my impediments.

The bottle landed on Zax as he prepared his question carefully.

"Does self-love require us to forget all the crappy things people do to us? For me, personally, if any of the bullies in our school hurt Flynn or any of you guys, I would want to punch their face." He had done a great job with his inner healing, still dealing with his anger issues.

"No, but we can choose to be empathetic, Zax. When people treat us with cruelty or disrespect, they are projecting their wounds and inner turmoil. The moment anyone lashes out or blames you for their unhappiness, they are operating from a state of separation, limitation, and insecurity." It had been a difficult concept to re-learn, especially when we were taught to react with similar behaviors in society. *Eye for an eye. Vengeance is mine. Hatred begets hatred.* It was the total opposite of love-consciousness.

I recalled my teachings. "I have learned that I can choose to take the high road and alchemize other people's density emissions with the truth of forgiveness. This powerful act alone can break cycles of generational violence."

"Each density trapped in the seven spinning spheres of our vortex offers a set of catalysts that must be integrated to cross the threshold toward our higher evolution." I continued to relay my thought process.

"Don't get me wrong, it doesn't justify cruel behavior or harm inflicted on another being. However, we can refuse to accept someone's memory of mistreatment into our cellular body for our well-being. This action stems from our heart center, and it liberates us from the perception of victimhood." I genuinely believed this was a vital lesson for humanity, from my humble perspective.

As I acknowledged my friends within the circle of trust, I vowed to empower them with as much information as I possibly could, to help speed up their ascension into the future timelines. It was up to them to accept the codes of the sacred Light.

My friends seemed very engaged in this game, absorbing every word like a sponge. Secretly, I was overjoyed that they didn't find my answers boring. It was incredible how much they had served the collective evolution of Gaia and the human race.

"So, are you saying that you forgive the shapeshifters, Ms. Rolland, and Ciakar for Conrad and Roma?" Alicia asked bluntly, testing my emotional resolve. She didn't beat around the bush.

"That's a tough one, Alicia. It takes time to process all the emotions of losing someone you love. I have learned that I can't control future outcomes, no matter how much I try." I swallowed the bitterness of regret, exhaling it out of my consciousness.

"However, I am working on relinquishing that negative emotional charge from my system," I explained honestly.

"In order to do that, I must trust the loving and intelligent Universe with an open heart, understanding there's a greater plan that we're not always aware of. I just know that when I'm ready to forgive them, I will continue to cultivate the energy of thankfulness," I replied, observing Theo's eye-roll at my response.

Whether they processed this information or not, it was my truth. *My truth.* I found my voice, and with this act, I awakened my Soul's self-acceptance of this reality. With every moment that I allowed myself to be grateful for all my experiences, I helped unravel the patterns of violence that permeated our planet with perpetual toxicity.

"This is how we evolve, nourish, and validate ourselves, and realize our true freedom as sentient beings," I continued to explain, taking deep cleansing breaths.

"Wow, Jo, that's pretty deep. I'm surprised by your answer. Maybe one day, I'll get to that place. For now, I'm still dealing with the aftermath of Rey's death," Nisha replied still processing her grief and loss.

"We weren't there, but from everything Alicia told me, that battle must have been epic. Are you okay with the way things ended on the island?" Nisha asked, no longer waiting for her turn in the game.

"It's been a tough lesson, but the Council and Roma have finally taught me that operating from anger or frustration over previous events doesn't help me or anyone around me. I feel the pain, don't get me wrong, Nish. I just choose to Release, Integrate, Surrender, and Embody the experience. We RISE and keep trekking forward, not choosing to suffer over the past. It's done. There's nothing we can do to change it, you know?" I responded with the confidence of profound celestial knowing.

The truth of the matter was that, if I chose to wallow in victimhood, no matter the obstacles or incidents that were presented to me, I would dim my inner light. It simply continued to perpetuate more shadow aspects into the planetary grids.

Conrad and Roma had risked their lives to clear these dark parts of the density veil that shrouded our world and held us all in captivity.

When we find our authentic voice and speak our truth, others could bask in its luminosity. This was how we transformed the planet and humanity, igniting our inner flame one Soul at a time, guiding our collective evolution.

"Wait, how do we know if you're answering correctly, Jo?" Flynn interjected. "You could be making this stuff up, and we wouldn't even realize it!" He laughed.

"Just use your discernment, Flynn. How do my answers make you feel? Does it insult your Soul, or does it resonate?" I asked, feeling cheeky.

"You could never insult us, Jo. Don't be ridiculous." Daphne laughed with her sweet, bubbly demeanor.

"Thanks, Daph, I appreciate you." I gave her hand a warm squeeze. The radiance and purity of her heart matched the brightness of the stars above.

"Let me put it simply. When we operate from our hearts instead of our inflamed ego, we become one with the sacred Light. We then allow ourselves to shine at full capacity, no matter the obstacles life places in front of us. It's all about the intention behind our actions and the space within that we emotionally react from." My heart desired to share all the knowledge and information stored within my upgraded software, instigated by the cosmic reboot. Much like a computer system.

My gut was telling me that my friends weren't ready to hear this metaphor. Tuning into my vibrational field, I continued to articulate my lessons with healing resonance carefully etched behind every energetic word.

"Our human existence will always operate depending on the state of our collective awareness. The ego wants to manage and maintain control of what it understands. If we let go of the fear of the unknown, there are no limits or liabilities in our reality. Trusting this inner light and aligning with our Higher Selves is the highest service we can provide our loved ones, humanity, Mother Earth, and the Universe." Taking a pulse of our inner circle with every breath, I realized the preachiness of my words. Perhaps it was too early for this depth of knowledge.

"Look, all of us are connected energetically. My happiness and your happiness are the greatest services to all. So, why wouldn't we choose happiness, right?" I chuckled, taking another drink of the sweet nectar.

I observed my friends as they processed the information downloaded from the ethereal realms. They didn't realize that I was transmitting healing light codes into their auric fields, further upgrading their physical structure by playing this game.

"Does this mean that we're celestial Earth Angels now?" Daphne joked, pretending to have wings to fly.

"Actually, Daphne, when you're a conscious being, you already realize that you have incarnated in this existence to achieve your full celestial potential. So, you are already on a trajectory within the energetic vortex of ascension, with every breath you take," Alicia answered on my behalf. It was nice to have another enlightened StarSeed in our group.

I smiled in acknowledgment. "Exactly. You're all becoming Angels with me, and I can't thank you enough for sticking by me and trusting me through this process."

"What about the fact that we still have issues that we're working on, Jo?" Theo asked, diverting his eyes. I could sense the density of shame that he still needed to release from his energetic spheres.

"Each of us came into this world with a specific amount of density in our physical form, Theo. The journey is to dissolve it by doing our inner work and aligning with our Higher Self." The words provided calmness and tranquility, soothing his nervous system, as evidenced by the changing hues around him.

"This is such an exciting time of renewal, guys! The arising of light through our system manifests through inspiration, creativity, moments of selfless actions. It transmutes any remaining shadow aspects that we retain in our Light Body from past trauma. Every time someone or something hits your t-spot, it's another opportunity to evolve. It's really about how open and receptive we are to serving the greater good, beyond the threshold of our personal gain," I replied, focusing my energy on Theo's heart center.

"What's the t-spot? We didn't learn about this in our comprehensive sex education class." Nisha laughed breaking the silence. I loved her sarcastic sense of humor, always diffusing the seriousness of the situation.

"Are you referring to Conrad, Jo? That was the most selfless act anyone can imagine." Nisha regained her composure, fully realizing the sensitivity of her question.

"Trigger spot. And yes, Nish, I will forever be grateful for him. Even though Conrad was an Arcturus Light Being sent on a mission, he has definitely transcended his mastery by saving my human life." I paused, quietly taking an energetic account of my emotional well-being. I missed Conrad every day on the Earth plane, but I knew his energy was guiding me in this lifetime. I couldn't wait for our next clairvoyant interaction.

"You don't have to be strong for us, Jo. After losing Rey, this must have been quite devastating for you. We're here anytime you need to talk or cry. No questions asked," Daphne probed, simultaneously wrapping her arm around me.

"I'll be all right, Daph, I just need some time to address the energetic charge from the loss and honor my emotions. Roma has taught me to neutralize my feelings by breathing through it, processing, and integrating into my heart space by releasing it." I acknowledged my truth, knowing that the pain would eventually dissipate as we all evolved in our physical bodies.

Although they were testing my ascension intelligence, I admired the incredible light projecting from their genuine care and love. We were healing each other, reflecting off our respective states of being in our progression.

These conversations were imperative for generating more Source energy within the collective, to provide us with the trajectory we needed as we shifted into the New Earth.

Working with my third eye enabled me to quantum leap into portals, catapulting my awareness into higher timelines. I permitted the Universe to infuse my emotional Light Body with more golden light codes by keeping calm and neutral.

I grasped this notion well. When we developed an awareness of our triggers by pausing, breathing, observing, feeling, and taking accountability, we removed their density from our body's storage capacity. It allowed us to generate more space to hold light within our human vessel.

This was the solution that would liberate each person from the antiquated programs and conditioning of the lower density reality that continued to perpetuate trauma-based response to every event.

The key to this enlightened state was to understand how to deal with our emotions. Society and our upbringing had designed us not to feel. We were programmed through learned behaviors to deny our true feelings.

We learned to develop or change the narratives in avoidance of the pain, to bypass its dynamic significance. These behaviors restricted and stopped the flow of the energies, rooting its grasp within our emotional Light Body.

The moment we attached to low vibrational frequencies of sadness, anger, or hatred and refused to accept whatever emotion arose within us, we pulled its potency into our being.

My feelings of betrayal and loss over Rey plus the grief from Conrad's death were not meant to be stored in my Light Body. The energy was designed to be courageously felt and honored in each moment, as it flowed through the processing and assimilation into my heart space.

The transmutation kept my human vessel unweighted from the densities that had slowed me down from ascending higher on this conveyor belt of life. The old patterns of energy leakage drained my light, but I had the ability and choice to fuel up my fields with every quantum moment.

What a revelation! I realized that this process would continue to be a constant challenge in our daily lives. It was a virtual game of balancing our old human ways of blame, shame, and perpetuated victimhood mentality with the new state of emotional wellness—a world filled with imagination and artistic expression.

The Council had taught me through my experiences that each of us had this inherent responsibility to manage our inner light fluctuations and maintain our boundaries on how we decided to engage with others energetically.

When there were dark clouds above us, we had the choice to radiate our powerful beams of light to diffuse the blocks and convert the darkness, in any situation.

Once we cleared the field, we transcended the contrast and duality existence. When we oscillated at a higher frequency vibration, our field developed into an extremely magnetic force of attraction, enabling us to manifest our desired reality from our heart.

As I continued to receive the downloads from the Galactic Council in energetic holographic zip files of psychic impressions, I translated that rate of sound-wave pulsations in a relatable and concise manner with my friends.

"So, how do we think the Celestial in training is doing, folks?" Zax broke the silence, diffusing the seriousness of the group.

"She's acing it, of course! Jo doesn't need us to validate her credits to advance to the next stage. I can tell how much she has matured with the amount of well-being, wisdom, and confidence she's exuding," Daphne stated jubilantly.

"Aw, thanks, Daph, I'm just so grateful to experience this with you, my Soul tribe. I think I finally have let go of my tribulations and old narratives. I realize there is no need to hold on to it anymore like a security blanket," I admitted.

"By appreciating each moment, I allow life's greatest miracles to unfold. I think it's important for us to love and value ourselves through all aspects of our lives. This embodiment will be my final stage of ascension." As I announced the next phase of ascent, another thought percolated in my mind's eye.

The seed of knowledge that was planted by the Council had finally bloomed, revealing bits of information about the global events that were about to arise for our world. No matter the obstacles that had faced humanity's darkness, I reaffirmed my intention and attention.

Whatever showed up for me in my trajectory, I would permit the energies to flow through my body, not allowing them to reside within me or identify with their vibrational texture.

I am not my emotions. I am not my feelings.

I blinked excessively as I finally grasped this concept that the perceived desolation was simply energy moving through my vessel for a software upgrade.

The energetic exchange of our connection with Source signaled the Universal quantum field that I was ready to embody my infinite potentiality. And as my path revealed itself, I understood my final stage of ascension at the Ascending Angel Academy. I anticipated my next mission from the Council with exuberance as my mind's eye projected the golden beams with violet hues at the end of the rainbow.

"Well, I'm not sure if I'm ready for another one of your galactic adventures, Jo. Not yet anyway. I'm still dealing with our recent escapades!" Flynn laughed nervously, bringing me back to the conversations.

"Don't worry, Flynn, you take whatever time you need. The road to recovery has lots of twists and turns, so don't rush your healing journey. Clear out your storage unit to create more light for your vessel to embody. You will receive everything your heart desires at the moment it's meant to arrive, through Divine will." I smiled through my response, my heart exploding with love.

"Besides, the ascension we are experiencing as a planet is a transmutation process of expansion. In scientific terms for us geeks, it's the direct consequence of the change in form when heat and pressure are applied." I could tell that Nisha appreciated my nerdy humor.

"Don't get me wrong, the change will be uncomfortable and perhaps painful due to the amount of intensity required to transform," I warned about the next phase in humanity's evolution. There was going to be a global pandemonium in our future timeline, but I kept this information to myself.

The world was about to be turned upside down from perceived notions of normalcy as Gaia purged and cleansed her wounds and transgressions perpetuated by humans. She was going to release the toxicity stored within her grids to progress into higher realms.

But for now, I wanted to celebrate our blessings.

"Never forget, my sweet friends, we are the anchors of Light, fighting conflict and exposing the shadows for the greatest planetary advancement known to mankind. Cheers to our sovereignty and to our next great adventure!" I raised my glass to toast my Soul tribe and our incredible experiences.

"Cheers to us, the Light Warriors of Earth! We are the divergent leaders of the shadow world, forging new pathways by tapping into our internal compass. We refuse to follow the zombified herd and abdicate our freedoms, to conform in conventionality and predictability!" Alicia asserted proudly.

"The Kick-Ass Light Ascending Warriors, you mean, refusing to be induced by the hypnotism of fearful thoughts!" Nisha smiled proudly, holding Alicia's hand.

"Ooh, yes, let's hear it for KALAW and our future escapades together!" Daphne giggled as she attempted to name our group, causing an uproar from Flynn and Theo.

"Geez, Daph, that's a lame name for our new superhero status. How about we work on that this weekend?" Zax grinned, fully engaged, and supportive of the idea. It was beautiful to observe his peaceful energy exchange with his best friends. His admiration and devotion to Flynn imbued his every human interaction.

"No matter what comes our way, I wouldn't want to experience this metamorphosis into the New Earth without you guys. I totally appreciate, adore, and love you all." I bonded with them emotionally.

We cultivated our reconnection with the mysterious Source of all creation by giving and receiving adoration frequencies. The transcendent revolution infused each of us with unlimited radiant life force energy of Love. It extended our heightened perceptions of beauty and magic, lifting us into our Higher Self-awareness. Our auric fields melded and swelled within our spheric bubble of grace.

I gave each one of my friends a warm embrace before they left, feeling nourished and enriched by the goodness of humanity.

The truth was that their love and joy was the greatest spark of nourishment that liberated my spirit for my daily existence in this realm. They reflected and mirrored my virtues, my morals, my integrity, and my lessons. I felt empowered with the resonance and could never imagine my life experiences without their Soulful energy exchange.

I was excited about the prospect of birthing more superhuman potential through physical human form. Once we initiated ourselves into the realm of service for others, we automatically drifted through the fourth-dimensional Earth plane, bypassing its timeline into the fifth dimension of creativity and celestial possibilities.

To continue this course, we needed to evolve to a place where mankind was completely untethered to the physical realm of trauma-based survival. This was the place where each person learned to master the gift of embracing timeless existence, preserving, and cultivating our collective creative energy.

Levitating, I giggled to myself as I witnessed this virtual holographic reality game from a higher perspective, by objectively observing the energies around me.

Once we all graduated from the ego layer of the three-dimension console of limited narratives and characters, we would be presented with an opportunity to co-create a higher realm that was outside of linear time.

Every obstacle and trigger presented events as a steppingstone. We just had to recognize the opportunity for advancement by allowing the catalyst to propel the upward surge of frequency within the energetic vortex of our auric fields.

Upon much reflection, my mission was not to fall for fake stories and deceptions of the external world. This new version of my Light Body had evolved from the old paradigms of fear-based conditioning that only functioned with the intent to paralyze my spirit.

I had to integrate my lessons and the missing dissonant frequency within my human vessel that was a conduit for the light. It was done by relinquishing control of future outcomes and acknowledging whatever resulted in my existence, accepting every situation and emotion with full accountability.

It was a great responsibility for my human form. If this required me to sever ties to anything or anyone that did not enrich my daily life, then I needed to prioritize my wellness above all else. As divine beings, we were responsible for our existence by honoring our truth. Each person on the planet was worthy of joy, inner peace, freedom of expression, and fulfillment. It was our Soul's inherent right.

By doing this, we were empowered to alchemize the lower frequency we held in our bodies into higher pulsations, sliding up the vibratory scale within our reality.

Roma.

I couldn't help but wonder where she was in this vast, magnetic Universe. Perhaps she had time-traveled back into the Lemurian timeline? Roma truly embodied the superhuman qualities that we all aspired to achieve on our journeys.

I recognized and respected that every person had a different vibratory signature that projected through their energetic field. It was unique, magnificent, and equally extraordinary. By celebrating our individuality, our planet and all living things with honor and integrity, we took back our inherent power from the Dark Forces.

When humanity fully opened our collective hearts through the willingness of giving without reciprocation or expectation, we operated from a place of wholeness. It signaled to the Universe that we were consciously choosing to expand our heart-center into the quantum field and were willing to create our reality by magnetizing the pureness of Source life force energy.

As my friends and I continued to connect on a soulful level into the wee hours of the night, I breathed in love and exhaled my gratitude for each waking minute. I found the beauty, magic, and pleasure in everything that was offered in the now moment.

This prepared me for the consequent blitz of celestial power headed my way as I prepared for my final mission. My physical body was ready to absorb the incoming golden rays from the Arcturus light force that was sent to enhance the best of humanity.

The cosmic time travel was becoming second nature for me now. The feelings of security, freedom, and peace were welcoming to my splintered Soul. I had learned so much on this ascension journey, with experiences that were beyond my wildest imaginations.

These celestial insights evoked other dimensions within my consciousness that could only be reached by mastering my thought consistency and integrating it with honorable, limitless, elevated heart-centered reactions.

"Welcome home, Beloved." The warm, familiar sensation emanated from the Council of Creation and embraced my being with gentle exuberance.

"You have done well in your second phase of ascension. We are quite proud of your choices and actions," they said, evaluating my mission. Watching myself and our experiences on the island played back on the holographic screen was a little unnerving.

"Thank you; however, I was unsuccessful in my mission to capture Ciakar and rescue Roma, our Custodian of the Galaxy," I replied with remorse.

"From the higher perspective, you have conducted yourself with great wisdom and bravery, Beloved. It's time for you to release all the restricted narratives encoded in your human DNA. This is your integration induction into an embodiment of the third stage of the Ascending Angel Academy," the Council responded in unison.

"I have passed the second stage?" I asked in bewilderment.

"You have graduated the Hall of Learning and Truth with grace and integrity," they replied. "While you were on the Earth plane recovering Roma and rescuing the captured StarSeeds from Ciakar, the Galactic Light System neutralized a security breach by nefarious forces. Due to Gaia's critical evolution into the fifth-dimension, planetary Light forces deployed a major offensive in the sublunar space against the Dark Forces that have been holding planet Earth hostage. We have emerged victorious because of your successful mission. Your cosmic reboot cleared the hold of the Draco entities within the current timelines." They continued to brief me of the unknown battle that was waged above Earth.

"With all due respect, we are still in danger on Earth. The Wizard of Bondage has escaped through another portal. What's preventing him from fulfilling the Draco agenda on humans?" I continued to question, perplexed by this discovery.

"If Ciakar decides to quantum leap into your timeline again, he will do so without the assistance and galactic power of the Draco Beings. The Custodian has also chosen to follow Ciakar's timeline hurdles to prevent another purgatory scenario," they reported. I was totally surprised to hear about Roma's next galactic mission.

"The cosmic clearing will take some time as the light code activations filter down into Earth's surface. Your civilization will begin to experience glorious energies of freedom as Gaia's crystalline grid elevates into gamma timelines. It will be a major event for humanity, as the grand ascension into the fifth-dimension is imminent. The Pleiadean Prophecy will be manifested as planet Earth elevates from the long period of cosmic darkness into the sacred Light." The Council radiated with luminosity and heart-centered love.

"A major energetic ascension portal will open in the Lemurian timeline as celestial alignment marks the Golden Age of Love. There will be a massive eruption of the grand solar flash, supplying magnetic white plasma light activations from the Galactic Core. The energy released from this compression will trigger another wave of the collective ascent of the planetary consciousness."

"Has humanity crossed over the rainbow bridge? Is everyone safe?" I asked, still concerned about the people operating in duality and fear-based systems.

"There will be many light code activations for those who awaken. Be prepared as the shadows of humanity are exposed into the Light. There will be a mass outcry for justice and false fearmongering as Gaia rids itself of the menacing fleas. Stay grounded in nature and continue your meditative practices to hold the space for this activation." They confirmed what I had come to understand.

A catastrophic event was about to ensue on planet Earth as a form of purging of lingering negative energies.

Although this information could be perceived as apocalyptic, I got the sense that it was the complete opposite. Humanity would be faced with another opportunity to take responsibility for their daily lives, without avoidance and inconvenient attitudes.

Each person was asked to level up, to expand their awareness of the higher realms and propel our civilization into a quantum leap. It was a precious gift for everyone to evolve in our engagement with one another, our societal structures, our planet, and to co-create new loving systems that thrived with equality and justice for all beings.

"You and the StarSeeds will help integrate and embody the higher frequencies into humanity's blueprint. You will continue to lead and expand the collective consciousness with the breath of life, ensuring that each human being takes responsibility for their actions. With our escape clause, everyone will have a chance to change how they operate and contribute to the world's challenges."

The Council referred to the admonitions of the Pleiadean Prophecy of the twenty-first century. There was a drastic imbalance of the Divine Feminine and Masculine energies within the quantum field of existence carried by each Soul.

Since everything in the Universe was interconnected through networks or grids of energy, these dynamic strings all intertwined at a single point within our solar system. Planet Earth projected a variety of holographic realities within the cosmic structure, and Gaia was the brain and heart of the Universe. Her wellbeing affected the future probabilities and realities of the entire cosmic realm.

The Pleiadeans discovered this essential wisdom about Gaia from a future timeline and named her the Crown of the Galaxy. The original prophecy was based on an apocalyptic parallel reality of our world if we failed in our mission to defeat Ciakar.

I suspected that Roma had this inside knowledge before she leaped into the black hole, supervising Ciakar and his evil plans. I didn't blame her for not sharing this information. The obligation for the entire Universe was too much to endure, even for the Custodian of the Galaxy.

It was why our planet was guided by the intelligent Light Beings from every ethereal realm. Within each possible timeline, whatever impacted Gaia and humanity, reflected on the galaxy, and eventually flowed into the cosmos. I was astounded to discover that the Council was trying to prevent a universal catastrophe.

As I processed the information, they continued to transmit their celestial wisdom. "Your species have been initiated, reconnected, and aligned to the frequency settings with our light codes that will evolve Gaia. Each person's DNA and heart cells will be resurrected into another multidimensional framework, to prepare for the massive collective upgrades."

My entire ethereal being radiated with explosive light arising from my heart center as they concluded their final session before my celestial commencement.

"This shift will assist Gaia and her inhabitants into the fifth-dimensional sphere of blissful existence. Only those who choose to live in harmony, peace, creativity, service, and co-creation will form an enhanced conscious community. Once again, humanity will have to choose how to evolve between the Atlantis and Lemurian timelines. Stand by for your final phase of ascension, Beloved. The golden embodiment of the Divine's expression is upon you. Many blessings of Light and joy."

The Council had announced my next mission, and I was filled with massive energetic enhancements, powering me with a surge of hope and transcendence. Their blessings illuminated my celestial light wings into full force, providing me with the magical powers of movement in the air, even on Earth.

As I returned to my teenage bedroom simulation in my human vessel, I immediately felt my heart overflow with love and gratitude for all my experiences and the present moment.

Even though Ciakar had escaped, I was resolute in my belief that justice would always prevail. Through the eyes of mindful empathy for our collective ego structure, I felt compassion as external forces continued their battle to slow down the awakening consciousness on a massive scale.

I graciously observed this trauma response of our society to a conditioned, divisive, outdated reality that campaigned to avoid the discomfort of its integration.

I comprehended that this sinister adversary was the ally of avoidance because the dualistic personalities of humanity rebelled against the intelligent and loving Universe. The survival-based ego was too fearful of losing control of future deceptive outcomes.

However, I had come to understand that the Universe was a rescuer as it continuously expanded its infinity and endurance. The love energy carried profound transformation that helped us unshackle ourselves from the illusive matrix, no matter how much despair was displayed within the virtual hologram of planet Earth.

With Conrad's guidance from the galactic realms, I was embraced by the Arcturus light force energy. As I basked in the comfort of this truth, I vowed to do everything in my power to ensure that our beloved planet averted the Atlantis timeline destruction due to artificial technology. There was already an imbalance in the natural world, causing humanity to become susceptible to diseases in the unseen realms.

The time had come for each human being to awaken from our collective dreamscape, liberating us from the nightmares of hardened existence.

I tapped into the energetic pulse of my emotional charge, focusing on each of the seven magnetic fields within my spinning vortex. I felt wholly at peace. My integration journey of truth had revealed many incredible insights of my celestial remembrance, graduating my prominence to an Earth Angel status.

Each of us held a role to fulfill our purpose in this incredible journey of life, resolving, clearing, and processing our respective inner traumas which was required for healing. I prayed that humanity would choose to ascend as a conscious community toward a better world that prioritized our innocent children and our natural world.

Unrestricted love was holding us all in every moment, with every breath, with honor, humility, generosity, appreciation, and truth.

These acts of service were all behaviors that Roma exemplified in her Soul, no matter where she chose to travel next in our exhilarating galaxy.

As I stared into the white and rose childhood vanity, I noticed Roma's beautiful reflection mirroring back at me. My eyes transformed with sapphire codes of light in remembrance, emulating the windows of her Soul.

I gulped the rawness of my emotions as sobs escaped from my throat, releasing the floodgate of tears. I surrendered fully to the broken fractures within my center as light filtered through the cracks. My heart yearned for her illumination and soulful connection.

I inhaled deeply, sending Roma all the intensity of love that sprang from my heart center. Wherever she roamed within the cosmos, I hoped my telepathic message reached her over the secure channel we created.

"We did it, Roma. Love anchors the New Earth templates of the Goddess Gaia. Love defies fear and transcends the separation and duality matrix. Love unifies all sentient beings as the true frequency of the Prime Creator. Love is the key to joining every individual being before we ascend as a collective. This is how we will navigate humanity to embody

the love consciousness of Lemuria, my beauty. I am certain that we will not repeat the history of Atlantis. We will not destroy ourselves with artificial technology. No matter the trajectory of my journey, our hearts will always be linked, transcending time and space, my treasured friend. Thank you for the gift of devotion and knowledge. I will miss you in every now moment, but I honor your journey. Until we meet again, my magnificent Soul mate."

I AM THE LIGHT, THE LIGHT THAT I AM.

❖   ❖   ❖

"Everything is everything, what is meant to be, will be. After winter, must come spring. Change, it comes eventually." —Everything is Everything by Lauryn Hill

AFTERWORD

In many spiritual cultures, it is believed that sacred fire burns low-frequency energies from the spirit and the lower levels of our consciousness. It consumes old, limiting perceptions that structures our thought patterns, controlling our emotional responses to life's experiences.

The emergence of truth and freedom, our divine birthright is the foundation for the global awakening and initiation. As we complete our Soul's karmic cycles, there is a metaphorical need to release the lodged energetic debris of our painful emotions, traumas, and memories that are necessary for us to transform.

Each life event is an opportunity for us to learn, grow, and elevate to a higher state of consciousness. The universe will continue to provide us with similar experiences until we choose to embrace the lessons, integrate them, heal, and evolve.

This clearing and purification process is known as a rebirth of our inner child's innocence, where our level of awareness expands as the old conditioning is eliminated.

On a collective level, this process aids our journey to fulfill our Soul purpose of connecting to the Source of Creativity within every one of us, assisting in our efforts to perceive the highest sacred truths.

We prepare ourselves for this experience of clearing and healing by holding steady in our daily intentions and actions, to express from our hearts, connecting us in a love-based conscious community.

We are cosmic Light Beings, manifesting in a human nervous system, an aspect of the divine force that transforms energy in multiple dimensions. We are facets of creation, entering this existence with pure consciousness, generating frequencies of unconditional love and bliss.

Our Souls choose to experience this reality for a purpose, for reasons unknown to us in this physical dimension. This may be done through Soul contracts or getting chosen for missions to guide the life and collective evolution of planet Earth and humanity through the Universal Law of Oneness. It starts with the gentle acknowledgment and loving acceptance of our essence within the human body we inhabit.

As soon as we enter the Earth realm, the mind begins to create an attachment to this reality through an identity known as the ego. The more masks and constructs we develop on our journey of life, the stronger the ego. It helps us to organize our existence to match our beliefs and experiences through our perceived lens.

The encounters we go through are meant to enlighten us, activate our pineal gland, and teach us lessons. This integration process enables us to overcome the obstacles created by low-frequency energies meant to derail us from awakening and transforming to achieve our Soul's divine purpose and potentiality. It is a remembrance of our sovereignty, our truth, that we were always meant to be powerful, autonomous Light Beings.

If humanity desires to create a new reality, a better, wholesome state of being, then we must direct our collective energy away from the dualistic, separative, and limited existence of our physical world.

We cannot continue to experience life through the veil of disempowered, conditioned beliefs of co-dependency, fear, disharmony, and conflict imprints. Our advancement toward a conscious community of wholeness, oneness, peace, diversity, and balanced existence is up to each one of us.

To achieve this evolution, we need to divert our attention away from contracting energy like greed, arrogance, comparison, judgement, and discrimination. We can only achieve this by clearing and healing our collective trauma stored within our emotional bodies. We can then evolve from our associations to every materialistic attachment that we have been brainwashed to desire. Where we direct our collective attention is critical as we invigorate that perception, person, place, or thing with our energetic pulsations.

We must find better, eco-friendly solutions to save our planet, using our vast expertise and intelligence to fulfill humanity's needs organically. And this starts with each one of us, making conscious choices on our consumption, taking accountability for our footprint for our children's future.

When energy expands, it creates a state of awareness within the non-physical realm through an experience. The increase in velocity or frequency when it speeds up moves the pulsations up the vibratory vortex of our auric fields into higher states of consciousness.

When this energy contracts, it slows down into a lower state of consciousness, back into the fight or flight density of pain and suffering. It is through this lens that we witness the events manifesting on our planet with our perceived realities.

As more cosmic light activates our DNA in our physical bodies, it increases the speed of our energy fields. This is known as ascension when we naturally move into faster or higher states of consciousness.

We become more aware of our Soul's remembrance and begin to recognize that we are powerful, sentient beings, with free will to choose and co-create our desired experiences.

The survival-based physical dimension is very dense, it holds polarity and duality. We are under the illusion that we are not free to create our reality, permitting external environments to dictate the quality of our existence.

With this ideology, relying on peripheral authority figures, educational, political, and institutionalized systems for our happiness, we start to become victims of attachments, dependencies, and expectations. We unwillingly give up our power to others through their control and manipulation.

Operating from the space of fear, scarcity, victimhood mentality, comparison, and greed divide us as a civilization. It's up to us to make the choices from love-centered space toward our highest good. This is how we become empowered, enabling us to contribute to humanity's transformation and form a better world for our children and future generations.

When we appreciate every now moment within the quantum field, we begin to rise out of our oppressed vibes. This takes a lot of courage and bravery since it's much easier to continue the comfortable narratives of victimhood or blaming others. We need to release the past, own our present moment, and take responsibility for the reality we wish to manifest.

Once each of us unites, heals, integrates, and embodies our Divine truth, we become empowered as a collective to be in service for humanity's highest good. We can choose to master our thoughts and act from our loving hearts with kindness, consideration, forgiveness, empathy, and compassion. This starts by taking action to save our beautiful blue planet Earth.

We can raise our awareness by informing ourselves to overcome self-serving divisive systems. Using discernment, we can decide how to contribute to environmental solutions as it resonates with our Souls. Mother Earth is manifesting all the dark attributes of humanity's energetic exchange that have been swept under the rug for generations.

Let's choose to shine our collective light and expose these shadows, acknowledge them so we can transmute them back into the light, no longer perpetuating the same patterns. This is our wake-up call to prioritize the health of our world for our innocent children, and the future of mankind.

To understand how we can make a difference, we should question everything and use our shrewdness. We have unrestricted access to information at our fingertips to understand our planet's circumstances.

Here are a few observations about the infestations currently occurring on our beloved home:

- Significant climate change factors that have contributed to new pathways for pestilence, disease, and a global pandemic. This also consists of severe flooding, drought, wildfires, rising sea levels, harsher hurricanes, volcanic eruptions, and catastrophic storms.

- New energy sources are being tested every day including wind and solar alternatives. The burning of fossil fuels is a major contributor to our air and environmental contamination. This affects our breath of life, which is essential for our existence and survival. We need clean energy consumption for humanity to endure on this planet. Mother Earth will evolve with or without us.

- Water pollution is a significant concern for our aquatic life as well as human health and well-being. Every sentient being should have limitless access to clean water with necessary minerals to nourish our bodies, no matter where they reside on this abundant planet.

- We all are aware that toxic waste and chemical elements are poisoning our beloved planet and all its inhabitants, which includes our children.

- We can all make a difference for our environment if we choose to recycle and reuse items. Waste management sites are becoming problematic with plastics overflowing landfills that are reaching capacity. Imagine if billions of people on Earth took action for their behaviors, how incredible the results would be?

There are so many other issues facing our planet. Ozone depletion, agricultural impacts, oceans and fisheries sustainability, and deforestation, to name a few.

Regardless of labels and beliefs, there is a higher intelligence that permeates and connects everything in our Universe, planet, and all living things. When we are misaligned and imbalanced, it triggers energetic blockages of the flow through our seven energy fields, which may contribute to pain, illness, disease patterns, and suffering.

This diminished energy flow may create distorted perceptions that allow us to be out of harmony with the natural laws and our true authentic identity. The spinning color wheel of our energy vortex draws in vital essence to maintain an aligned and harmonious state of being for our mental, emotional, physical, and spiritual health.

As an aspect of the Divine Source of Creation, our human emotional bodies are an expression of our free will, thought memory, feelings, and experiences that contribute to our reality. Ensuring balance and integration of our emotions assists us on our journey to become an empowered, self-sovereign, conscious community.

If we choose to acknowledge our present moments with blessings of gratitude, we can experience a greater range of joy, peace, fulfillment, and bliss in the boundless potentials of cosmic love.

We are all connected within this intelligent, loving Universe. Where there is light, we can always have hope to exist in coherence with our planet through the alchemy of kindness and service for the greater good.

Love is the most powerful force in the Universe. It can heal the world, inspire others, and bring us closer to our Higher Self. It is eternal, a never-ending gift to ourselves and to all that we truly adore.

The concept of self-love may seem small, but it can explode and embrace the whole Universe, throughout every timeline, reality, and dimension, as infinite love remains in a constant perpetual motion.

Please, take only what resonates with your Soul, always use your discernment, and follow your instincts and intuition; they will never steer you wrong.

From my heart to yours, I love you and honor your journey. I hope you enjoy the uplifting and inspiring poetry for inner peace, nourishment, compassion, and fulfillment. With gratitude and grace, many blessings.

SPINNING COLORED WHEEL

Root Center

Let's weave together energetic fields,
within our bodies that magnetically yields.
Vibrations regulating organ function,
with our immune system and emotion.
The first field in the spinning, colored wheel,
governs our sexual organs that may need to heal.
With estrogen, progesterone, testosterone,
compounds compared to entanglements of a clone.
We see red as we experience an inflamed life,
through the base of our spine, sharp as a knife.
Managing our survival hormones instinctively,
reproduction, elimination, sexuality, distinctively.
A tremendous amount of artistic energy,
when in balance, creativity flows in synergy.
Providing grounding, confidence, and serenity
in our empowered state of sensual identity.

Sacral Center

The second spinning wheel of life
operates smoothly without strife.
With consumption and eliminations
using digestive enzymes and extractions.
It's related to social networks, structures,
relationships, family, and cultures.

This orange field governs our intuition,
self-esteem and worthiness in addition.
When in balance, we feel secure, safe,
Loved in any environment without strafe.

Solar Plexus
The third spinning color wheel
located in the pit of our gut that needs to heal.
Governs stomach, intestine, spleen,
liver, bladder, adrenal gland to be clean.
The kidneys too, with a hue of yellow band
oversee will power, self-importance that is grand.
Impulse control, drive, aggression,
competition, dominance, and egocentric intention.
When in balance, we eventually overcome,
the wounded Souls that we have become.

Heart Center
The fourth spinning color wheel
is powerful energy when we feel.
Located in the center of the chest,
behind the breastbone, it beats the best.
Green governs our generous heart,
lungs, and growth glands from the start.
The oxytocin created stimulate,
a healthy immune system without debate.
It's associated with various emotions,
love inspired when in energetic motion.
Embodying unity and trust,
gratitude and compassion are a must.
The place that houses our Divinity,
the color of earth, it's our spirituality.
When in balance, we are caring,
feeling whole, fulfilled, and daring.

Throat Center
The fifth spinning color wheel
is a vortex of blue that will appeal?
Located in the center of our throat,
articulates our truth with authentic note.
It governs the neck, calcium, thyroid,
salivary glands and parathyroid.
It's responsible for our metabolism,
expressing our reality through this prism.
When in balance, we communicate,
using our voice, operating from a pure state.

Pineal Gland
The sixth spinning color wheel,
is a purple light of the cosmic reel.
Known as the third eye in spirituality,
it governs the door to higher dimensionality.
Shifting our perceptions as we awaken,
through the density, illusion, do not mistaken.
When this center is open, we can see,
through the physical veil where we are free.
Tuning into higher frequencies, riding the wave
beyond the five senses, evolving and brave.
When in balance, we become aware,
lucid, observant, and conscious with flare.

Master Field
The seventh spinning color wheel
rests above the head, with hues of indigo and teal.
It includes the pituitary, master gland,
cascading down with a swirl of a magical wand.
The coherence of this spiral to our Root,
provides us the greatest experiences that will suit.
Our highest level of consciousness originates,

in balance, harmony, and flow where divinity relates.
When we become activated, we feel worthy to receive,
insights, epiphanies, from the unified field we believe.
We access the data, memories through a
quantum leap,
evolving and ascending our mastery, no longer asleep.

GLOSSARY

Ascension: this process includes three stages, initiation, integration, and embodiment. It is the spiraling upward motion within the human auric energetic vortex fields. It raises the pulsation/vibrations of light and frequency rhythms within the human body, to align with the Higher Self aspect of Source.

Aura: there are seven layers of energetic spheres surrounding the human body vortex, also known as chakras. The first field is the etheric layer which is closest to the physical body and is connected to physical health, pain, and pleasure. The second field is the emotional or astral aura plane, which extends up to three inches away from the body. The third field is the mental layer, which sits three to eight inches away and is related to ego, values, and beliefs. The fourth field is the astral body, encompassing the love layer. It's correlated with the heart chakra, connecting the three lower auric planes to the three higher ones. The fifth field is the manifestation layer, the spiritual aura plane. It reflects spiritual health and connects to the wider universe. The sixth field is the celestial layer, which corresponds to intuition and is linked with the third eye. Finally, the seventh field is called the ketheric template or the "I Am" layer, which is the potential, fully integrated and embodied connection with the unified quantum field Source and divinity.

Awareness: it is the state of being in every now moment, self-informed. The old paradigm explained that consciousness was rooted in mind. Science and esoteric philosophy suggest that consciousness is pure awareness, before perception, before thought, before mental activity, and is the basis of nature, existence. Perception is the result of many mental activities, but awareness results from one mindful activity.

Consciousness: it is the energetic divine expression, an aspect of the "One I AM Source," "the Prime Creator" and "free will" that characterizes our Souls. It transcends time and space and is multi-dimensional. It is a combination of perceptual experiences (such as colors, sounds, smells, tastes, etc.), sensations and feelings (such as hunger, thirst, happiness, sadness, fear, pain, pleasure) and cognitive processes grounded in emotions through life events (such as attention, thinking, memory formation and recall, etc.).

Divinity: it is the state of all existence that is believed to come from a higher power, the unified quantum field, such as God, Supreme Being, Prime Creator, or spirit. Our Souls are an expression of the Divine, an eternal aspect of Source experiencing life based in truth, while material things are regarded as transient and founded in illusion.

Ego: it is the imaginary identity, mask, of an "overstimulated nervous system" or shadow of self that operates in survival mode—the root cause of pain and suffering due to childhood trauma. The primary function of the nervous system is to help maintain a sense of linear order through the multi-dimensional nature of life. It is a conditioned tendency to get lost in an inflamed personality or inflamed emotional state due to an inflamed nervous system. When your consciousness is limited through patterns of overstimulation, the nervous system deletes from your perception anything that contradicts your strongest beliefs.

Empath: an overly sensitive individual, highly attuned to the emotions and energy of others within the collective. They can easily take on the emotions of others as their own, including the collective auras of the planet, through porous boundaries, and may end up absorbing the pain and stress that is not their own. Empaths are sharply intuitive and are adept at reading people and situations beyond just surface-level impressions. Intuition is the filter through which they experience the world. Due to their giving nature along with their keen insight into the human psyche, they tend to be natural healers.

Energy: it is the study of forces like love and gravity, motion, vibration, and frequency, which can take many forms. Moving objects have kinetic energy while resting objects have potential energy (the objects will move if resistance is removed). Einstein's famous equation, $E=mc2$ shows the equivalence between mass and energy. Nikola Tesla states that energy, frequency, and vibration hold the secrets of the universe and that we are all part of one quantum energy field.

Enlightenment: it is the unification and "full comprehension of existence" or the actual experience of our own shifts in consciousness. It is the remembrance of our Divinity, as we expand our states of consciousness and elevate our higher self through the energetic electromagnetic fields around our physical bodies. One such definition for spiritual enlightenment is the complete dissolution of one's identity as a separate self with no trace of the ego-mind remaining.

Essence: it is our personal style that transcends all of our stories and narratives. In some respects, essence and soul are almost the same thing. The terms are often used interchangeably; however, the essence does not animate the body; it is the quality of how you express the stories you live through. The core essence is your Soul's distinctive fingerprint, what makes you uniquely "you." It is what separates each person in their individuality. It drives our soul and is the engine which our spirit revolves around. Essence follows us no matter which forms we may take. To see and accept the essence of another is to have power in how you work and flow with another. To embrace your style is to never work against yourself. Understanding your essence will help you flow with more grace in life.

Existence: it is the factual state of being or having objective reality, referring to the ability of an entity to interact with reality directly or indirectly. Science states the only things that exist are matter and energy, that all things are composed of material, that all actions require energy, and that all phenomena (including consciousness) are the result of material interactions. In every moment of existence, you have free will to choose, to identify with sensations and the knowing of experiences and are free to express yourself with pure awareness.

Flower of Life: it is a sacred symbol that shows up in temples, churches, and revered texts, from early Egypt to the Kabbalah and Christianity. It consists of overlapping circles that create symbolic connections to the Seed of Life. Made up of nineteen complete spheres and thirty-six arcs in a large enclosing circle, the Flower of Life is considered "the perfect form."

Light Warrior/Worker: the flame carriers; they hold the light energy of this planet in balance to help shift it into a higher level of consciousness to illuminate and enlighten the world. Some lightworkers, such as spiritual teachers and psychics, take on the role of energy healers to raise the collective state of consciousness around the world. They can manifest, create, or control things with their thoughts, attention, and intentions. They also have an innate ability to transmute low vibrational energy into light, to heal and make those around them feel safe and comfortable, exuding vibrational frequencies of their inner light, warmth, love, and joy.

Metatron's Cube: it contains all known geometric shapes that exist in physical matter, from snowflakes to the human eye. Thirteen equal circles extend with lines to twelve outer rings. It represents our body within three-dimensional space and time. This symbol is a reminder that your creative energy will find its way into the world.

Pineal Gland: also known as the third eye, it is a small, typically cone-shaped structure at the center of the brain, located between the eyebrows. It arises from the roof of the third ventricle, enclosed by the pia mater and functions primarily as an endocrine gland secreting melatonin. Most people sense they are not living from their highest potential, operating instead from the subconscious mind. The third eye gives us an intuitive perception of the Universe and the world beyond the five senses, providing self-awareness and celestial intelligence. It represents the point at which the body receives energy (transmission of frequency) from the universe that keeps our lives sustained. We use our perception, our consciousness, and our senses to gain awareness of energy transmissions via information and data.

Physical Universe: it is all of space and time and their contents, comprising all quantum energy in its various forms, including gravity, electromagnetism, radiation, and matter, and therefore planets, moons, stars, galaxies, and the contents of intergalactic space. It is an existing matter and space considered as a whole, the cosmos. The Universe is believed to be at least ten billion light years in diameter and contains a vast number of galaxies: it's been expanding since its creation in the Big Bang about thirteen billion years ago.

Sacred Geometry: they are symbols that carry sacred energy, and reflect the organic shapes found in the Universe, nature, in cellular structures, and in fractals. They are the icons for the universal truth, creation and all existence.

Solfeggio Scale: consists of vibrational sounds of music, in rhythmic patterns that use the power of frequencies of the 432-hertz and 528-hertz scales and are directly associated with DNA repair. Music based on these tones can be used for healing by activating our pineal gland in our mind and positively affecting our emotions.

Soul: it is the energy that transcends a person's being. It incorporates the person's thoughts, will, desires, emotions, and their ability to reason. The Soul is the heart of the body; it does not die since energy cannot be destroyed. It is an immortal part of a person that transcends death and goes on to a higher existence or reincarnates back into the third dimensional reality.

Spirit: it is the spark of light, the living radiant life force in the body. It is the reason why we are living and moving around. It is the source of power and control for both our body and soul. When we die, the spirit—the living force—leaves the body. Hence the body dies. The spirit stops existing, while the soul moves on. The spirit is often considered to be the spark that animates a person's spiritual story before it returns to the light.

Spiritual Awakening: it is the conscious awareness of remembrance and reconnection with the Divine through self-realization, which is ultimately one and the same. It also dissolves the illusion that we were ever separate from that oneness. It is the process when our consciousness expands and opens into a new expression, recognizing our true nature. It moves us into alignment with the divine and shifts us toward our most authentic way of expressing our higher self and fully living.

Spiritual Bliss: comes from being totally aligned and integrated with your higher self, your soul, your divine truth, your mind, and your body, and in harmony with the universe. The dictionary defines it as supreme happiness, utter joy, and contentment, dwelling in paradise or attaining nirvana. It is a state of being, not an actual place, free from pain, worry, and suffering.

Universal Law of Energy: states that everything is energy. This includes humans, our cars, and our houses and all that's in them. We are all made of atoms. Energy is neither created nor destroyed; it is the cause and effect of itself. Energy is always evenly present in all places.

It is in constant motion and never rests. Energy is forever moving from one form to another, and change is its only attribute. There is a frequency or vibration of energy that fills the Universe. This energy is not only beneficial but also essential to all living cells, whether human, plant, or animal. Human beings utilize this energy with their mind. Every thought is transmitted by this energy. Every aspect of life in the physical realm depends on this basic energy.

Universal Law of Perpetual Transmutation of Energy: it is a constant state of motion and transmutation. The law explains that the non-physical level of life is always moving in the physical form. The physical level of life is the manifestation of the non-physical. If we understand that energy is forever moving into form, and we know that our thoughts, ideas, and feelings are energy, it is easy to follow how the images we hold in our mind most often materialize in our daily lives. If we wish to exist in harmony with this law, we must always be aware of our thoughts and feelings. If we choose to react in a negative pattern from past behaviors, we can acknowledge them, honor them, and choose to process them, resulting in a positive state of being.

Universal Law of Vibration: it is also known as the Law of Attraction, as it explains that everything vibrates; nothing rests. Our thoughts are waves of energy that penetrate all time and space. Our feelings are our conscious awareness of vibration. The specific relation of the law of attraction here is that energy that is on the same frequency will resonate and attract. The energy that is not on the same frequency will repel. Our physical reality is but a manifestation of our own, unseen, internal reality. To live in harmony with this law we need to remember that our feelings are our conscious awareness of our vibration. Our objective is, when we are not feeling well to become aware of what we are thinking. To change the vibration, we can improve it by thinking of something pleasant.

Universal Law of Attraction: it is a constructive or positive use of energy that raises the level of consciousness of humans and in turn, raises our vibration rate or frequency. Every individual has a different rate of vibration. All of humanity's global problems are created by our thought projections. What we emit from our collective mind in the form of thoughts, we magnetize and receive back into our energetic fields. Spiritual growth requires the transmutation of all negative thinking, which dissipates "the life force" or vital energy.

Universal Law of Rhythm: it explains that everything goes through cycles, yet everything has a rhythm, a pattern. What may sometimes appear to be random is very orderly. The tide goes in and out, the seasons come and go, night follows the day, and so, you too have your moods swing back and forth. We know that by law, the swing will change, and things will get better. We can be on a natural downswing and still feel good.

Universal Law of Polarity: it states that our three-dimensional physical existence has an equal and opposite divergence, and one does not exist without the other. We don't have an inside without an outside, no dark without light, no up without down, etc. It proves there is no bad without good. Therefore, in every situation that might be considered relatively bad, we always know there is also good, even if we do not quite see it. Knowing this can be really reassuring in any given experience.

Universal Law of Relativity: it explains that all things are relative. Nothing is good or bad, big, or small until we relate it to something else. Everything in life just is. There is no high or low, fast, or slow, except by comparison. We can use this law to heighten our self-esteem. We will then become aware of how special we are considering the truth.

Universal Law of Cause and Effect: it means that for every action, there is an equal and opposite reaction. Energy returns to its source of origin. Whatever we send into the Universe comes back. Therefore, when we say kind things to everyone and treat everyone with compassion and respect, it will all come back to us in abundance.

Vibrations: they are the rates of frequency or wavelength that oscillate through dimensional levels when we expand or contract our consciousness. High vibrations are generally associated with positive qualities and feelings such as love, forgiveness, kindness, compassion, and peace. On the other hand, low vibrations are associated with darker conditions such as hatred, fear, greed, judgment, comparison, and depression. The higher our vibration is, the more in touch we are with our higher self, inner "god/goddess," divinity, Soul consciousness, wholeness, universal harmony that describe our true nature. This also means the lower our vibration is, the more out of sync we are with our higher truth and being, and therefore, the more suffering and conflict we experience in life.

WORKS CITED

Online Research Sources: http://www.ascensiondictionary.com/ https://evolveconsciousness.org/consciousness-and-polarity/#polarities

Bartzis, Andrew, The Galactic Historian, Contract Revocations, https://andrewbartzis.com/

Dispenza, Joe. *You Are the Placebo: Making our Mind Matter*. Carlsbad, CA: Hay House, 2015.

Talbot, Michael, and Lynne McTaggart. *The Holographic Universe: The Revolutionary Theory of Reality*. New York, NY: Harper Perennial, 2011.

Tolle, Eckhart. *A New Earth*. Penguin Books, 2015.

ACKNOWLEDGEMENTS

"Dear Fear, I acknowledge that you intend to conjure sinister thoughts and emotions during this global pandemic. This non-empirical delusion causes anxiety about a future outcome that doesn't yet exist. I refuse to perpetuate this form of irrationality. I reclaim my power and sovereignty from your potent influence."

— LALI A. LOVE

Thank you, God, and the Universe, for all my blessings and for all the abundance that is yet to come. I embrace every moment with an open and loving heart, including all my experiences and lessons for the evolution of my higher self.

I would like to extend my heartfelt appreciation to all my esteemed colleagues and writer friends who have generously embraced my stories and encouraged my writing journey. Specifically, I am incredibly thankful to the members of the Queer Indie Alliance for their loving support and inspiration. They are beautiful souls who embody love-centered unity by creating a "diverse, inclusive, and supportive community of radical acceptance".

I am grateful to be blessed with the unconditional love of my family, friends, and colleagues. A special acknowledgment to Halo, Mario, Ash, Steve, Anya, and Rashmi for reading my advanced reader's copy. I feel truly blessed and honored to have received your endorsement.

To my heart and soul, you both inspire me daily to be the best human in this existence. Keep forging your creative and authentic paths, as you illuminate the world with your brilliance. You can manifest whatever reality your heart desires. Thank you for your generosity, uncompromising love, and motivation. I honor your journey.

Existence, Consciousness, Bliss.

ABOUT THE AUTHOR

Lali A. Love is an award-winning author of visionary fantasy, thriller, and metaphysical poetry. She has received the Global E-Book Gold Award, the Elite Choice Gold Award, the Book of Excellence Award, Queer Indie Youth Award, and the International Reader's Favorite Bronze Award for quality and powerful storytelling. Lali lives in Canada with her husband and two beautiful children who are her greatest source of joy and inspiration.

Lali aspires to write uplifting, inspiring poetry, and gripping, thought-provoking, character-based novels that relate to modern day issues and invoke an emotional response in her readers. She has researched and studied epistemology and metaphysics to further her understanding of the Universal Laws of Energy. As an intuitive, alchemist, and energy healer, Lali has been called to embody the light, anchored in love, kindness, and gratitude, for the betterment of humanity.

With humility, compassion, and grace, Lali intends to help elevate levels of consciousness for the highest good, empowering individuals to seek their authentic truth. She is an advocate for self-healing journeys, self-actualization, equality, diversity, unity, women, and children.

BOOKS BY THE AUTHOR

Heart of a Warrior Angel: From Darkness to Light

In this metaphysical thriller, Lilac Noble must face the traumatic experiences of her childhood before she can conquer the dark entities that have wreaked havoc on her family. On this epic journey, Lilac undergoes the destructive process of spiritual enlightenment in order to lift the veil of darkness and shame that has obscured her youth.

As Lilac unlocks painful memories of abuse, she uncovers menacing secrets feeding the evil within her generational bloodline.

With the unconditional love for her family, Lilac finds the courage to discover her inner truth, vulnerability, and healing, as she awakens her divine light and overcomes her debilitating fears of the past.

A heart-wrenching and gripping tale of a family's rise from poverty, oppression, and abuse. Spanning two continents and three generations, this inspirational novel portrays the best and worst of humanity and shows how the "tiniest spark of light can overcome the darkness of any magnitude," through forgiveness, compassion, and the most powerful force in the universe–Love.

The De-Coding of Jo: Hall of Ignorance Book 1

What would you do if you accidentally discovered a mysterious, holographic portal into the cosmos, hidden in the basement of your high school's library? Would you take the leap of faith?

The De-Coding of Jo: Hall of Ignorance is a meld of fantasy, paranormal and science fiction, with a strong appeal to young adult readers (14+). It is the first book of the Ascending Angel Academy series, incorporating plot-driven and coming-of-age stories of diverse, gender-inclusive teenagers struggling with self-identity and a sense of belonging.

When a demonic parasite turns her classmates into an army of sleepwalkers, sixteen-year-old Jo must confront her celestial identity and reveal the mystery of existence. With the help of her best friends and a Galactic Compass, Jo unleashes the cosmic powers of creation to prevent the Lord of Darkness from enslaving all of humanity into obscurity.

Will she be able to decode the artificial system in time to save her friends and the sacred Light?

The Joy of I.T. (Infinite Transcendence)

The Joy of I.T. is a non-fiction, transformative anthology of ingenuity and inspiration as we shift into higher states of conscious community. Featuring a collection of forty poems, artwork, mantras, and affirmations, this book will motivate, enlighten, and cultivate your senses with visually stimulating vibrational frequencies of love.

A wonderful gift idea for the holidays or special occasions, The Joy of I.T. may be enjoyed as a coffee table book or by your bedside table for a boost of mystical adrenaline, guiding your journey toward self-mastery, harmony and infinite transcendence for the well-being of all.

Ananda: Poetry for the Soul

Ananda, the bliss within, is an inspirational poetic sonata for the evolution of the Soul. With harmonic verses, each healing poem provides therapeutic, meditative, and transformative reading for self-mastery.

A handbook for the wellbeing of the Soul, with messages of hope and transcendence imbuing each page and highlighting the interconnectedness of humanity.

"When we operate from the space of heart-centered consciousness, every Soul becomes our mirror and our teacher. We are all connected within this web of radiant life force energy called Love." —Lali A. Love